To Kill a

PRESIDENT

A Novel

GEORGE L COLON

iUniverse, Inc.
Bloomington

To Kill a President

iUniverse books may be ordered through booksellers or by contacting:

iUniverse
1663 Liberty Drive
Bloomington, IN 47403
www.iuniverse.com
1-800-Authors (1-800-288-4677)

ISBN: 978-1-4620-5938-6 (sc)
ISBN: 978-1-4620-5937-9 (hc)
ISBN: 978-1-4620-5915-7 (e)

Library of Congress Control Number: 2011918129

Printed in the United States of America

iUniverse rev. date: 10/26/2011

For Ryan

For Ryan

CHAPTER 1

New York, 1950

On the East 138ᵗʰ station's platform, Osvaldo Cotto searched the two long lines of steel gray tracks for the Third Avenue El, which was running late.

A dull light appeared, and in a few seconds, a string of ashen cars sputtered into the station. The doors of the El's car opened and he fought the rush-hour passengers climbing in. He still remembered the meek immigrant from a culture of respect, a poor *jíbaro* farmer from a cane field, who allowed others to push on a crowded train. But he'd since learned to shove these eleven years and push back the forces that had driven him. The empty spaces on the yellow rattan seats disappeared, and he stood for the ride into Manhattan. He glanced at the posters lining the walls of the car: the cartoon figures of the Piels brothers extolling their beer, Jackie Robinson of the Brooklyn Dodgers endorsing Chock full o'Nuts coffee, and a smiling bellhop with a last call for Philip Morris cigarettes.

But he tuned it all out.

1

Don Pedro would soon order the party faithful to execute Operation *Huracan*. The barber Arcadio, Don Pedro's right hand man in Puerto Rico, had sent secret communiqués through party operatives here in New York.

Resting his back on the car's closed doors, he became tired of reading his newspaper, the Spanish language daily *La Prensa de Nueva York*. The fighting in Korea dominated the headlines. On the sports pages, the New York Yankees had taken the first game of the 1950 World Series from the Philadelphia Phillies. But he reserved his greatest interest for the photo of the President of the United States with General Macarthur at their recent meeting on Wake Island in the Pacific.

A smiling Harry Truman shook the General's hand, and according to the caption, congratulated him for his brilliant landings in the North Korean port city of Inchon, outflanking the communist forces. Osvaldo stared hard at the image of the President. And he wanted to shout it out to these impersonal New York commuters, their faces hidden behind the quiet anonymity of newspapers, refusing eye contact.

"We're going to assassinate the President of the United States. We're bringing the war of the Puerto Rican people here, to the United Sates—to you. You occupy our island. *Yanqui*, get out."

The train now passed into Manhattan from the Bronx, and he stared at the East River below the Third Avenue Bridge. He'd crossed his Rubicon and there'd be no turning back.

He was ending this phase of his life and beginning the new one he'd prepared for years.

Although he'd report for work as usual at the Achilles Metal Works, polishing handles for ladies' pocket books didn't serve his purpose in life, but it did pay a decent wage that allowed for a nice apartment in the South Bronx. Yet a higher purpose called. He'd give up the good life for the cause—the cause of the Puerto Rican people. The party now called. And it sunk in that he'd never see his beloved Puerto Rico again.

But I'll ride life's journey forward, not backward, he thought.

Yes, he was going to kill the President of the United States.

Feeling warm, he took off his fedora and brushed back large spinnaker ears and the thin hair of a receding hairline. He studied the Third Avenue Bridge. *How do you blow up a bridge?* Somebody else would work out the details.

And how do you assassinate a president? That job was his.

He had experience with assassination. And as the El approached the Manhattan coast, his memory journeyed back to Puerto Rico, 1936.

He'd shadowed American Police Chief Francis Riggs for the two assassins, Hiram and Elias, who were waiting nearby to kill the Colonel for his recent murder of unarmed demonstrators against American rule at the University of Puerto Rico. At the command of then American Governor of Puerto Rico, Blanton Winship, appointed by then American President, Franklin Roosevelt, the Colonel ordered the police to open fire on Osvaldo's nationalist comrades opposed to the foreign rule of these gringo intruders, especially the sugar companies who worked to death the poor *jibaros*, or farmers, in the cane fields of the land and who stole the wealth of their island. Police killed four university students and professors. He bore the American people no ill will. Perhaps if they knew how their government, bankers, and sugar companies treated Puerto Ricans, they too would be angry and put a stop to the oppression.

He kept vigil outside the Cathedral of Old San Juan, where the Colonel attended mass, and when it ended the Colonel walked down the church's front steps, shook some hands, and got into his car. Osvaldo walked away and lit a cigarette, the signal.

Elias and Hiram, decked out in suits to conceal their weapons and white fedoras to hide their faces, walked toward him. Passing by, they didn't acknowledge him. Osvaldo wanted to look back but resisted, as instructed, and ran a few paces. Shots rang out. Then screams. More shouts. He heard the car brake. More shouting. Women in mantillas and men in white hats and *guayabera* shirts, a curious Sunday crowd, rushed toward the scene past palm trees. Should he keep walking? He couldn't resist. And besides, it would have looked suspicious if he'd not run to the scene.

Throwing away the cigarette, he doubled back. The Colonel, rosary in hand, blood staining his white uniform, his face in agony, lay dying in the back seat of the car. A bullet had pierced the bible in his hand. Another was

3

found in his head. Elias and Hiram ran away. Too late. The guards quickly overpowered them.

Osvaldo melted into the crowd and disappeared, his job done.

It had been doable.

But now, he needed to kill a President—the President of the United States.

CHAPTER 2

Washington, DC, 1950

A car pulled in front of Blair House, temporary home to the President of the United States while the White House underwent its first major overhaul since the British burned it down during the War of 1812.

Chief Athanaeus Bernard Howland of the secret service got out at the main entrance, hands on hips, and his steel gray eyes surveyed the scene. Wooden guardhouses at opposite ends of Blair House manned by alert guards smartly dressed in blue uniforms protected its two side entrances. The cherubic Bill Loring, head of the White House Police, appeared and saluted him.

"The boss is coming, sir."

"As you were, Bill," the Chief commanded.

The Chief inspected the green canopy extending from the main entrance, ten steps high, to the sidewalk. On the steps, protected from the sun by the canopy, Officer Jim Eagleton held his watch. His intensity satisfied the Chief. Eagleton's eyes, like movie cameras, continuously scanned the steady procession of strollers in front of Blair House. Along the sidewalk, a black iron picket fence protected the grass and the flowers from the passersby.

The Chief long ago learned to tell the tourist from the Washington, DC, resident: the locals didn't look at the house, but the tourists stopped to read the plaques on the fence. These readers worried him most. They came close to the house—too close, sometimes. The bronze plaques, turned green with years, commemorated the former residents of the house, the Blairs, friends and advisors to presidents, cabinet members, and Civil War officers.

Three more policemen came out of the side entrance and posted themselves on the sidewalk. Some strollers stopped in front of the house, sensing someone important about to appear. Two Cadillac limousines drove up to the house and Loring blew his whistle. The cars pulled up slowly in front of Blair House, and the crowd grew excited. Four men in plain clothes got out of the first car and positioned themselves around the second car. Two more men got out.

They opened the door for a dapper gentleman, with snow-white hair and rimless glasses. The old gentleman adjusted his brown double-breasted suit and his white Stetson hat. He sported a cane and brown, white-tipped shoes.

"It's the President," somebody said in astonishment.

"It's Truman," somebody else added with equal surprise.

All eyes stared at the President of the United States as he made his way to Blair House, flanked on both sides by the four secret service agents. A few people surged forward, hands extended, but the secret service and police kept them back. Then the President stopped suddenly to shake hands with a man and two little boys duded up in cowboy suits.

"Hello, young fella." The President took the hand of the first boy and patted the other's head.

Chief Howland removed his own wide-brimmed hat and unbuttoned his gray pinstripe suit. A drop of sweat rolled off his closely cropped hair, and from his back pocket he removed a neatly folded handkerchief, wiping a short gray crew cut. He held his breath and looked not at the children but around him at the crowd, all potential assassins to the Chief.

"You really the President?" one of the wide-eyed, freckle-faced boys asked.

"I was the last time I looked. I'll check again. Tightwad Republicans might budget me out of the fiscal year. Think we can do with less. Maybe we don't need a president."

That elicited chuckles from the crowd, but not the straight-faced secret service. The President shook a few more hands. The Chief stood behind him.

"Hello, A. B.," the President turned to greet him.

"Afternoon, sir."

The President leisurely made his way up to the main entrance and greeted Jim Eagleton on the top step. Officer Eagleton saluted smartly, momentarily taking his eyes away from the crowd.

"At ease, Jim." Mr. Truman shook Eagleton's hand. "You're out two bits."

Eagleton smiled. "Yes, sir."

The Chief frowned, briskly following up the steps, relieved when the President was inside. "What was that about?" the Chief asked.

"The boss and I have a bet," Eagleton answered. "I say the good weather won't last into November. He says it will."

"I see."

"He's a regular guy."

"Yes, a regular guy. But I need your eyes always on the crowd, Jim."

"Yes, sir," Eagleton blushed.

Back in 1923, his own superiors assigned the new agent A. B. Howland to look out for President Warren G. Harding's assassin. He failed and still blamed himself for Mr. Harding's assassination—for the death did not result from natural causes, as the official investigation concluded. Although it behooved him to go along with the ensuing cover-up and keep quiet, the whole affair still haunted him. The secret service came close again to losing another president— Mr. Roosevelt—in 1933. For that close call he also took responsibility. Chief Howland became distracted on that day in Miami when Mr. Roosevelt, then President Elect, appeared with the mayor of Chicago. Although he heard the

7

assassin's words, he saw, too late, the gun and heard the shots ring out. "Too many are hungry!" the assassin shouted.

The first words Mr. Truman spoke to Chief Howland at their first meeting also rang out. "God damn it, I want to see the people and want them to see me." The Chief had done his best to oblige after the death of the wheel chair bound Mr. Roosevelt.

But the general laxity with security needed to end, he knew. The Chief hated these crowds and the fact that the men liked Harry Truman a little too much. This chummy relationship could lead to laxity and disaster. One needed to keep a certain distance from the subjects one protected. Although he couldn't change this chemistry, he needed to change procedures.

The car drove him the few blocks back to his Treasury Building office as Blair House receded in the background.

A small, elegant residence, it struck a handsome pose on the southeast corner of Pennsylvania Avenue, across from the White House. Four stories tall, Blair House stood anonymously among a row of other mansions. According to people, it had a touch of the Georgian and the Neo-classical style of the early nineteenth century—whatever that meant. Chief Howland knew nothing of architecture. He was just a cop, a good cop. Before that, he played baseball.

"I want to see the people and want them to see me, Chief."

He yearned for presidents in wheelchairs.

And he needed more men.

CHAPTER 3

San Juan, Puerto Rico, 1950

Gregorio "Goyo" Tejada drove his old red Dodge through the brick and cobbled streets of old San Juan. Making his way through the Plaza de San Francisco, he drove north on the dimly lit streets, *Calle* Luna and *Calle* Sol. Steering his American car through the narrow streets of the capital, he sucked in the balmy, musky air of the old city. Nineteenth-century iron streetlamps lit his way past the old Spanish houses with overhanging balconies. Goyo Tejada sped up to the Plaza de San Jose, where he stopped and parked.

The German Luger strapped in its holster to his shoulder inside his white suit was oiled and ready to use. Goyo Tejada used it well. That's why little Arcadio Diaz, the barber, had summoned him.

He straightened his tie in the rearview mirror and wondered what to say if Arcadio asked what had kept him. Certainly not the truth: a beautiful dark woman whose perfume clung to his clothes after they'd frolicked all afternoon. A smile broke over his handsome face, exposing a gold tooth and straightening out his thin pompadour. Taking off his white hat, he pressed his fingers over his pomaded black hair.

"Arcadio wouldn't ask," he said, stepping out of the car.

The shops around the plaza were closed and all was quiet, except for the *coquis*, the tiny frogs whose customary songs filled the night. In the dim light coming from a barbershop's door, two figures stood guard before barber's pole, discouragement against customers. They stared. He returned their look and strode past the guards, who nodded.

A large grimy mirror inside caught the confined space of the small shop with worn barber chairs with dangling leather strops inside. A young man sat in one chair, reading a days-old newspaper. His suit, too big for him, and a wisp of a mustache budding from a virgin upper lip pegged him as not much older than twenty. He put the paper down and nodded.

"*El Barbero?*" Goyo asked.

"In the back," the young man answered without emotion, studying him.

A small man appeared from behind the curtain. "Goyo, we agreed to meet at six." A small man, Arcadio still wore a white tunic. Gray, unkempt hair overflowed from his head and a growth of at least three days speckled his face. Goyo thought the barber in need of his own services. The barber's brown eyes looked annoyed. "It's past eight. When I say six, it's six."

"Don't tell me anything," Goyo turned and faced Arcadio, giving the barber a long, hard look.

Arcadio's face twitched. "I'm not telling you anything." The barber's eyes met his. "Don Pedro is asking—through me." He picked up a razor.

Goyo put his hand through his suit and felt his gun.

The barber picked up some combs and barbers tools and rearranged them on the counter, along with the razor, then stepped back.

Goyo gave him his back and walked to the counter. He inspected a dirty basin with smeared faucets and toyed with the lather dispenser. Picking up some scissors, he trimmed his mustache, poured witch hazel into his cupped hands, and rubbed it on his face, never taking his eyes off the barber through the mirror.

"Gregorio, Julito." Arcadio turned to the young man, who nodded and twirled his modest mustache as he studied both men. "Don Pedro says the time for sacrifice has come. Many enemies of the Republic of Puerto Rico need to be eliminated. First, there's a *Yanqui* lawyer whose presence on our island is unsuitable to our cause."

Goyo turned, looked at Arcadio, then at Julito, and back at Arcadio.

"Don't worry. Julito is young but good in this business. College student. University of Puerto Rico. We can speak in front of him. Julito, Gregorio. We call him Goyo. Goyo here can shoot a garbanzo bean off a coconut and not graze a hair on the shell."

Julito nodded indifferently.

"What's so important about this gringo lawyer?" Goyo asked, still sizing up Julito.

Arcadio explained the lawyer was buying land for his bosses in Chicago, who were planning to build a canning factory in Rio Piedras. His name was Howard Saunders. Goyo studied a newspaper clipping with the lawyer's picture that Arcadio handed him.

Saunders was staying at the new Hilton in the Condado section, where the party had planted Julito as a busboy and bartender. Arcadio explained Julito could drive a car and knew the island well.

"A car picks up the Gringo every morning around nine and brings him back to the hotel by six," Julito said. "He has dinner in his room, then works until eight. Walks out to the lagoon at the end of Ashford Avenue and swims near the Dos Herman's Bridge. He likes to dive from rocks there. Don't know why he doesn't swim in the pool like other gringos. It's isolated out there, nothing but construction equipment. They're building more hotels for the *Yanquis*. You can get off a shot without being seen."

"Too risky," Goyo said, picturing the area in his mind. "We need to be quiet."

"I prefer shooting the *maricon*," Julito insisted. "You can climb the rocks and get him before he knew what happened. We could leave the car near there unseen."

"The guards minding the construction equipment will hear a shot. We'll have to shave this gringo quietly." He drew a carved ivory case from his suit and fondled it for a few seconds. A deft pull of the wrist produced a long, sharp razor that pirouetted in his hand.

Julito tugged at his modest mustache. "That'd be too bloody."

Arcadio thought for a few seconds. "I agree, Goyo. Don Pedro wants to send the *Yanquis* a message that they can't buy out this island from the people. But a slit throat is bad for world opinion."

Goyo nodded. "We'll do it your way." He turned to Julito. "What else can you tell me?"

"He's usually by the rocks for a swim about 9:15 and back in his hotel by ten. He never fails. Might have a drink at the poolside bar. Brings up prostitutes he picks up on Ashford."

"I see. You just point him out to me, college boy, and drive us out of there. That's what 'we' means. I'm frank. I work alone. That way there're no fuck-ups. You work with me, careful who you talk to and what you do. Understand?"

"Call me Julito, not college boy. You understand that, I understand you. I've heard of your exploits, Don Gregorio. You'll soon witness mine."

Goyo stared, then nodded. "Yes, *Julito.*" He stressed the name and his eyes stresed the sarcasm. "We'll need a few days to prepare." Julito said they'd follow his movements for a few days. He told Goyo to be at the Hilton around ten the following night. That's where he tended bar and Saunders stopped for a drink after his swim. "Walk in to the poolside bar, sit in the bar. Order a drink. When Saunders walks in, I'll say, 'Drake has sailed into the harbor.'"

"Drake has sailed into the harbor.

"You work it out," Arcadio instructed. "When it's done, we'll meet in the south. Go to the safe house. I'll contact you there in a few days. Long live a free Puerto Rico."

"*Viva Puerto Rico libre,*" Goyo answered, and he left.

He got into his car and drove out of Old San Juan. He worked best alone and depended on no one since his brother Arturo's death. He knew human frailties to be dangerous. Greed. Envy. Stupidity. And above all, the need to talk. Julito was young. College boys talked.

Once again, the party called on him to continue this struggle and he'd answer the call. "Drake has sailed into the harbor," Goyo repeated. He knew of the English pirates and corsairs who'd long ago sailed the waters of Puerto

Rico—and how they'd been pushed back into the sea. But he'd take something for himself out of life. Money could be made, he'd discovered, by dealing in certain commodities the tropics produced and gringos wanted—and which the authorities frowned upon.

CHAPTER 4

Goyo Tejada sat at the Hilton pool bar. "Bartender, double Chivas and soda."

"Yes, sir." Julito served him without ceremony or recognition, then radiated toward the other customers.

He drank slowly and studied the pool lounge's fancy decor. No one danced to the medley of big band tunes piped in from a music room. Occasionally swiveling around, he watched the Americans splashing in the water. Others drank and laughed. A few Puerto Ricans mingled with them. He hid his dislike for the patrons with occasional polite smiles. *Rich men and Gringo lovers*, he decided, feeling comfortable with neither. But the money in his pocket and his expensive brown suit entitled him to drink here. It was far from the mountains near his native Ponce after his father's death, when life grew hard.

Among this luxury, he now recalled those years.

"Another drink, senor?" Julito asked, tugging at his modest mustache. Goyo looked up. "He's here." Julito motioned subtly to the right. "Drake has sailed into the harbor."

Goyo sipped his Scotch, then turned casually.

He caught a glimpse of an American man in a red bathing robe and sandals and recognized Saunders from the newspaper clipping Arcadio the barber had shown him. A Puerto Rican woman in a green bathing suit, with an upturned nose and hazel eyes, entered with him, and the two slipped into a cozy corner table. Goyo returned to his drink and after a few sips turned again casually to study the couple ordering drinks. Goyo nursed his own drink and studied them, laughing and holding hands. The American's informality surprised him, as he'd imagined him to be more formal and serious.

After twenty minutes, Saunders came to the bar to shake hands with some men, and Goyo saw him up close. Handsome, thin, and fit, with blue eyes, he hardly conformed to the image of fat businessmen depicted in nationalist propaganda posters. His graying blond hair and lines made him about forty. Saunders chatted with the men and returned to the girl. After a few minutes, he paid his check and they left.

Later that night, Goyo met Julito by the Dos Hermanos Bridge near the hotel and they walked on the beach. Julito explained he'd entered Saunder's room with a passkey and examined his papers. Saunder's client, Illinois Canning, pursued a land deal for a factory site in Puerto Rico. An old woman refusing to sell her property held up the deal.

"These gringos are buying up everything," Julito said.

They watched Saunders for several days. Julito continued to track him in the hotel and Goyo observed his movements out of it. A car picked him up around ten and shuttled him on his business trips. On Sunday, Goyo followed him to the pier, where Saunders boarded a fishing boat. At the casino, Saunders cast his dice as Goyo cast his eyes on him. And of all his activities, none proved more regular than his nightly swims on the beach by the secluded rocks. *These swims kept him fit*, Goyo thought.

They'd kill him on the beach at the first opportunity. Goyo would hide behind the trees and wait for the gringo to return from his swim. While Saunders dried himself on the rocks, Goyo would approach quietly from behind and shoot him while Julito waited nearby in the car. Saunders didn't come the first night. On the second night, streetwalkers roamed near. He slipped out of the beach, careful the whores didn't see him.

On the third night, a moonless sky and an eerie silence rewarded their vigil. Goyo waited quietly behind a palm tree. Saunders approached. The gringo climbed the small rocks and stripped to his trunks, then waded into the water and took a quick swim. He returned to the rocks and dried himself facing the sea. Approaching silently from behind, Goyo climbed quietly on to the rocks. He stood and aimed calmly as Saunders turned. He gently squeezed the trigger. A bullet flashed out and struck Saunders in the head. The gringo slumped, then dropped on the rocks.

Goyo felt none of the emotion he felt the first time he killed a rival bootlegger for pay. He had qualms a year earlier in Caguas when he gunned down an American engineer. Now he marveled how routine it had all become, even though he could remember a time when he still respected God's commandments as taught by priests and his mother, especially the one that said, "Thou shall not kill."

Yet he put these speculations quickly out of his mind.

He looked around, thinking he heard female voices. But the night was quiet, except for the rhythm of the waves and the *coquis*, the tiny frogs chanting in the night. He walked quickly to the car where Julito waited, and they drove out of El Condado.

Goyo sensed Julito's tension and took the wheel outside San Juan. On the coast, they exchanged places again and Julito drove through the valley of Caguas. Goyo kept watch, his gun ready. But they met no roadblock and no police, only night and stars and the singing of the *coquis*. When morning rose, they'd crossed the treacherous mountain pass and were in the south.

CHAPTER 5

Police Officer Fulgencio "Papo" Obregon of the Metropolitan Police watched in fascination the early morning waves creep on to El Condado Beach, then withdraw. Each roll of the waters produced a fresh deposit of sea life and dyed the yellow sand khaki. The waves edged up to a line on the sand, then retreated, as if frightened by the body they'd deposited there. The dead man, chalky white from the loss of blood, wore only swimming trunks—and a hole on the side of his head.

His friend Martin Lanza and another officer had summoned Papo at home that morning with news an American had turned up dead on the beach. Papo's vacation was on hold, and Pietri of Homicide needed him. Although primed for days off in the mountain, murder piqued his fancy.

Papo took off his New York Yankee cap, a reminder of a Bronx childhood left behind on his parents' return to Puerto Rico. He preferred New York's colder clime better but had long since adapted to tropical weather. He felt warm in dungarees and in his tropical *guayabera* shirt that loosely fit around his robust frame.

He put his cap back on and took off his sunglasses, placing them in one of the four pockets of the *guayabera*, then wiped his large mustache with his hand, breathing in the scent of salt and sand mixed with moisture. Above his round nose, his large, intense black eyes studied the crime scene. A small crowd of gawkers gathered behind the police cordon a few feet from the body and stared at the unfolding drama. Papo knew people curious by nature. Murder, though not unknown, was rare in Puerto Rico. Having investigated a dozen, Papo knew they usually resulted from personal feuds, jealousy, and other silly reasons. But dead Americans were new to him.

A newspaper photographer snapped pictures. The crowd buzzed in awe. Each move by the detectives produced more *oohs* and *ahs*. Uniformed officers watched the crowd and checked IDs.

Pietri of Homicide, overdressed in a blue business suit and looking self-important, as usual, examined the body. He turned, saw Papo, and frowned. When he finished his examination, he walked away, giving Papo his back. Pietri always looked down on him and no doubt resented his presence here, a vice officer intruding on the domain of Homicide.

When his turn came, Papo again took off his Yankees cap out of respect for the dead and made the sign of the cross. He'd seen this man walking through the Condado section. Although he no longer believed everything the Irish nuns taught him long ago in a Bronx church, he still thought life precious. He knelt, and examined the man's wound, grayish and raw. He knew the killer fired at close range. The victim went for a swim while the killer hid behind the rocks, surprising the gringo when he returned. The killer walked back to the road and got in a car, probably with a waiting accomplice. Someone must've seen something, a tourist, a *puta* walking in the night, or a John.

Papo knew this area where the night ladies walked. Very well.

He himself picked up a streetwalker one night near here and found himself going back, incomprehensively falling in love. He went to her nightly before returning to his wife. This sad affair led to a brawl with an American sailor, Papo's arrest by military police, and the temporary loss of his gun and badge as well as an administrative assignment. He wondered if Saunders, too, had tried the fare.

An expensive gold wedding band remained undisturbed on Saunder's finger. The carved initials HS and JS conjured up the wife, a beauty no doubt, a blonde like Jean Harlow or Mae West. He wondered about any children; being a father himself, Papo often feared not being there for his little girls. A wallet still had fifty dollars. It all intrigued him. More questions would be asked, but by the boys in Homicide, not him, for his beat was vice. And besides, he was going on vacation.

He watched his partner and best friend, Martin Lanza, stop to talk to Pietri from Homicide. Tall and slim, and for that reason called El Flaco, Martin still looked as he did when they first met ten years before, except for a sprinkle of gray now dotting hair once completely black. Their beat was the fringes of Condado Beach, where they worked the tourist section in plain clothes, keeping the pick pockets, pimps, and prostitutes a respectable distance from the new hotels. El Flaco wore his customary white suit and a plain blue tie. Papo hated suits and thought his preference for dungarees and comfortable *guayaberas* one reason promotion eluded him.

El Flaco came over.

"So what'd you find out, Sergeant Lanza?" Papo said. They'd discovered they'd both lived in New York early in their careers and spoke English, sometimes annoying their colleagues. "Who is he?"

"A *Yanqui* lawyer from Chicago. Buying land for his client, Papo." Martin explained he worked for a canning company from Chicago investing in Puerto Rico. They needed the property of a Senora Dominguez, a widow. Saunders offered good money. Even the Puerto Rican government pressured her, wanting the jobs Illinois Canning would create. She was coming around, despite a house full of memories. Two nephews, sole heirs, didn't want her to sell. Saunders had been close to a deal.

So what does the brilliant Captain think?"

"Pietri thinks it's somebody who didn't want the deal carried through. A relative, maybe. The senora's nephews had a stake in it. He's pursuing that angle."

"What about his out-of-court activities?"

"We talked to the hotel staff. The man liked to swim every night. Had a whore he was pumping regularly."

21

"I'll pick her up," Papo said playfully. "I know every *puta* working this precinct. Your captain may not know how to pick up a prostitute, proper gentleman that he is."

"You're too hard on Captain Pietri. Watch it or he'll cut your balls off. You're temporarily assigned to Homicide. The vacation's on hold." El Flaco said Papo would look for the whore and report to Pietri. After questioning the lowlife, Papo would then talk to tourists, as he spoke the best English in the department. Pietri wanted a report tomorrow morning.

"Tomorrow morning? He's optimistic."

"I'm telling you what he told me. I'm leaving, Papo. My orders are in. They're sending me to Penuelas in the south in a couple of days. I think I'm going to like it there. I have to clean out my things. Then I have to get back to Pietri."

"I'm going to miss you, Martin."

They agreed to meet the next evening at the Cafe Sazon, an old haunt on the beachfront. El Flaco warned him not to step on toes and left. Lifting the sheets, Papo took another look at the body. He'd seen Saunders strolling through the beach area and wondered who else might've seen him, too. Did he bring about his own death, or did it come unwittingly from external circumstances, like waves from the sea that rolled against the base of the sea wall surrounding old San Juan? The wall pushed them back.

Papo held back the tides of social misfits rolling up against the tourists, a life once envisioned differently.

CHAPTER 6

"I went up to Howard's room one night," the whore Lupita told Papo after he rounded her up near the beach on the Condado with information supplied by the hotel manager. He interrogated her in the modern, spacious police headquarters in the New San Juan.

"How'd you meet him?" he asked, his large black eyes probing her pretty hazel ones.

"The hotel people made the arrangements," she continued, the hazel eyes meeting his without shame or remorse. "They provide that service for their guests, you know." She winked. A fine looking, thin white woman with high cheekbones, light brown hair and a funny, upturned nose and pointed cheek, she explained calmly and without remorse as she filed her nails. "Slept with him that night. He asked I be only with him during his stay in San Juan."

"Where'd you go when not in bed?"

"Took me dancing at the *El Tropicolo* night club. These gringos have no rhythm, you know." She smiled. "I had to lead him. He faked the steps well.

23

Took me to dinner. We walked on the beach, mostly. He went swimming by himself, for the most part out in the lagoon."

"Pay you well?"

"None of your business," the hazel eyes rose indignantly."

"See anybody following him?"

"No ... wait. There was one fellow, a slender man with a moustache. Came close to us in the casino. Had a gold tooth."

"Why does he stand out? "

"Don't know. Saw him two or three times. Got a feeling he was studying us, for some reason."

Papo jotted this down in his notebook. "Don't disappear. We may have to call you in again."

"This time I worked for free. I'll charge for my service next time."

"No, you'll work for free."

Lupita was clean—of murder, anyhow, and trafficked only in sex.

He next interviewed the old wrinkled cab driver with the drooping gait who took Saunders on legal errands. "At your service, Officer," he said when asked to sit. He doffed his cap respectfully and held it nervously in his hands during the interrogation.

Where'd you take the departed?"

"On his legal errands. Went to the offices of the Puerto Rican government, mostly. Took him and his whore places."

"Which whore?"

"The pretty one with the up turned nose and pointy chin. Never did find out her name."

"Where else?"

Took him on his fishing trips and to the casino."

"What you talk about?"

"He spoke little Spanish and me, less English. Just enough to get him to his destinations."

"See anybody around him?

"Saw lots of people."

"Think. Anybody seem out of place?"

The cab driver thought. "Wait there was one man—tall, slender man with a moustache. Pompadour. Saw him a couple of times, in fact, hanging around the casino and on the dock when I dropped him off on one of his fishing trips seemed out of place."

Papo perked up. "Think hard."

"Yes, saw him later up close. Asked him for a cigarette. Smiled, flashed a gold tooth, and gave it to me."

"What brand?"

"Marlboro."

"Thank you. You can go now. We may call you back."

The ship captain kept on a mariner's cap decorated with anchor when called. "Took him fishing a couple of times. Didn't catch much. Somebody caught him." He smirked.

Papo probed but got nothing else out of the old sea dog, his sunburned face weathered by sea and sun, hard and resentful. "See a tall, slender man with a Pompadour?"

"No."

"Try to remember."

"I greeted Saunders on my boat. Saw nobody outside. Can I go now?" he asked, annoyed. "I'm losing money."

"You're free to go. You may have to come back."

He got up, angry, and left without ceremony.

The hotel staff revealed little, though the troubling case of the missing busboy-bartender gnawed at Papo. Was it another tourist? None of the mostly gringo guests had much to say either, and Papo's sixth sense said no. Did it relate to his business in the States?

Papo eliminated Dona Dominguez' nephews, although Cesar Pietri conducted the interrogation, separately, with their lawyers present. Papo watched from the side. Two spoiled rich boys who loved women, booze, and casinos and quickly squandered an inheritance acquired slowly by a dead father. Although he was opposed to their aunt's dealings, their interrogation convinced Papo they lacked the heart and motive for murder.

"And where were you on the night of the murder?" Pietri asked.

"I was with my mistress," the first nephew insisted, looking Pietri in the eye. Fat and clean shaven, he wore, like his brother, an expensive white tuxedo when they'd both been pulled out of the casino. "You can call her in. She'll back my story. I'll just ask you be discrete in this matter. I also have a wife."

"Mistresses do lie," Pietri said. "But we'll talk to her. Of course, you could've hired somebody to kill him."

"You'll have to take my word I did no such thing."

The second nephew also well fed and also with a clean upper lip, acted cool and collected when interrogated separately. He took long drags from an expensive English cigarette through a gold filter and blew out rings of smoke with his answers. He'd been at the Tapia Theater the night of the murder, as Pietri later corroborated. The second nephew also repeated calmly he'd not hired anybody to do the job. Neither owned pistols; both claimed they'd never fired a gun.

Despite their lawyers' protestations, Pietri held them under suspicion of murder.

In police headquarters the following day Papo examined files of criminals recently arrested. Under the comfort of its overhead, electrical fans, he went through mug shots of the *putas*, pickpockets, perverts, gamblers, bootleggers, confidence men, and narcotics dealers arrested the last five years in San Juan. Papo personally arrested some of them, and he hoped a picture might trigger a buried memory. Somebody saw something in the Condado area the night Howard Saunders died. But nobody slender with a gold tooth and Pompadour jumped out. He placed his notebook back in his pocket. Rubbing his large eyes after methodically studying the pictures, he knew none of San Juan's low life killed Howard Saunders. He returned all the mug shots to their metal cabinets.

And after talking to yet more tourists, he discovered that three different people had seen a slender man with a mustache and gold tooth around the crime scene. Two prostitutes placed him near the rocks. One of the *putas* also saw Howard Saunders.

On the wall of police headquarters, Papo studied a photo of Governor Luis Munoz Marin, next to a photo of President Harry S. Truman. In profile, the Governor's long nose jutted out prominently. His slicked, dark hair combed to the side and a wisp of a mustache gave him the appearance of a benign Adolph Hitler, or perhaps a more serious Charlie Chaplain. He'd learned from department gossip that the Governor himself followed the investigation and Papo concluded murdered gringo lawyers bad for business investment. "Only time he cares is when they kill Americans bringing money bags."

Pietri pressed him early for the report the next day. "It's not ready," Papo told him, adding none of the low life around the Condado did it. "They'd have taken the wallet," he explained. "Wasn't a tourist, and not the nephews. Let them go. There's a slender man out there with a mustache. The *putas* told me. Look for him."

"Don't stick your face too deeply into this investigation, lover boy. You've stuck it already in the wrong holes. I'll decide who we'll look for. I want a report. Then you're through with me. You go on vacation, then back to vice."

"I've done penance for that sin, Captain. Don't mean to disrespect you, but you have no right speaking to me that way. I've put in my time in this department, and I've done my job and have always followed orders."

"Not always, Obregon. Don't protest too much. Don't ask questions. Don't want to know about these *putas* or I'll bring you up on insubordination charges." He walked away.

Cesar Pietri's words stunned him. In Pietri's tone, Papo read more than an assertion of rank, and a raking over his shame with the whore Manuela. It carried an arrogance born of a lighter shade of skin, a straighter chin, and a nose chiseled more finely than Papo's own rough hewed features. It came from schools attended closed to the lower classes—and social circles advantageous to promotion in the department.

The authorities, Papo knew, tolerated prostitution. Like sugar, tobacco, and coffee, Puerto Rican women comprised another commodity sought by tourists and locals. So long as whores remained on the fringes of El Condado and the shantytowns, they were safe. But the police rounded them up once they spilled into areas that raised the public ire.

Being part of this investigation would prove his worth in this ungrateful department and allow him to take control of his life. But seeing how the higher-ups ignored the facts puzzled him. A man was seen near the murder site, a tall, slender man with a mustache. Homicide called him a John after a whore, or maybe one of Dona Dominguez' nephews, but Papo knew better. They certainly weren't slender. With the many slender men with mustaches in Puerto Rico, he'd be difficult to find.

Finding the missing busboy would be easier. The hotel staff accounted for its whereabouts that night. The busboy quit two days before the murder and disappeared.

That evening, he got together with Martin Lanza for a last supper. Martin, leaving in a couple days for his new post in Penuelas, met him at the Cafe Sazon by the sea on the fringes of the Condado.

Like a good deal of new San Juan, the Cafe Sazon quickly rose out of cement and concrete. A few seashells and tropical landscapes decorated its walls and transformed it into a cozy haunt. Papo studied the few natives and the American tourists and servicemen sitting comfortably in leather seats and sipping Daiquiris and piña coladas. They listened to the current love songs of the tropics, mixed with dated big band sounds from the States coming from the jukebox. He observed furtively the *gringa* women in long skirts and bobby sox.

He shared with Martin his hunch the slender man was tied to the murder. He knew the identity of the busboy but couldn't reveal it to Pietri or his best friend, Martin.

"What's this dead gringo to you?" Martin shrugged it off. "Submit your report. Throw it on Pietri's lap."

"This is my chance to prove myself in this department, Martin. I'm telling you, three different people saw a slender man with a mustache and gold tooth around the crime scene. Two prostitutes placed him near the rocks. One of the *putas* also saw Howard Saunders. The whore he was pumping recalled seeing him. So did the cab driver."

"Let it go. Eat your food, already."

"Shit, Martin, try to understand."

"Eat your food."

Papo tasted the rice and beans with avocado salad, then savored morsels of richly spiced roast pork. The plantains he spread liberally with *mojo*, the white garlic sauce he loved, before washing them down with three bottles of beer.

Martin ate half a ham and cheese sandwich and ordered fried plantains. Eating only two, he left the rest to Papo, who finished them for him. He glanced at the newspaper, the English language *San Juan Star.* "The Americans are beating the Communists, Papo. They say the Chinese army's across the border in Manchuria. If they cross the Yalu River into North Korea, World War Three may start right then and there."

Papo glanced at the headlines. Somehow, the Korean "police action," as the papers dubbed the war, seemed far away and unimportant. He couldn't imagine the world going to war over Korea." I see my Yankees won again," he changed the conversation.

"The election's coming," Martin said.

Papo said nothing. A Republican, he wanted Puerto Rico to be a state of the union, the forty-ninth, though he feared Alaska and Hawaii would get there first. Martin opposed statehood—and independence—favoring the island's status as an American territory. "Support Governor Luis Munoz Marin and the Popular Democrats. Your family does. You'll go places in the department … But tell me, how are things at home?"

Papo remained silent. Martin probed.

"Strained," Papo finally offered. His wife Marisol spoke little and refused to sleep with him since his affair with the prostitute.

"Tell me about it. Manuela was her name, right?"

"She worked the fringes of El Condado. One night she appeared, coiled around a tree."

"You should've kept walking."

"I did. She asked me for the time. I gave it to her. But she kept appearing night after night." Papo described her alluring, diaphanous dresses pressed tightly against dark skin. Her curly hair, straightened with pomade, seemed to shine. The large, dark eyes probed his seductively. She moistened her red lips.

He stopped one night and talked to this country girl not long removed from the mountains. She lived in a shanty on the outskirts of San Juan and there he bedded her, knowing the possible consequences, and incomprehensively he found himself falling in love. He, a married man with small daughters. Although no stranger to lust, he'd thought himself the master of his feelings.

29

A police officer called to crack down on prostitutes, he shouldn't have gone farther.

Evil tongues told Marisol.

Martin, who'd counseled him during the ordeal, suggested church and a priest and sermonized that men were allowed but one woman. When they strayed, they might be forgiven—but they needed to seek this forgiveness.

Papo no longer had religion but hoped for forgiveness.

"Be gentle with Marisol. Spend more time at home. Win back her love. Forgive and forget this girl. God will judge her. Healing will begin."

Papo mulled this *consejo* over, like the good advice Martin had always imparted.

"Only wish we had more time, Papo. Wish I could take you with me to Penuelas."

Calling the waiter over, Martin started to pay the check and left a dime tip.

Papo stopped him. "It's on me." He gave the waiter a dollar and told him to keep the quarter change.

"Still extravagant," his partner chided.

Outside, Martin added last-minute *consejos* and promised to stay in touch. He again admonished he do his job and not step on toes, adding a last warning against young whores. "Leave them to rich men and American soldiers. Remember, I'm your friend, Officer Obregon." The two embraced. Martin stood at attention and saluted.

He returned the salute and they parted.

Papo felt a strong tropical breeze that relieved the oppressive heat across the old fortified city of San Juan but not the turmoil in his head. He watched the sun slowly melt behind the distant line where the tropical skies met the blue waters of the Caribbean. But the scent of the sea had grown stale and even the whistling chants of *coquis.*

He again cursed his enemies and his basic honesty. No, he'd not rise in the department. Forget Homicide. Yes, some how he'd lost control of his life, which had been shaped by forces beyond his control. Convinced his enemies in the department impeded his advancement, he believed other policemen, better connected ones, got promoted. His statehood politics made him as much an outcast in the politically sensitive police department as the fanatical nationalists. One needed to be a member of the Popular Democrats to advance these days. For unlike his grandfather and uncles, and unlike a nationalist brother, he favored statehood for Puerto Rico.

And he took no dirty money, like others who looked away from wrongdoing and performed favors for extra pay. Shunning this practice made him, ironically, a pariah of sorts. Although his father's side helped, he came from wrong social circles on his mother's side. His chances of making homicide and rising in the department receded.

But this challenge out of the ordinary pleased him. The vacation would wait.

And he'd mend relations with his wife Marisol.

But to further complicate it came this slender man with the mustache.

And the busboy.

"Where's Julio Obregon," he asked the Hilton's manager. The officious manager in a tie and shirt looked puzzle. "Don't know. He quit without giving notice."

That busboy was his half-brother. This information he'd leave out of the report.

CHAPTER 7

Goyo and Julito hid for two days in the hills of the south. Julito knew the way to an abandoned shack off a dirt road, a few miles from Ponce. They covered the car in thick foliage, erasing its tire marks from the road. There they awaited word from the barber Arcadio.

They found two sleeping mats and an old wooden table in the shack, along with bread, hard salami, and warm bottles of soda. An outhouse provided for their needs and a small pump turned out water with exertion of muscle power. They arrived, exhausted from their long drive, before noon the day after killing Howard Saunders. Having eaten, they'd slept several hours, venturing out only at night.

They'd spoken sparingly at first, mostly about directions, then about cars, American movies, and women. On the second day, Julito told him he was seeing a young woman named Lola with a small baby boy from another man.

Goyo mentioned he was married, but not that his wife, Consuelo, had left him and gone to New York with their small daughter, Ivelisse.

Julito expounded his political philosophy. The Americans would be kicked out and the new order would begin. Firm, but benevolent Latin authoritarianism would then guide their ignorant countrymen, so corrupted by Nordic values. "The new political order would shed them," Julito vowed. "The wealth will be equally distributed."

Goyo didn't ask how. He understood authoritarianism from the time his Uncle Justo, his mother Altagracia's brother, forever pointing his finger in Goyo's face, proclaimed authority over their household when Goyo defied him. He didn't know what Nordic meant, but assumed it related to gringos. "Wealth will never be distributed equally," he said. "You'll always have rich and poor."

"But national sovereignty spreads out the resources of the nation more equitably." Julito continued to rant about economics, imperialism, and the exploitation of one nation by others in history.

Goyo said little. Intellectuals, he thought, always ran the sociological and political shit they studied in college. He was happy when Julito finally shut up.

On the third day before dawn, a messenger arrived from the barber Arcadio with word Don Pedro would see them. Julito drove.

Morning rose through the mountains, and Goyo saw the sun's rays filter slowly through the brush. Rain had fallen on the sierra and trees pregnant with plantains grew in abundance. The aroma of moist earth and the scent of coffee beans ripening on their vines filled the air.

"It's a bitch getting through these mountains," Julito said.

The *jibaros*, the farmers of the mountains, risen early to the music of the cocks, rode to the fields on horses and donkeys. Straw hats protected them from the relentless sun. Their sashes held the sharpened *machetes* their ancestors used to clear the brush and earn a living from the land.

"Get the fuck out of the way!" Julito shouted. "These *jibaros* are slow." He turned to Goyo. "When the revolution comes we have to modernize. We're still walking in the nineteenth century and we better start running if we want to catch up to the world."

The *jibaros* pulled to the side to make way for the lumbering car. They stared curiously at them, holding the reins of the animals awkwardly. "Good morning, brothers," Goyo greeted. Julito ignored them. "Yes, we must modernize," Goyo agreed. He'd been to New York and Havana and knew his countrymen were behind. But he resented Julito's city airs. "Don't disrespect them. An offended *jibaro* can cut your balls off before you can cock your pistol."

Julito said nothing.

A rich college boy, Goyo thought. "Probably never struggled in life." To him, nature offered a mere obstacle to be overcome on the way to the hacienda and the *jibaros,* mere statistics and sociological abstractions.

But for Goyo, the *jibaros* and the mountains were home, his roots, like the fruitful plantains, firmly planted here. Nearby his father, Don Hortencio Tejada, seeded the land that gave birth to Goyo and his siblings: Arturo, the eldest, and the girls, Tanya and Tata. When his father Hortencio sold the land to the sugar company the family moved to Ponce where his father died.

From his brother Arturo, a nationalist, he learned to use a .38 pistol. Police gunned down Arturo in a rally in Ponce one Sunday. But the guns skills served Goyo well. Running bootleg rum and in Cuba, he learned of the lucrative marijuana and cocaine trade.

When the police stopped him one day with a shipment of liquor and arrested him, the party and Don Pedro helped. So when Don Pedro asked through intermediaries to kill an American engineer, he did.

The engineer worked outside Caguas. Goyo staked out his movements for several days from the vantage point of a small hill near other rocks the engineer surveyed for a road, never getting close to him. Goyo made out his cowboy hat and boots. He shot him as he left work late one night, still feeling a small measure of remorse, but less than he'd felt when he shot the rival bootlegger. The party gave him money and smuggled him to Florida, then New York, where he stayed weeks. When he returned, his wife had fled to New York with his daughter. He vowed to find her.

The party gave meaning to his life and he felt he belonged to something.

They arrived at an old Spanish hacienda in the mountains. Arcadio waited for them in the courtyard, clean shaven and odd out of his barber's tunic. "You did your job well. Was it clean?"

"Yes," Julito said. "Nobody saw us, except a couple of whores."

"Good. Don Pedro will see you soon. Wait upstairs. Make yourselves comfortable. We'll talk later."

They waited in Don Pedro's cluttered study, a large table strewn with writings in the middle and on the side, worn law books stacked haphazardly on a shelf gathering dust.

Don Pedro Albizu Campos entered and greeted them. "Good to see you safe. You've served the cause well."

"Good to see you, *Maestro*," Goyo shook his hand.

"*Maestro.*" Julito kissed Don Pedro's hand.

He seemed gaunt and thin to Goyo, who knew him from the time he came to his brother Arturo's wake. Goyo remembered a younger, glowing Albizu, immaculate in a suit and bowtie. Now, he wore slacks, a white *guayabera* and slippers. His brown skin had lost its luster and appeared ashen. The bushy mustache and coarse hair, slicked down with pomade, was almost white now. Age lined his face after his time at the federal prison in Atlanta, Georgia. Inciting the demonstrations leading to the Ponce Massacre, where Arturo died had exacted its toll.

But fire lit his eyes, which glowed undimmed, like the first time Goyo heard him speak years ago. The three sat around the table and chatted about old times. The pleasantries done, Don Pedro grew serious.

"The struggle begins soon." He waved his right hand emphatically as he always did. "We'll stop this phony election. A win by the Popular Democrats places in grave danger our people's way of life. I have another favor to ask. A shipment needs to be picked up and delivered—arms from governments abroad sympathetic to our cause. We won't allow the elections to take place. We'll hit police precincts and government buildings."

"We rise?" Julito asked, his eyes lighting up. "No more legal nonsense, *Maestro?*"

"We rise. My lawyer days are over." Don Pedro spoke of Harvard Law School and his journey through American courts and the League of Nations seeking self-determination for Puerto Rico. "The haves control the courts. The have-nots must seize their own destiny." He turned to Julito. "Arcadio will instruct you. Now excuse us. Gregorio and I must talk."

"Long live a free Puerto Rico." Julito thrust up his right arm and hand in salute and left.

Don Pedro turned to Goyo. "I have another request—a mission calling for sacrifice." He paused.

"I'll do my duty, Maestro. Where?"

"New York."

"New York?"

"Yes. You've been there?"

"Yes. My wife's there.

"I didn't know."

"She left me and took my daughter."

"I see. You will take the struggle to the *Yanqui* homeland. Arcadio will explain. In New York speak only to Osvaldo Cotto and Manuel Landia. Tell them to unleash Operation *Huracan* after the attacks here. Liquidate '*El Hombre Verdadero*'. When the time comes they'll explain. We'll need your prowess with a gun. Tell them under no circumstances to come to Puerto Rico. Their job—and yours—is there."

"Operation *Huracan* after the first attack. Liquidate *El Hombre Verdadero*. Who is this *Hombre Verdadero, Maestro*?"

"An enemy of the Republic of Puerto Rico. Cotto and Landia will reveal his identity."

"And Operation *Huracan*?"

"That too they'll explain. Go, Gregorio. Arcadio will instruct you. Long live a free Puerto Rico." Don Pedro embraced him.

"*Viva Puerto Rico libre*," Goyo, too, raised up his arm in a stiff salute.

Downstairs, Arcadio waited. "You leave in three days from Isla Verde Airport and will land at Idlewild Airport in New York. Julito will get instructions about the arms pick-up. You'll hitch a ride with him back to San Juan tomorrow. Two more men will accompany you. When you get there, go to the travel agency on the marina. Ask for the ticket under the name of Rafael Lullanda. One of our operatives has the ticket for you, and false identity papers. There will be five hundred dollars. You'll get an address in the Bronx where you can go. More instructions will follow you there. Questions?"

"No."

TO KILL A PRESIDENT

"Then good-bye, Gregorio. Good luck. Long live a free Puerto Rico."

"Viva Puerto Rico libre." Goyo left with Julito.

A ticket to New York would take him closer to Consuelo and his daughter—with five hundred dollars in his pocket. He'd serve the cause already and wondered how much loyalty he still owed Don Pedro, no longer the strong, dynamic figure who had inspired him at that first rally but a fragile, broken man. He'd again serve his leader and the party and deliver the message to the faithful in New York. But he'd also serve himself.

CHAPTER 8

The Third Avenue El dropped Osvaldo Cotto on Eighty-Sixth Street and Third Avenue in Yorktown and he walked, as he'd done these eleven years, to the Achilles Metal Works on First Avenue and Eighty-Second Street. There, he took off his tweed sports jacket and sweater, adjusted rimless glasses, which his coworkers said gave him a scholarly appearance. He donned an apron and removed his gray fedora, revealing a rapidly receding hairline.

He'd give his boss Mr. Rifkin notice today, after work. The old Jew had treated him well. Mr. Rifkin called him a master and considered him his best worker, polishing as many as seven hundred metal pieces a day. But polishing handles for ladies' pocketbooks didn't serve his purpose in life, although it did pay a decent wage that allowed for a nice apartment in the South Bronx's comparative affluence. His fellow Puerto Ricans lived largely in poorer tenements of East Harlem, Hell's Kitchen, and the Lower East Side.

Yet a higher purpose called—the cause of the Puerto Rican people coming before all else.

He'd soon tell his wife and two stepdaughters he was leaving again—perhaps for good—and leave them a fair sum to live comfortably for a while. Then Ana and the girls would carry on without him. Perhaps they'd meet again in Puerto Rico—or in heaven.

Osvaldo had secretly begun emptying his locker when told to begin planning for *Huracan*. Sunday, he'd meet with Manuel Landia, Nationalist Party chief in New York, to begin finalizing plans.

For now, he removed a blue Pan American Airlines travel bag and placed in it a calendar from Melendez' Bodega on East 138th Street in the Bronx with a tropical landscape, the first nine months torn off. He also packed a print of the mountains of his native Jayuya, careful no one noticed. And two books, a Spanish translation of Carlye's *History of the French Revolution* and one of Gibbon's *The Decline and Fall of the Roman Empire.*

Drills and small tools purchased out of his own pocket he'd already packed.

With his coffee and a butter roll, he took in the customary pleasantries with the other metal polishers.

"Morning, Mr. Cotto," the mostly Eastern Europeans and Jews greeted him with a respect not granted other workers, who went by first names. They told him he resembled a college professor more than a metal polisher. As he was white, some were surprised he was Puerto Rican.

As he'd done these eleven years, for eight hours, save for a half-hour break for a lunch of white rice and beans kept warm in a thermos, he buffed metal and other fixtures for women's pocketbooks and compacts for makeup. Proud of his skill, he normally tamed the simple technology required, managing the electrically powered buffer applied expertly to unpolished, clouded items: chrome, nickel, enamel, supplied by runners wheeling in steady bins of jangling metal, who then collected his finished pieces, transmuted into shiny works of art. But today, concentration proved hard and he slowed down. As the cacophony of machines whizzed and vibrated incessantly around him, so did his mind with jangled thoughts.

And he began polishing still clouded ideas into a well-buffered plan.

Osvaldo had recruited three men. One had served in the *Yanqui* army and could fire a pistol. Two others could not, but Landia had told him over the phone the party was sending a fourth man to teach them. Osvaldo himself could handle a gun. They would kill the President of the United States to publicize the plight of the Puerto Rican people. He bore the American people no ill will. But they needed to know how their government, the bankers, and the sugar companies treated Puerto Ricans. Killing their President would show them and set a panic through the country. Puerto Rico could then break away, an independent country, to seek its own destiny.

He knew the President took morning walks through the capital. Perhaps Osvaldo and his men could surprise him during one of these walks before his guards could react. And he'd read in the papers Truman worked in the White House, chauffeured back and forth to Blair House, where he lived while they refurbished the White House. They could rush his car during one of these commutes.

At five, he placed the last of the handles in the collection bin and removed his apron. Through the locker's mirror, he studied his receding hairline as he combed it. His hands brushed back his large ears. Straightening his tie, he donned the sweater, sport jacket, and fedora and sought out the old man.

Mr. Rifkin, in the white shirt and black suspenders never shorn, made the rounds after talking to some potential buyers.

"Yes, Osvaldo?"

"I have something to tell you. I have an emergency back home in Puerto Rico. I'm afraid I have to leave. In two weeks."

"You're quitting on me."

"I'm sorry."

"The pre-Christmas rush is on. Orders are picking up. Why are you doing this to me?"

Rifkin had given him a job, treating him almost like a father, and he felt sorry he was quitting. "Sorry," he repeated.

"You Puerto Ricans are irresponsible. You ran back home after making a few *pesos*."

Anger began to overtake Osvaldo. "Insult me, my family, or my mother long in her grave, but don't insult my country."

"You don't even have a country," the old Jew dared. "You're a colony."

Osvaldo stared long and hard at the old man. "We have a country, and we'll be free."

Rifkin proclaimed America his country and said he'd never return to his native Russia.

Osvaldo contained his anger, picked up his blue travel bag, and left.

CHAPTER 9

Chief A. B. Howland drank his third cup of coffee of the morning in his Treasury Building office, sleeves rolled up and tie loosened. He put down a finished a report for his boss, the Secretary of the Treasury, on a large oak desk and picked up a folder, marked PRS, summarizing the latest threats on the President. The Protective Research Bureau also collected intelligence and communiqués from FBI and other law enforcement sources.

One unsigned letter from Iowa scolded the President for recognizing a Jewish state and wished all Jews finished off. Such comments had become common since Mr. Truman's recognized Israel in 1948. But this one added, "I'll finish you, too. And I have just the oven to do it, Harry Jewman." Agents in the Midwest were already tracking it down, as well as another, also tinged with threat, protesting the bombing of Hiroshima and adding that history would condemn him for this act of genocide.

"Don't give a good goddamn about history," Mr. Truman once told him. "Did what was right to protect our boys, who the Japs would've slaughtered if we'd invaded. Saved a lot of those damn Jap bastards, too."

Another, addressed to Harry "Stupid" Truman, also hinted at retribution.

The Chief culled through reports on communists, American Nazis, and their progenitors, the old German Bund members, anarchists, and southern hate groups unhappy with Mr. Truman's integration of white and Negro servicemen in the armed forces.

One FBI communiqué perked him up. In New York City, the Puerto Rican nationalists were stirring and informants reported increased meetings, anti-American rhetoric, and condemnation of the President. Puerto Rico came under the secret service's radar back in the thirties after nationalists assassinated an American police chief and attempted to kill a judge. Their leader, one Pedro Albizu Campos, hurled verbal attacks and threats upon Mr. Roosevelt when jailed back in the thirties. After a decade in jail, he now roamed free, released four years earlier in '46. In Puerto Rico itself, though, the nationalists seemed quiet. This fact he found puzzling. *They're too quiet*, he thought. He knew of a coming election there for delegates to a constitutional convention to determine the island's future political status. *Damn people. We should just cut them lose and tell them to fend for themselves.*

He needed to infiltrate his own men into their meetings.

But right now they were tied up protecting Margaret Truman, the President's daughter, making a second appearance on Ed Sullivan's *Toast of the Town* show soon. The "really big show" formed the number one topic of conversation in White House, secret service and even Department of the Treasury circles. Everybody was getting this new commodity called TV. The Chief, too, finally bought one for the performance. But the security nightmares these shows posed kept him up at night. Soon she'd be back in Blair House and his agents, rather than watch the crowd watching Margaret Truman at the CBS studios, could watch Puerto Rican Nationalists.

He needed more men. Thirty more men would do the job for the American people. The Chief sipped his coffee and mentally tallied the dollars and cents for more agents, administrative assistants, and slightly higher operational costs. Congress needed to allocate $200,000, and he vowed to pester the lawmakers until he got it. "Can't protect presidents *and* run anti-counterfeiting operation on a shoe string," he'd told his boss, the Secretary of the Treasury.

"Don't know what the hell is wrong with those cheap assholes in Congress. They better cough up the money or we're going to lose another president one of these days."

The Chief even asked Mr. Truman to put in a good word for the secret service with his old pals in Congress. After all, only he, of all men, saw the President of the United States at will, without appointment or prior notice. "Take your cards and play them," an inner voice said. He picked up one of five phones on the oak desk and pressed the intercom.

"Yes, Chief," came the feminine reply.

"Barbara, get the Secretary's office on the phone."

"Yes, Chief."

"Tell them the report's ready."

In a few minutes, the phone rang again. "Chief, I spoke to the Secretary's office. He's been detained in the Federal Reserve. They'll call as soon as he gets back."

He put down the phone, next to a picture of a dead wife and a wedding photo of his daughter Julie and her Air Force captain, now a major. Along with the limited bric-a-brac needed to project a proper sense of power, he permitted himself only an old baseball from his playing days, yellow after twenty-five years.

"What could be so damn important in the Federal Reserve?" he wondered. He spun the taut, round cowhide slowly in his palm His resume boasted none of the politician's arts: over the shoulder whispers, intrigue, lobbying, backslapping, horn tooting and sudden secret meetings. He'd always played by the rules and stepped on few toes. He needed to step on a lot more and stop playing nice.

The latest report by the White House contractor Mr. McAdams spoke of costlier renovations taking longer than expected. Just after the '48 election two years earlier, a piano sank through the floor of the family sitting room while the First Daughter rehearsed for a concert. Only after this potential tragedy did the Chief realize the serious structural defects plaguing the presidential home.

These delays were bad news. While Mr. Truman, the First Lady, and their daughter loved the cozy mansion, the security problems it posed and the growing lunchtime crowds kept the Chief up at night.

He got up and stretched, hands on hips, and looked out the window at the Washington, D.C., panorama. In the distance he saw the Capitol, the Mall, and the White House. Yes, the White House.

"I want to see the people and want them to see me," Mr. Truman's command echoed constantly in his mind.

But at least he'd finally shaken the physical malaise that lingered after his recent return from Wake Island, where he'd accompanied the President, gone there, halfway around the world, to meet with General Douglas Macarthur.

He sat down again and glanced next at the yellow files stamped CONFIDENTIAL with daily progress reports from the six branches of the secret service. The folder marked COUNTERFEITING SECTION grew bulkier each day. Counterfeiting was on the rise in America, and the economic threat it posed to the nation was one priority. Four other folders held pressing matters. But he examined first the one marked WHITE HOUSE DETAIL. It contained his foremost concern: the protection of the President of the United States and his family.

Two memos from the White House Detail summarized the President's activities for that day and outlined the following day's schedule. Tomorrow, Sunday, the President went to church and caught up on sleep, though it mentioned the growing crowds outside Blair House and Mr. Truman's continued practice of shaking all hands.

Chief Howland put down the folder. A drop of sweat rolled off his closely cropped hair and fell on the desk. From his back pocket, he removed a neatly folded handkerchief, wiping the short, gray crew cut.

In his years with the secret service, the Chief had brushed against assassins, cutthroats, and forgers. Once a gang of counterfeiters he infiltrated discovered him and nearly killed him. But protecting Harry Truman posed his biggest challenge.

He discovered how serious a task one eventful morning in 1945, shortly after Mr. Roosevelt's death, when Mr. Truman disappearance act panicked the White House Detail, who discovered him later, taking a morning constitutional down Pennsylvania Avenue—alone. "Don't shield me like some goddamned cheap South American dictator from the next coup," Mr. Truman shot back when chastised.

Despite his misgivings, the Chief accommodated the President's morning strolls, and long ago stopped advising against them. He assigned four agents to accompany him, taking the precaution of sending an unmarked car with agents and machine guns to shadow the President—without Mr. Truman's knowledge.

He'd end the general laxity with security. The Chief would insist. No, he'd put his foot down and damn well insist. The presidential limousine would no longer stop so Mr. Truman could shake hands with friends. Or strangers.

The phone rang. "The Secretary canceled, Chief. They'll get back to you."

"Thank you, Barbara." He hung up. "Hmn. Goddamn him and his stupid fiscal affairs."

And again, in his mind, he saw Mr. Harding's mistress, Nan Britton, sneaking into the White House, escorted by his secret service colleagues. The young A. B. Howland's first job had been to look out for Mrs. Harding, should she suddenly appear at an inopportune time. And again he saw President Warren Harding's assassin as he had every day since 1923.

CHAPTER 10

St. Mary's Park provided a safe place for Osvaldo Cotton's secret Sunday meetings with Manuel Landia, who brought news from Puerto Rico. From a hilltop a respectful distance from the few picnickers and strollers out on a cool morning, Osvaldo surveyed the park's greenery, remembering his talk with his boss Mr. Rifkin.

"You don't even have a country," the old Jew's words rang in his head. Puerto Rico was a colony. "My country is America. I will never return to Russia," the Old man had continued. *As if anybody wanted to return to Stalin's shithole.*

Then he saw Landia climbing a pathway up the park in a black business suit and matching hat. Osvaldo lamented Landia always wore suits, whether chairing meetings, or, as in years past, defending clients in court before disbarred by the federal government for refusing military service during the war and doing time in prison for Selective Service violations.

Osvaldo, dressed in a windbreaker and Brooklyn Dodgers hat, saw clouds in the sky and awaited Landia's instructions, hopefully before rain infiltrated their meeting. Fear of wiretaps limited their telephone conversation to calls from public phones at designated times. From the hilltop, Osvaldo scanned for FBI agents and possible undercover Puerto Rican policemen surveying them. Under a microscope as they were, Landia should've dressed down and not bring attention in this working-class Bronx community.

When he got to the top, Landia caught his breath. "We move soon. Spoke to the barber Arcadio."

Osvaldo too needed to catch his breath. "When?"

"In under a month." He unbuttoned the jacket and loosened his tie. "To coincide with the elections back home first Tuesday in November. My gut says Don Pedro will move a day or two before. They'll disrupt the elections there." He swept the air with one hand and clasped his waist with the other. "We'll disrupt things here. The Barber is sending someone with instructions." Landia coordinated cells working on *Huracan*. Two worked in the open, organizing a mail drive to inactive members and another making picket signs for planned demonstrations in front of the United Nations and Congress.

Two others worked in secret.

One, led by Jose Robles, El Indio, would plant pipe bombs in populated New York venues. During the war, Indio trained for demolition, but drinking and brawling landed him not overseas but in the stockade. He hated the army and blamed the *Yanqui* officers for his troubles. Now, he assembled pipe bombs in a basement apartment in a Bronx tenement.Osvaldo coordinated the other cell. It would kill "El Hombre Verdadero"—the President of the United States. A man from Mayaguez who'd served in the *Yanqui* army in Panama and knew automatic weapons volunteered. Another, from Ponce, owned a car and would drive them to Washington. But the third, a family man with children, at first showed interest, but lately expressed doubts.

"Who's the Barber sending?"

"Gregorio Tejada. He'll join you."

Osvaldo knew that name. "Yes, he's good with a gun. Ladies' man. Lots of women trouble."

"Yes."

Tejada's latest ex-wife hailed from the town of Jayuya, like Osvaldo. "Heard of her parent's complaints."

"When I have more details, I'll give you a car to meet Tejada's plane," Landia continued. "I'm arranging for him to stay in a safe house here in the Bronx. Chucho Cabranes will cover the expenses."

Chucho, the party secretary-treasurer, worked the accounts and kept official—and secret—books. Osvaldo suspected he was a homosexual.

"And the guns?"

"I'll arrange to get them through a secret contact in the Spanish secret service. Chucho will work out the money. When they're ready, I'll contact you. I'll call a meeting after Tejada arrives. In the meantime, we'll stay in touch through the two public phones." They shook hands and Landia took his leave. Osvaldo saw him descend down the path and followed him before he disappeared into the park.

If not for stepdaughters, he'd put Tejada up in his own apartment, as he'd done Don Pedro after the Maestro's release from prison in 1946. But he'd not let this womanizer near the girls.

The threat of rain receding, Osvaldo walked down from the hill and sat on a park bench. He watched the picnickers, out in numbers now, and a pickup softball game had just started.

He'd do all the party commanded—including die for the cause. An attempt on Harry Truman was a suicide mission. After traveling to Washington, the four of them—or three—would cross paths with the President on one of the early morning walks he took in the capital. They had a shot. They themselves might die.

But he dreaded most telling Ana good-bye after their life together these eight years. He'd also leave the girls from her previous marriage. After a first, unfaithful wife in Puerto Rico, Ana had stuck by him. But something bigger than personal happiness called.

And staring out at St. Mary's greenery that hid for a few reflexive minutes the Bronx's intruding urban landscape, Osvaldo had visions of the land.

He saw his Papa ruined by *Yanqui* politicians in the pocket of the sugar interests that passed laws wiping out the market for Puerto Rican sugar. Debt ridden, his father, like other small farmers, lost the land to the Eastern Sugar Company and the *Yanqui* banks, which consolidated the small plots into huge, mechanized enterprises, reducing the need for labor.

51

And Osvaldo remembered the below subsistence wages paid by the new masters of the land. He and others migrated to the city. For him, hard work awaited. And a woman's infidelity. The party provided a home for him.

But now he had doubts about the men he'd recruited. Once, back in 1936, they'd been hungry—and angry at Colonel Francis Riggs' murder of their comrades. He never doubted Hiram and Elias' resolve, and they gunned down the Colonel. They were also angry in Ponce, back in 1937, where they gathered one Palm Sunday to again protest after the police quickly captured Hiram and Elias and murdered them in their San Juan headquarters without trial. Governor Winship and the American authorities cracked down on his nationalist brethren, jailing El Maestro Don Pedro.

That day, he'd counted fourteen policemen in gray who menaced the demonstrators with machine guns. An officer spoke to the large crowd gathered on the plaza on this Palm Sunday through a bullhorn. "This march is forbidden. Do not proceed."

Morales, a bespeckled parade organizer, came to the front of the marchers. "We'll stop here while we talk." Under a white flag, Morales and three others approached the police. After exchanging words, Morales returned. "Governor Winship has withdrawn the march permit and has ordered us to disband."

"Bullshit," they yelled. "Fuck them. Let's march."

The procession started and the crowd broke out in the national anthem *La Borinquena*. "*La tierra de Borinquen donde he nacido yo ...*" They sang first the conventional lyrics about Columbus' enchantment with the new land of *Borinquen*, as the original Taino Indians called Puerto Rico, and then the more militant lyrics extolling the *Borinquenos* to arise from their slumber and defend their rights. They had awakened. They were marching. They would defend their rights—and perhaps die for them.

"Look, more policemen," someone said. "On the side."

"More on the right."

A wall of gray now enveloped them.

Then the first shots sounded. Next to him on his right a man's head exploded like an overheated glass jar. Blood and gray brain matter oozed down his torso like spoiled marmalade. "Mother of God!" Osvaldo screamed.

Another bullet fell the man behind him. Somebody else dropped on his right. He heard screams.

"They're killing us, *companeros*. Stop!"

"No, onward, *carajo*. Show these lackeys and their *Yanqui* masters we're not afraid."

The march pressed on. More shots rang out. Marchers slipped on the blood now staining the cobbled streets. Total chaos broke. Osvaldo felt crushed glass beneath his feet. Morales' glasses. The march ended. Panic ensued. People ran. Several onlookers fell, including a woman, a bullet through her chest.

Osvaldo stopped and turned. He felt a sharp, burning sensation on his arm. He touched it and saw the blood staining his shirt. He slipped away. Sympathizers treated his wound.

Then came the exodus from Puerto Rico on a ship of the Marine Tiger line to New York. He mopped floors, washed dishes, and worked in factories under cold, impersonal bosses before the kindly Mr. Rifkin gave him a chance.

Now they some were no longer angry—or hungry—but well fed in New York.

But he was still angry.

A new day is coming, he thought, tears in his eyes. Although he'd not enter the Promised Land, he'd help bring it about.

CHAPTER 11

Papo began his search for his half-brother, Julito, in at the home of his brother's mother, widow of their common father. Papo's own black mother had served as their father's mistress. The snubs endured from Mary, the once slender, stern stepmother, now stout and matronly, lay in the past. Although she never sparked love in him, Papo had long extinguished his hate. Wrinkles hardened her once radiant face, now as white as flour, like the hair. Yet softer eyes greeted him, as well as a heart, once hardened by infidelity, now thawed.

"I haven't seen Julito in a while," Papo said. "Neither has the family. Been wondering where he is."

"Is he in trouble?"

"No, no," he lied. "Just want to see him and find out how he is."

"Your brother shows up whenever he wants for a meal, then disappears for stretches. I try to get him to talk about his activities, but he's always evasive."

"Do you know any of his friends?

"He's seeing a *dark*-skinned girl, Lola."

In the lowering of the eyes he read not just disapproval but the nuances of social pretension and racial superiority not yet shed.

"I see."

"Can I get you coffee?"

"Thanks," he forced a smile.

While his stepmother got the coffee, he pondered his brother's possible role in Saunder's murder. Julito was born after their father left Papo's mother, to return to his legitimate wife, Mary. Papo lived in New York at this time with his mother and stepfather after their father's death. His grandfather tried to unite the siblings when Papo returned, but though Papo bonded with his older brother, Lucho, who worked with his uncle in the printing shop, Julito remained distant and shunned him. Papo came to realize color and illegitimacy played a role. Although never developing emotional ties, Papo knew his brother's mind. Julito didn't live in the real world, but as a child, in a fantasy, now rekindled by college books and nationalist rhetoric.

When she came back with the coffee, he pressed on. "What about his other friends?"

"Let's see. There is a Federico and a Jose. Those are the only ones I know of. They're nationalists. He does talk about the nationalists and kicking out the Americans. We need the Americans and we've argued about that."

"Yes, I know," Papo said. "It's just a passing phase. He'll wake up one day."

Papo didn't tell her how he'd resented not only his politics but also his sibling's high allowance and stylish living, while he himself did with less. The nationalists provided an outlet for his brother's fantasies. Had he kept watch on Howard Saunders in the hotel? Yes, Papo was convinced, though he doubted he'd shot Saunders. Who did? The slender man with a mustache and gold tooth two prostitutes placed near the rocks? These thoughts he kept from his stepmother.

"Do you know the last names of this Federico and this Jose?"

She thought long and hard but couldn't come up with any.

"Any idea where they might be."

"At the university, I think.

They made more small talk, and then he thanked her and took his leave.

At the University of Puerto Rico's registrar's office, his badge gave him access to his brother's schedule. He took the precaution of taking off his New York Yankees cap, lest it offend the anti-American crowd there. Tracking down the professors, he discovered Julito hadn't attended classes in a while.

A suspicious sociology professor not only spoke of Julito's political views, but sympathized with them and questioned Papo's motive. "You look nothing like your brother."

Another, a bearded professor of literature enjoying a large meal at the faculty cafeteria, had no information either. He called him a Sepoy, a term unknown to Papo, who assumed it a negative term for police. In high-sounding language, the pompous old fool even suggested police had no business on a college campus.

"I keep order on this island, sir," Papo hit back.

"You oppress our people and do the bidding of your *Yanqui* paymasters."

"Good day, professor," Papo left. *Damn perfumados*, he thought, remembering his stepfather's term for useless intellectuals, after their preference for French colognes, who ran their mouths instead of doing honest work.

Students loafing in the student center also proved suspicious.

"What do you want with him, policeman?" an unpleasant fat girl with a crooked lip asked.

"I'm his brother."

"*You?* Ha."

None claimed to know of Julito's whereabouts. Nobody knew a friend named Federico. Many Joses studied there. He left.

They'd all be cutting sugar cane instead of classes without Americans, he thought. *Give them independence for a week and let them live on sociology and political science.*

After his long day, he drove home to Toa Alto. His wife, Marisol, gathered plantains outside their home. She turned, unceremoniously, and continued pulling them off the tree. Papo gave her a nod but got none in return. But at least she was still there, after threatening to leave him. His daughters Carla and Natalia ran out and kissed him.

"*Bendicion,*" they asked for their benediction in filial piety.

57

"May God bless you and the Virgin keep you," he gave it, kissing and tugging at the ponytails. The thought of losing his girls filled him with fear. Papo sensed their impatience and they broke his hug to run off and play.

In the bedroom, he unbuckled the ankle holster. The.38 service pistol never left his side except at home. He placed the holster in a closet's recess and locked it with a key always on his person inside the house. He washed and got a beer, downed it in three gulps, and opened another. In the living room, he sat in an easy chair with the newspaper, sipped the second, and lit a cigarette.

Marisol entered. "You want dinner?

He searched for a thaw in her demeanor but found none. "Yes." He yearned to talk but didn't know what to say.

He'd loved her at first sight when Martin Lanza introduced them at a policeman ball. He proposed the next day. "Think it through," Martin had cautioned. "Don't be rash." Martin often chided his impulsive nature. But her dark, sparkling eyes and warm smile filled him with love. In a nice dress, with makeup and combed hair, she still stimulated passion. In soiled aprons and unkempt hair, her plainness struck him, now that she rarely dressed. But taking her for granted, this woman who'd born him daughters and kept his house well scrubbed, he again realized how much he loved her. And though sorry he'd hurt her, he was even more sorry he couldn't express it.

The paper, full of the coming elections, said nothing about the murdered lawyer, a fact he found curious, and again he concluded dead American lawyers were bad for business.

In the dictionary, he looked up the word "Sepoy" and discovered it referred to native troops used by England in the nineteenth century to police their colony in India. "Son of a bitch," he thought.

His eldest daughter, Carla, called him for dinner. Papo ate two plates of rice and beans and four pork chops, with a heavy helping of fried plantains and garlic sauce. He washed it down with two more beers.

The girls ate slowly and sparingly, and only after prodding by their mother. Dark like their parents and maternal grandmother, they inherited the straight conquistador nose of the white Obregons.

"And what did you learn in school?" their *papi* asked. Looking at each other, their dimples rose playfully.

"Nothing," they declared in unison and laughed.

Papo laughed too, then got serious. "I'm going to drop in and talk to your teacher."

They too got serious. Later, he tucked them in and kissed them.

After washing, he went to the bedroom and climbed into bed, waiting for Marisol. She checked the girls, now sound asleep and readied herself for bed. Although he hoped she'd again sleep with him soon, he knew it'd not be tonight. She slipped under the covers in a couch on the opposite side of the room, shunning his bed since learning about the whore Manuela. "You won't stick it into me after where it's been," she'd declared then. It'd been more than a month—almost two. But at least he was grateful she still slept in the same room. And again, he pondered what had possessed him to be unfaithful.

Manuela still appeared to him in dreams, still coiled like forbidden fruit around the tree, still alluring in the diaphanous dress pressed tightly against her young body, her dark eyes still probing seductively, and her moistened red lips still beckoning his. Yes, he was a man. But good men needed to control their passions.

He fell asleep. Manuela didn't show.

CHAPTER 12

The next day, Papo called on his grandfather, Bonifacio Obregon, the elder, widowed, and long retired from the printing trade. As a young man, his *Abuelo* Bony dabbled in nationalist politics and flirted with Don Pedro Albizu Campos's nationalists in the twenties. His government contracts ended abruptly. Then, one night, hooded men broke into the shop and smashed his presses. But it was Don Pedro's calls for heightened violence that caused his break with the nationalists in the thirties.

His grandfather, and not Soledad, the maid, appeared behind the iron gate. Papo remembered a time when the old man walked straight and deliberately, always with purpose—on two feet. Now, his cane served as a third leg. But the slower gait still communicated purpose. He hurried and let in his grandson.

"*Bendicion, Abuelo.*" Papo kissed him.

"May God bless you and the Virgin keep you." His grandfather embraced him. They walked to the house.

Don Bony served as surrogate father after a car crash took his eldest son, Bonifacio the younger, Papo's father. He helped Mary rear Lucho and Julito,

61

his half-brothers, and Papo's own mother *La Negra* Inez, raise him. White now covered Don Bony's head, eyebrows, and mustache, like freshly fallen snow in Spanish Harlem and the South Bronx. There, mother and son saw hardships their first winter. Don Bony's remittances, with Inez' labors, saw them through those times, gray now in his memory.

Inside Don Bony's Spartan living room, a large radio stood, as on a throne, in front of a rocking chair, kept company by two chairs. "Soledad isn't here," Don Bony said. Without his dentures, the words rolled around his mouth. "Go, make yourself some coffee. Got to finish my necessities. We have serious things to talk about."

Papo got the coffee in the kitchen, already brewed, and braced himself.

Their grandfather changed his politics and supported Luis Munoz Marin's platform of postponed independence until Puerto Rico pulled itself up by its own bootstraps. President Franklin Roosevelt, fed up with nationalist violence, threatened to turn Puerto Rico loose without a cent. Don Pedro Albizu Campos welcomed the idea, but Don Luis deemed Puerto unready for independence—or the statehood championed by the island's Republicans. Don Luis' Popular Democrats proposed a middle ground called commonwealth. The shop pumped out campaign literature for the Popular Democrats and when they won, Don Bony's fortunes rose.

His grandfather returned. "Your brother's been packing the sociology he reads in school and the shit nationalists feed him. He worships Don Pedro. I too followed Don Pedro, but he's a bitter man. Hate and resentment consume a man." They both thought a few seconds. "Now your brother's packing a pistol."

Papo thought the old man's dentures loose. "A pistol?" Papo sprayed out the word *pistol* slowly. "Why didn't you tell me?"

"You had your own troubles."

"No, you should have come to me." He dreaded Julito's tie to Howard Saunders' murder—and to the slender man with the mustache and gold tooth.

"Told your Uncle Ciro and your brother Lucho. They can't find him. Julito talked about fighting the *Yanquis* who took our land. He'll wind up bitter one day, just like Don Pedro." His grandfather offered his pet theory: that

Don Pedro suffered from a racial complex resulting from the union of a black servant mother and white, merchant father who sent him to Harvard where his grandfather believed his problems began.

Americans, ever funny about race, rejected him socially.

In 1917, he became an officer and got command of Negro American troops. The white officers' quarters and social clubs were closed to him. Never once firing on a German, he spent the war unloading ships and sorting out cooking details.

"That does something to a man," Papo mused. It was subtler in Puerto Rico, though here too, people suffered indignities. Although opposed to political violence and the nationalist political agenda, for the first time Papo felt empathy for Don Pedro. "What else did Julito say?"

"He found school a waste of time. 'Irrelevant to the cause' were his words. Told him not to take his politics too seriously and that he needed to earn a living. 'Can't eat sociology and political science,' I said. Or work in the Hilton all your life."

Papo surprised the old man when he told him Julito quit his job and that a visit to the college and chats with friends produced no results.

Don Bony mentioned the girl Lola with a small child fathered by another man Julito was seeing. She lived in El Fanguito and Bony produced an address on *Calle* Mira Flor. "Find her, find him—before he does something stupid. He's your brother, remember that." His grandfather's stare and ensuing silence spoke what Papo knew to be on the old man's mind: that they were brothers, the flesh and blood of his dead son. The thoughts stirred emotional scars.

"I need a drink. Get me a drink."

His grandfather returned with a bottle and glasses and served him a drink that warmed him—good *canita*—bootleg rum, the kind he confiscated from non-relatives. "It's good to talk, son. I always felt guilty we didn't do right by you."

"Yes, you did, *Abuelo*. Yes, you did. I tried with Julito. Even went with him to a nationalist rally. But what do I say if I find him? 'I'm your brother. Stop it'? We've argued. He's set in his ways; I'm set in mine."

"Always thought of yourself as more American than *Boricua*. But we're Puerto Ricans. And Obregones. First comes family, then Puerto Rico, then America, and then the police."

"I'll find him. Maybe I can track down this Lola. Give me another drink." Bony poured him another.

"And Marisol and the girls?"

"Fine. Marisol was sick, but she's better. The girls are getting big and beautiful."

"And the thing with the young whore? It's over?"

"Yes."

His grandfather's eyes probed, but Papo evaded his glare.

"I know you're a man. I had desires, too. Thank God I no longer do. It's a relief when the urge leaves you."

"I can hardly wait," the grandson mused, only half sarcastically.

They discussed the murdered *Yanqui* lawyer and Papo revealed his part in the case, troubled by the little press coverage, confiding in the old man his belief Pietri and the police brass headed in the wrong direction.

"I've followed it on the radio. Dead Americans are bad for American investment." His grandfather, too, took a shot of *canita*. "The Governor's holding back the press."

"Some poor *Boricua* gets it, and Don Luis doesn't care. But threaten Americans bringing money bags, and he does." This time he released the full force of his sarcasm.

"That's right, Papo. Don Luis has a tight rein on the police. And he's gagged the press. Can't scare American investors or tourists."

Papo well knew the American presence provided the family's livelihood. He took his leave.

"May God bless you and the Virgin keep you." His grandfather gave him a *bendicion*. "Find Julito. Get the gun."

Papo headed not to El Fanguito but to Uncle Ciro's. Dressed in white pants, a white *guayabera*, and white shoes, his uncle dabbled in spiritualism and worshiped the saints. He never dirtied his clothes, delegating work to his son and others. Papo told him of his concern for his brother, and tugging at the customary religious beads around his neck, Ciro went in search of him, hoping to find him in his girlfriend Lola's home in El Fanguito.

Papo knew his way around El Fanguito, the Little Mud Hole. A shantytown of wood and tin shacks, it sprung up around the lagoon sometime in the forties when the great hurricane devastated the sugar fields and mills and set off a migration of farmers and unemployed laborers from the hills and valleys to the capital.

He once walked a beat there with El Flaco, Martin Lanza. Police business took him there often, but Papo feared being recognized and his brother tipped off about the manhunt. Papo left and later returned to check with his uncle.

Ciro, his white garb sullied by El Fanguito's mud, reported he'd not found Julito, although he'd tracked down the girl Lola. He tugged at his beads. Papo thought this belief in the spirits was futile. He believed in God and went to church on Christmas and Easter with Marisol and the girls but believed God's intervention in man's affairs was limited. More remote were the saints. One needed to pull one's own strings in this world.

Ciro described the shack Lola shared with younger siblings after her parents' death. Her dirty-faced child, clothed in a soiled, torn T-shirt, stared wide-eyed, his tiny penis dangling between his legs. "Just a young country girl tasting life too early," Ciro explained. Suspicious at first, she proved polite and claimed no knowledge of Julito's whereabouts. "Said she'd contact me."

"What does she look like?" Papo asked, imagining the bad impression she'd make on Julito's mother Mary, who no doubt feared the affair would "ruin the race."

"Beautiful." Uncle Ciro smiled, describing her dark skin. "Big pretty eyes. Ample set of breasts and an ass to match." His tiny eyes gleamed. Although in tune with the spirits, Ciro, a favorite of the ladies before an expanding waistline and balding head lessened his appeal, never neglected the flesh. "The scent of the woman will bring him back. We just wait."

Papo left, fearing other policemen might hone in on Julito. He needed to find him first. And not just for Don Paco's sake. He needed to find the slender man with a mustache and gold tooth one of the *putas* saw near Howard Saunders.

CHAPTER 13

Chief Howland tried relaxing on a Sunday evening. In pajamas in his Georgetown apartment, sparsely furnished with bare essentials, he brewed himself a fresh cup of coffee. Then he settled into a comfortable sofa to finish the *Washington Post*. Putting the paper down, he turned on his new television set, just delivered—a tiny metal box atop a simple wooden cabinet purchased to hold this new contraption—and flipped the dial to the CBS channel. Enduring endless commercials, he waited for Ed Sullivan's *Toast of the Town* show to come on.

He still mulled over in his head the latest reports from the Protective Research Bureau. Agents in the Midwest were still on the trail of the writer of the threatening letter from Iowa, addressed to Harry Jewman, protesting the President's recognition of a Jewish state and wishing that all Jews would be killed. "I'll finish you too," the letter added. "And I have just the oven to do it." The second letter was tinged with threats, protesting the bombing of Hiroshima, and its origin proved more elusive, as did that of the other one addressed to Harry "Stupid" Truman. There was no news about the Puerto Ricans.

He had also found troubling the daily report from the White House detail: Mrs. Truman slipped out of Blair House to go shopping without informing the secret service. Tomorrow he'd confront the President and demand the Truman women refrain from leaving the residence at will without serving reasonable notice. After a token apology for the inconvenience, he'd limit their activity in and out of Blair House. What a group of women, beginning with the fiercely independent First Lady.

"We're restless Missourians," Mrs. Truman made clear early. "We won't be cooped up like cows in a barn." Her ninety-year-old mother, Mrs. Wallace, also moaned and groaned, especially about "the damn doctors up in these parts."

Then there'd been Mr. Truman's late mother, a peppery southern dowager, who very early before her death refused to sleep in the Lincoln Bedroom. "Won't sleep with no damn Yankees!" she screamed one day. Although never bumping into Mr. Lincoln's ghost during the old pre-Blair House days in the presidential mansion, the elder Mrs. Truman still haunted him.

And besides the older women's challenge, there was the daughter: a concert pianist-singer! Not even the hair-raising late-night pursuits of the Roosevelt boys compared to the rigors of protecting a television star in the many road hotels and concert halls, with potential assassins watching from the seats.

Music came on and Ed Sullivan appeared to the applause of the studio audience.

"Good evening ladies and gentleman, the big, brawny MC with closely cropped hair said, rubbing his hands. "Tonight, we have a really big show for you."

Looks like a labor goon, the Chief thought. More fit to work over recalcitrant dockworkers on strike than entertain people. After the opening jokes, Sullivan ran down the evening's bill.

"And also back for an encore performance we have in store for you an even bigger treat. Ladies and gentleman, the First Daughter of the United States is with us tonight. A big round of applause, please, for Miss Margaret Truman." The audience complied.

The Chief watched the first two acts, then endured more commercials.

"And now ladies and gentleman, the First Daughter, Miss Margaret Truman."

Margaret appeared to great applause in a flowing white gown. Her piano accompanist prompted her and she opened up.

Beautiful dreamer, wake unto me,
Starlight and dewdrops are waiting for thee
Sounds of the rude world heard in the day,
Lulled by the moonlight have all passed away . . .

Flat, the Chief thought. Attractive, yes, in her flowing gown, but flat. Had she not been the President's daughter she'd not be there. Not pretty, either, no matter how much the father pined. She favored her mother, with her long Wallace nose, and would no doubt one day look just like her.

Miss Truman sang one more Stephen Foster song, and the recital over, the Chief turned off the television and went to bed.

At least the Trumans proved wholesome types, without too many apparent skeletons—except for the suicide of Mrs. Truman's father, kept well under wraps by the family. Otherwise, there was little to hide. Although some insisted Mr. Truman had Jewish blood from a grandfather named Solomon, there was no truth to the rumor, as the family had impeccable Christian roots. Opponents also brought up his connection to the corrupt political machine of the Pendergast brothers of Kansas City, but that also was no big deal.

Not so his first President, Mr. Harding.

There had been not one but two mistresses. One, Nan Britton, bore him a daughter out of wedlock during a secret tryst in the White House closet. The Chief had watched out for the First Lady. Affairs were not new to presidents from Mr. Washington to Mr. Roosevelt. The Chief had commanded his men to shield from the public—and Mrs. Roosevelt—Mr. Roosevelt's mistress, Lucy Mercer. There had been others. The prior First Lady—herself not free of sin—found out, and in fact had her own flings. Mr. Truman, the Chief was certain, was an exception.

And with Mr. Harding, there was also the matter of unknown progenitors.

Did Mr. Harding have Negro blood? Yes, the Chief believed. His enemies raised the issue during the 1920 election and rumors of a Negro great-grandmother had made the rounds in Marion, Ohio. He knew Mr. Harding paid off Negro relatives through intermediaries and heard from fellow agents quotes from Negro relatives that "Cousin Warren be pass'n." Mr. Harding hardly put this issue to rest by once asking, "How do I know one of my ancestors may have jumped the fence?" It remained for future historians to make these revelations public; his job was protecting presidents.

Falling asleep, he floated back in a dream to the Palace Hotel in San Francisco, 1923. He'd accompanied the presidential entourage on a cross-country trip that took them to Alaska and back to the west. He again led Nan Britton into the room in the dream. And again he saw Mr. Harding's assassin leave it. Too late. Mr. Harding was dead.

The alarm clock woke him from this recurring dream.

CHAPTER 14

When Chief A. B. Howland arrived for his lunch date, Mr. Truman washed upstairs, and in the dining room, the First Lady, already seated, finished a slice of bread.

"Afternoon, Mrs. Truman."

"Hello Chief," Bess Truman said. "Please sit."

"Thank you."

"How's Julie?"

"Fine. Spoke to her yesterday—and the major." The Chief brought her up to date on his only daughter, Julie, recently married to an Air Force captain newly promoted to major. "They're flying high. Not as high as your television star, but well, thank you. Saw the recital last night. Margaret was wonderful."

The First Lady smiled. "Yes, wasn't she? Well bring your star by and her flyboy. We see a lot of *you* but little of *them*."

Taken aback, his eyebrows rose. He stifled a frown and managed a weak smile.

Her mischievous eyes left his and concentrated on another slice she was buttering, although he caught them spying him to gage his reaction.

He found Elizabeth Truman plain and unremarkable, save for the large, prominent nose that conferred character, if not looks. Wisps of white hair now overtook the gray and hinted at her sixty-five years. Her dress, a subdued black and white polka dot, respected both fashion and the delimiters of age, position, and a full, matronly figure.

"How's Mrs. Wallace?" he finally managed.

"Resting. Hayes is serving her."

Mrs. Truman's mother, Madge Wallace, faced hip surgery and rested upstairs. The doctors expressed confidence in a speedy recovery. Her widowed mother's needs, the Chief knew, often came before the President's. And accustomed to second place in his wife's affections, Mr. Truman never complained, not even in his Senate days, when Mrs. Truman often left him to the loneliness of the capitol to return to Independence, Missouri, to care for her mother.

Hayes the white haired Negro butler appeared in a white jacket and white bow. "May I begin serving, Mrs. Truman?" he asked in his customary refined speech that matched his manners.

"No. We'll wait for the President."

"Very well, Madame."

The Chief knew the First Lady always waited. She waited the nine years from the time Mr. Truman declared his intentions to the time he made good on them. She waited for him to succeed at farming, then banking, then business. Mr. Truman failed at all. All the waiting confirmed for his Wallace in-laws, who'd looked down on the former farmer, an inability to care for her adequately. Then, she waited for her Captain Harry to return from war in France.

The Chief rose when the President entered and sat next to his wife. "Hello, Chief. Hello, Boss." The President placed a kiss on the First Lady's cheek and held her hand. Mr. Truman once confided he'd fallen in love in grade school. It was manifest he'd loved her since, for he'd never seen a man lavish so much affection on a woman. Although the Chief had loved his late wife, outward display had diminished over time.

Bess Truman blushed but didn't return the President's kiss. A shy person, she no doubt felt as embarrassed now as she had been with the first kiss. Yet the Chief knew she came through in the pinch, submerging her hatred of Washington politics and the public spotlight to hold the Bible for him when he took the oath after Mr. Roosevelt's death. She stood next to him on his whistle stop campaign when he came from behind to beat Dewey in '48. But Chief Howland understood the ordeal for this private, unpretentious woman, to expose herself to gossip columnists and critics.

"Margaret call?" The President asked.

"No." Bess' eyebrows rose. "Three whole days since she's dropped a note."

"Well, you know I'd rather have grandchildren than a singer, but what's a fellow to do? Wonder how Joe Stalin handles these things, huh, Chief?" The President winked. The Russian dictator also had a daughter. "How's Ma?" He turned to the First Lady.

"Asleep."

Hayes returned. The President said he'd "strike a blow for liberty" and Hayes poured him his bourbon and water. Then he served their roast beef and potatoes and left.

"And how was your day, dear?" Bess asked.

"The Chinese army's north of the Yalu in force."

"Doing what?"

"Don't know. Macarthur thinks it just a bluff."

"Don't do anything stupid, Harry," Bess said. "It'd be a terrible war against the Chinese."

"There are no good wars. Know firsthand."

"Pa and Ma got caught up in one, too."

The Chief said nothing, familiar with Mrs. Wallace's experiences in southern Missouri during the Civil War and its ordeal for the Wallaces, rebel sympathizers.

They ate the rest of the meal in silence.

The First Lady went to check on her mother.

The Chief followed the President up to the conference room. Mr. Truman went into the adjoining sitting room and up the stairs to his bedroom. The

Chief waited in the sitting room, on a Chippendale chair, resting his feet on a Persian rug in front of the marble fireplace adorned with sparkling brass irons and pokers. The Blairs, who'd lived here, had loved material things—and power. Around this fireplace, he imagined them wheeling, dealing, and entertaining Washington society. Here their portraits still hung, for they'd been vain.

How unlike the Trumans, Harry especially, a hell of a guy, the most human of the men he'd protected. Although respecting Mr. Hoover and Mr. Roosevelt, both with a common touch of sorts, a social barrier existed he never breeched. But Harry Truman was the common touch, of the people and from the people. Lacking all pretensions, Mr. Truman told earthy jokes that made his men laugh. The Chief feared they grew too close to the President.

"A. B., let's talk," The President came in.

"Yes, sir. You read the White House contractor Mr. McAdams' report. Renovations will take longer than planned. It's bad news. I'll sleep better when you're all back in the White House. There, we'd be able to protect you better."

"Actually, I like it here, A. B.," he smiled. "Not much room for entertaining, but it's cozy. Bess and Margaret love it."

"I know. But it's again time to talk security." The Chief didn't smile.

"I was hoping it was strictly a social call, A. B."

"Sir, you need to cooperate more with us." His look hardened. "I realize Blair House inconveniences us all—you, Mrs. Truman, and your daughter. But you must restrict your movements during the rest of your stay here."

"We're restless Missourians not used to being cooped up like cows in a barn," he repeated an often used line.

The Chief conceded the difficulty but once more listed the letters the Protection Research Bureau received everyday threatening the first family. "A lot of demented people out there. Armed people who'd love you—or your women—for targets."

The President sat back a moment in thought. "People really want to kill Harry Truman?"

"No. They want to kill the president of the United States. Like Zangara in '32." Zangara often came up in their discussions.

The Italian immigrant Giuseppe Zangara lived in Florida and planned to travel to Washington to kill President Hoover. But when President-Elect Roosevelt arrived in Florida, Zangara found it easier to kill a president there. He missed Roosevelt narrowly, killing instead Chicago's mayor, Anton Cermak, next to Mr. Roosevelt, who delivered a speech from his car. "It's the office, not the man." The Chief stood next to the car that that night in Miami, distracted by one of Mayor Cermak's jokes. And he remembered the assassin's words. "Too many are hungry," Zangara self-appointed spokesman for the world's downtrodden screamed before firing. The mayor's agony as he slumped in the back seat remained stamped in the Chief's memory.

Mr. Truman's eyes widened. "Interesting. But work around us. My wife and daughter have strong characters. Ma too. You know, not even the President of the United States tells them what to do. A. B., I commanded an artillery unit during the first big one. Had the loudest, most insubordinate Irish sons of bitches you ever saw. But when Captain Harry gave an order, they jumped. My women I can't command."

"I must insist, sir," the Chief countered.

"I command the Armed Forces. I have the power to blow up the world. But I can't command my women. The paradoxes of power, eh? Wonder what Joe Stalin would do? So what now?"

"Mrs. Truman gives the secret service half an hour's notice before leaving. The car doesn't stop in front of Blair House during lunch. It's hard controlling the crowds. It goes straight into the garage below."

"You dampen a good day."

"And we don't stop the car to shake hands on the street. We do have specific threats. Everyday our Protective Service Bureau receives letters from potential killers out there. Most are just crazies, but we can't discount them."

The President reluctantly agreed, but he asked the secret service be less intrusive. "I feel like Al Capone surrounded by gangster bodyguards— sometimes like a cheap South American dictator shielded from the next coup." The Chief had heard these lines before. "It's hard enough being in this prison. Don't make it worse."

"I'm sorry."

"Thanks for looking after my little girl. But don't hem us in."

The Chief again apologized and took his leave.

And again he returned to Bayfront Park, Miami, February, 1933. Again he saw the gun and again he heard the Italian immigrant. "Too many are hungry!"

Too many indeed.

A woman's purse hit the gunman's hand, spoiling his aim. But for a purse, they would have lost a President.

No. One couldn't be distracted by the subjects one protected.

CHAPTER 15

The winding loops and curves through the mountains lay behind them, and the dirt road ahead ran through lush tropical lowland. Goyo made good time to Santa Isabel, steering the old Fleetwood past interminable palm trees. Next to him, Julito slept, but not the two men in the back seat. The barber Arcadio had instructed they pick up the men in Penuelas near the southern coast.

They'd loaded three heavy crates filled with arms in the trunk, under the eyes of a third man, a Spaniard by his accent, then left Penuelas and now headed for outside of San Isabel on the southern coast for a rendezvous with another man, named Juan. They'd continue to San Juan where Goyo's plane to New York waited. Their luck held. Large, menacing clouds hovered above, and then drifted off toward the coast.

"Storm's coming," said one of the men in the back, the nervous one with the sneer whom Goyo dubbed *El Loco* for his edginess.

"Calm down," the other man said. His name was Chiche. He wore a fedora, smoked incessantly, and scratched his hand constantly.

"I'm sick of sitting."

"We'll be there soon," said Chiche, who continued scratching.

"Psoriasis," Goyo concluded. *He needs a good shampoo*, he thought silently to himself.

Goyo's thoughts drifted back to Consuelo and the green eyes that sparkled the first time they met his in Jayuya. He'd soon return to New York and find her and their daughter.

The sound of the sea rose, and out of night's blackness, Santa Isabel appeared, its lights flickering like a match next to the volatile waters. It slumbered, oblivious to the waves pounding the sea wall.

"What's that?" El Loco jumped.

"Police," Chiche said, still scratching.

Ahead, a car's headlight appeared to their right and a flashlight shone directly in front. Julito next to him awoke. "I'll talk," Goyo commanded. "Just relax I'll do the talking. Probably a routine stop. Hurricane watch, I think." He slowed down and made out two blurry figures in gray uniforms. On the shoulder of the road, to their right, a police car, parked perpendicular, blinked its lights. A patrolman on the left side of the road, hand raised, ordered them to stop. A second in front came toward them, his flashlight trained on them.

The first approached from the driver's side, the second from the right. "Get out of the car, please," the first one ordered.

"May I ask why, officer?"

"Just get out of the car, please," the policeman insisted, his hand on his holster. Goyo complied.

A soft rain began to fall.

"Next time, do as you're told. License?"

"It's not what you say, policeman" Goyo recognized El Loco's voice. "It's what we say." Goyo turned, saw a flash, and heard a shot. The policeman staggered and fell. The second dropped the flashlight and went for his gun. Another bullet from the right passenger window dropped him, too.

A shot flashed from the police car.

"I'm hit," Chiche cried out.

Goyo fell to the ground and crawled to his car's rear. Two more shots rang out, missing him. Goyo slipped behind the car, gun drawn. The left rear door opened and El Loco crawled out. Goyo peeked around the back end. Two shots flashed from the police car, aimed at El Loco, who returned fire four times, his gun now spent. The policeman shot once.

Unseen, Goyo crawled slowly to the car's front, gun drawn. Pulling the safety, he got to his knees. Keeping his nerves steady, he studied the situation, then aimed at the driver's side, emptying nine rounds, then got up slowly.

"Chiche's dead," El Loco yelled.

Goyo examined the body. The scratching stopped. He turned to El Loco "You're stupid. They just wanted the license. We might have talked our way out. Why'd you shoot?"

"Because I hate them. Let the revolution begin here. Long live a free Puerto Rico."

Goyo glared at El Loco, who glared back. "We got to leave," Goyo said. "Let's pull Chiche from the car. Julito, check the police car."

Pulling Chiche's dead body out, they laid it on the side. Goyo told Julito to drive the cop car off the road.

Goyo and El Loco dragged the bodies next to it. Julito shook.

Goyo examined the dead policemen. The other stirred. "This one's breathing."

El Loco reloaded, pumped two more bullets into him. "Not anymore."

Julito checked the squad car and returned, more shaken.

"What happened?" Goyo asked.

Julito trembled. "He's dead."

Goyo and El Loco looked. A bleeding head and arm protruded through the rear window. They examined the dead man, a tall, lanky sergeant.

"What's this *flaco* to you?" El Loco asked.

Julito stood dazed. "His blood's on my hands."

Goyo pulled the dead skinny sergeant from the car, drove it to the side of the road, and wrapped bushes around it, wiping it for prints.

They drove off in a steady rain.

CHAPTER 16

Early morning clouds had already cast their gloom when Papo saw the American and Puerto Rican flags at half-staff outside headquarters. Terrible news waited inside: three policemen and a third unidentified man died outside Santa Isabel. Rumors flew and tension rose until the official communiqué came.

Sergeant Martin Lanza fell, with the others, while on hurricane alert. They stopped a car with two or three individuals, who for reasons unknown, opened fire. An eyewitness in Santa Isabel saw an old Fleetwood and remembered two suspects loading crates on to a second car shortly after the time of the shootings. One rumor hinted at a political connection. Some whispered the officers searched for arms believed shipped to nationalist sympathizers.

Papo reacted in disbelief, unable to comprehend a world without Martin Lanza.

But reality set in, devastating and hard. Martin Lanza was dead. His *compadre* and *amigo* was no more. He felt alone in the department. The political angle scared him. He pulled a handkerchief from the pocket of his *guayabera* shirt and wiped tears from large eyes swollen red with grief. He found his composure when Pietri asked for the report. Papo stalled.

"Don't have it. Martin Lanza was my friend. I need more time."

"Sorry, Obregon. Martin Lanza spoke well of you. Let's catch the bastards who did this. Wrap up the Howard Saunders case. Write something down, sign it. Then take a vacation. Mourn."

Pietri's kindness caught him off guard. "I want in on this one."

"No. You're drained—we all are—but you were close and won't think straight."

Papo promised the report in a couple of days. He'd leave the missing busboy out and if questioned later, blame this lapse on grief.

Later, Uncle Ciro called. Julito surfaced, dirty and hungry, at Lola's shack. "The girl said he'd come see me." When Papo arrived at Ciro's house still later that afternoon, his grandfather also waited. "Sorry about your *compadre* Martin Lanza," the old man offered.

Papo nodded. He studied the crucifix on a wall, overlooking Uncle Ciro's shrine, draped in white linen and decked with statues of the Virgin Mary and the African deities Chango and Yemaya. Saint Barbara held center sway on the shrine. Ciro's offering of water, rosary beads and burning candle paid homage to her image, bearing sword in one hand, chalice in the other, a crown on the head. Papo knew the candle invoked divine protection for his brother.

But not even the saints would save him if Papo's worst fears proved true.

His brother arrived, thin and gaunt, with Uncle Ciro. His grandfather hugged him. Papo trained a long, cold stare. Julito averted his eyes.

"So, brother," he addressed Julito, "You pack a pistol and run around with nationalists. Swear before we continue you didn't kill Martin Lanza."

"I swear," Julito said, remorse in his tone, not looking him in the eye. Reluctant tears finally flowed from eyes swollen with emotion.

"Men cry. I've cried. I cry now for my best friend. So who killed him? You? I'll turn you in myself." Papo came toward him. Julito's eyes grew fearful.

"Martin was my brother." Papo's eyes glared. "A brother in deed, not name."

"Now, now," Uncle Ciro said, coming between them, pushing Papo back.

Julito summoned courage and spoke. "Brother, on our dead father's grave, I didn't do it. Goyo killed Martin."

"Who?"

"Gregorio. They call him Goyo. That's all I know."

"Gregorio *who*?"

"Don't know."

"Who killed Howard Saunders?"

"Gregorio. Don't know his full name."

"And you helped him? You're an accomplice. For that alone you'll go to jail. For killing a policeman ..."

"Help me!" Julito sobbed. "I haven't been a brother, but help me. I don't want to die."

"Yes, your brother will help you," the old man said. "But help him."

"How did Martin die?" Papo pressed.

"We were headed for Santa Isabel to deliver arms."

"From who?" Don Bony asked.

"From Don Pedro."

Papo looked at his grandfather, and the old man at him.

Julito described their rendezvous on the coast with the Spaniard and told them of rumors of a submarine off Ponce. He heard also of Argentineans and blond men speaking a guttural language delivering arms in a speedboat.

Don Bony pegged the Spaniard a Falangist, known to Papo as agents of Francisco Franco's fascist government—Spaniards settling in Puerto Rico, some before 1898. They supported Franco during the Spanish Civil War eleven years earlier, before the FBI rounded them up during the war for pro-German sympathies.

"Didn't think too many remained in Puerto Rico," Papo said, thinking all deported by now.

"They're still here." His grandfather explained Franco harbored dreams of a new Spanish Empire and sphere of influence and undertook this adventure to support Don Pedro's. Ciro assumed the blonds to be Germans, working for General Peron of Argentina, who loved to pull Uncle Sam's beard. "Peron gets arms from Franco and ships them here. Sends his Nazi expatriates on these adventures. They get bored hiding in the Pampas."

It all amazed Papo. People said Franco saved Christianity from the communists, but he didn't think him a saint. Papo remembered seeing picture of the Spanish dictator, a former cavalry officer, in newsreels during the Spanish Civil War just a few years earlier. One, of the former cavalry officer in his boots and riding pants saluting Adolph Hitler, stood out in his mind. Although he understood his motivations, it puzzled him Franco would risk the diplomatic repercussions involved.

Of Argentineans, Papo knew only of their tangos and of the pretty way they said *Che*. He'd always pegged General Juan Peron as a tinhorn dictator, one of the many that plagued Latin America.

But Nazis were evil. He thought it unimaginable Puerto Ricans would deal with them no matter the motive. Shocking—no, scary. Could it all be true?

"Go on."

Two men, Julito continued, Chiche, and a nervous one they called El Loco, loaded the crates. They drove to Santa Isabel. There the police stopped them and the nervous one gunned down the first cop. The man named Chiche killed the second. Julito, petrified with fear, never shot his pistol. Gregorio emptied his gun into the police car and killed Martin. "Gregorio and the nervous one pulled the bodies off the road and told me to check the car. I saw this tall, lanky cop. A sergeant. It was Martin."

Papo stifled a sob.

"We left. It was pouring. We connected with a man named Juan, delivered the crates, and abandoned the car, hitching a ride back here with this Juan."

"And Howard Saunders? Julito told him the whole story from the time he met this Gregorio in Arcadio's barber shop to the Saunders' hit.

"So, brother, this is the end of your fantasies and readings. But you weren't playing at sociology and political science. This was real. What can I do, fly you out on a magical plane? You helped this Goyo kill my friend. Give yourself up."

"No, help me."

"God Almighty, he's your brother," Uncle Ciro said. "You can't turn in your own brother."

"He can turn himself in. Do it soon, before they get these *cabrones* and they tell on you."

"We have to hide him," Ciro insisted.

His grandfather cried with Julito.

"Where do you hide a man who's killed a cop—three cops?" he asked. "This island's small. You can kill gringos, but not cops. Maybe his best shot's giving up."

"Before I died, I wanted to see you all united and happy," Don Bony said. "Now I'll just die." His grandfather's eyes swelled with emotion and without dentures the old man looked pathetic as he spoke.

"Send him to the mountains," Uncle Ciro said. "He can stay with Cousin Nicolas. We'll work out an alibi and say he was there all the time. With the help of Santa Barbara and the saints, he'll be all right."

Papo thought. "It's risky. If they find out I'm involved, I'll be an accomplice. I'll lose my job, maybe wind up in prison."

"We'll protect you," his grandfather insisted, regaining his composure. "I'll take the fall and say I helped him. They won't know you're part of this. Keep quiet. We'll do the rest."

"We have to risk it," Uncle Ciro added. "We can't sell him out."

"He's involved in four murders. It's not worth trying. They have an eyewitness. Maybe we can get him on that magic plane to New York. It's feasible. Your son Guillermo in the Bronx can take him in. He needs to go far."

His grandfather sobbed harder now, and Uncle Ciro looked grim.

Memories of the past slights by Julito and his mother, Mary, surfaced. Once again, Papo remembered his brother's painful rejection and that his stepmother had once barred him from her house and publicly failed to acknowledge him. Pedro Albizu Campos had suffered indignities at the hands of gringos. Had his white relatives also slighted him? Papo looked long and hard at his brother, who averted his eyes. Turning him would be easy. But his grandfather's pain moved him. Papo agreed to their plan but wouldn't drive Julito to Cousin Nicolas. His cousin, Jancinto, Ciro's son, it was decided, would drive him at night.

"I'll find this *cabron* who murdered my friend."

"You're not thinking straight," Ciro insisted. "Nobody knows about your connection to all of this, Papo. Let the powers that be deal with it."

"Who? The saints, Uncle?"

85

"You know what I mean. The police. Those not emotionally involved in all of this."

"Your uncle is right, Papo," the old man pleaded. "Listen to him. Don't be rash."

"I'll kill him myself," he vowed, and started to leave.

"No don't be rash," his uncle pleaded and tried to block his way.

"Get out of my way, Ciro. I'll do what I need to do. You take care of this." He cast a last look of contempt at his brother, then left.

CHAPTER 17

Family and officers in gray uniforms packed Martin's *velorio* in Tao Alto. Papo sought out the widow Gricel but had trouble getting close to her as relatives and friends surrounded her.

She seemed to be holding up well under the ordeal of the wake. Her beauty had always come through despite a pockmarked face, thanks to a full figure, vibrant black hair, and a lively smile that spoke volumes. Now she'd grown fat after bearing Martin three children and the pockmarks had grown worse. Her hair, dotted with gray was in disarray. Grief now muted the smile. Seeing him, she waved him over.

"Gricel, I'm here for you."

"Ay, Papo, Papo, Papo," she broke down in sobs. "Why him? How could such a thing happen?"

"There, there."

"He was so proud when he made sergeant and with his new post. And look. Dear God, why?"

Relatives came between them and Papo, unable to answer, backtracked.

He paid his respect to Martin's parents. His mother, a shriveled septuagenarian, her face hidden by a wet handkerchief, cried. His father in an ancient white guayabera shirt too tight for him, just stared. His wrinkles, weather beaten in the tropics, then frozen by his years in the cruel New York winters, showed the many cares of his years.

"I'm here to share your grief," Papo offered.

The old man nodded and stared vacantly.

He looked for Martin's children but didn't see them.

Papo approached the coffin in the living room, kneeling before the body and crossing himself before the cross above on the wall. He stared at his dead friend, dressed in police gray, who seemed unreal, like a large wooden toy soldier.

Atop a makeshift altar draped in white next to the coffin, candles burned next to Lazarus' likeness, a halo around the statue's head, crutches in the hand. Dogs at his side licked the saint's wounds. An old lady dressed in white with her back to the mourners sat in front of the shrine and chanted the rosary.

"May God take him from her pain ..." the old woman recited.

"And take him to his rest," came the chorus of mourners.

The candles' flames, nudged by a sudden window breeze, bent but glowed defiantly.

Papo stared, hypnotized.

His mind wandered to the early days. Martin, already a veteran with three years in the department, became his godfather and gave him *consejos*, those valuable tips, a new cop needs. They walked a beat in the shantytown and played dominoes and drank beer when they were off duty. Reckless with money and often broke, Papo borrowed from Martin, who never denied him. Martin served him as social mentor.

Returning to Puerto Rico as a young teenager, Papo adjusted slowly. His halting Spanish made him socially awkward, and in school the other kids laughed at him. Somebody even left a *"Yanqui go home!"* sign on his desk. His mother, Inez, and stepfather, Chago, understood his plight and soothed him, but the *bodega* they ran in Santurce occupied them day and night.

His good English proved valuable in high school, and his large size led his teachers to urged him to join the police department, which he did on a whim, surprising his stepfather and mother, who'd assumed he'd study law and enter politics. They chided him, as they often did, for his rashness. By then his Spanish improved, but he still felt socially awkward. And though growing closer to his brothers, he confided his intimate thoughts to Martin, who introduced him to people and guided him through the subtleties of Puerto Rican society. Through Martin, he met Marisol and, besides best man, served as his firstborn's godfather, making them *compadres.*

When prayers finished, he stood solemn in front of the body. He'd find this killer and kill him. His own life he'd place on hold until he'd found this *cabron,* this Goyo.

"By Jesus Christ and his mother the Virgin, I will find who did this," he vowed out loud. The mourners stared. "By Lazarus and Santa Barbara and all the saints in heaven, I'll not rest until I've brought to justice this *carbon.*" He sensed his colleagues scoff and felt Pietri's frown. But he'd not feel the breeze or the rays of the sun until his killer was in a jail cell or a grave.

He'd found a purpose

CHAPTER 18

Following his brother Julito's tip, Papo began his search for the mysterious "Gregorio" in La Milagrosa, an old colonial complex, once part of El Moro Fortress, now separated by modern structures. It housed San Juan's pre-1945 police records as well as an I-Section with a secret political files. He knew his way around this complex, as it had been home for more than a month during the dark days after his involvement with the prostitute Manuela.

Manuela had declined his plea to be his alone and continued plying her trade. One weekend, the American navy washed ashore, a white tide seeking women as waves seek the shore. "What's this?" Papo confronted Manuela and a sailor outside a hotel.

"Fuck off," the sailor, a sun burned red head, came at him and they exchanged blows. Papo knocked him to the ground, but the bruised sailor quickly got up and landed a blow before military police separated, then arrested them both, turning Papo over to his own authorities. He handed in his gun and badge.

They handed him, pending a review, an administrative assignment in La Milagrosa. There he answered phones and alphabetized and re-alphabetized records of criminals arrested before 1945. Sergeant Tomas Alarcon, a jolly, fat fellow, kept an eye on him and addressed him as a son.

"*Mijo*, rein in your passions. You're impetuous," Alarcon counseled after Papo detailed his fight with the sailor. "Son this, son that," he said, feeding him *consejos*, morsels of fatherly advice.

The Spaniards had built La Milagrosa three hundred years earlier to store supplies and later converted it to a prison. When Americans built larger, modern jails, they converted La Milagrosa into a records room, and during the autonomy of the late 1940s they turned it over to native police bureaucrats now filling more positions in the colonial administration. The damp, musty smell of time permeated it.

The I-Section with the political files was off limits without the special permission he lacked. He had no time to maneuver the maze of bureaucracy to get it.

But he'd made friends in La Milagrosa.

Officer Carlos Perez stood guard in front of the I-Section. Its files contained records of nationalists, communists, socialists, Falangists, and such people of interest. Anybody who raised suspicions during the war had his picture here. Although familiar with their content, Papo never had cause to look through these files. But he'd struck an acquaintance with Carlito during his month stay at the fortress, and they chatted often when neither had work.

Short, barrel-chested, and dark like him, Carlito, who never smiled, did little save inspect the special passes needed to see the files.

He knew also the archivist Clarisa, with the pudgy nose. He'd known her well. Her light brown hair, now prematurely gray, once fell playfully around his face and the bright brown eyes lit up with each encounter. Clarisa ended it before he met his wife, Marisol.

Carlito Perez and Clarisa would ask few questions, but Tomas Alarcon, his fat supervisor during his time there, would ask many. Despite Alarcon's good nature, Papo fancied himself too a prisoner while here, and Alarcon the jailer. So he waited for noon, when Alarcon took his customary two-hour lunch and siesta.

Carlito flashed a rare grin when he saw Papa, exposing the bad teeth that made him stingy with his smiles. "Back already?" He laughed.

Clarisa looked up. An indifferent tug of the lip went for a hello and she went back to her records.

"Carlito, I need to see some files."

"You know I can't, Papa. I'll get into some serious trouble."

"Come on, let me in."

Carlito's eyes, perplexed, studied the archivist Clarisa for a long time, and then him curiously. He again stared at her, then at him and nodded as if understanding. "I'll pretend to go to the bathroom. You go in. Then I'll say you sneaked in without my permission." He got up and Papa followed. Carlito took his time in the bathroom, unsmiling and sparing Papo the flash of bad teeth that came with a smile this time mercifully stifled. Papo went back and slipped into the room.

Clarisa, perplexed, challenged him. "What do you want?"

"Somebody in those files."

"No. You can't come in here. If you're a gentleman, you'll leave now."

Their fling, now long receded in their memories, might still open doors. His eyes search in vain for some acknowledgement of this past, but her eyes, now dim, offered none.

"You know, Clarisa, you ignore our past love. I've never forgotten. Nobody knows. I've been a gentleman and gentlemen don't tell. I can forget I'm a gentleman."

She thought for a minute. "I'll turn around and pretend I didn't see you." She didn't probe when told he looked for a suspect in a pressing case.

Though he felt disapproving stares and heard whispers, no one else challenged him and he went through the dusty drawers in search of all Gregorios.

A damp and musty smell of age awed and spirits seemed to linger here.

Papo flipped through dossiers of men charged with political offences and studied their photos: assassins, anti-American demonstrators, lawyers, journalists, and university students—all alphabetically arranged by decade in wooden cabinets. He began with the first drawer—from the turbulent 1930s.

Antongioni, Angel, attempted to assassinate the American Governor of Puerto Rico in 1938. Arsuaga, Anibal, shot the windshield of the federal magistrate who sentenced Pedro Albizu Campos to prison for the Ponce massacre. Beauchamp, Elias, and his companion, Hiram Rosario, gunned down Colonel Francis Riggs, Insular Police chief, and were executed without trial by police, touching off riots and the trouble in Ponce. Casellas Torres, Jesus, drove the car as his partner Arsuaga fired on the magistrate.

Finishing, the Zs, he'd found five Gregorios, all too old, fat, or small. The forties files contained few cases. Papo knew the high alert during the war years permitted the authorities great powers to go after nationalists and Falangists, long before Pearl Harbor, as early as 1939. Most cases after 1940 involved refusal of military service. Two Gregorios failed to match.

Papo sensed these cases rife with illegal searches, false arrests and confessions, beatings and executed nationalist detainees. He himself abused rights. Once he beat a robbery suspect in handcuffs who called him *chato* and *maricon*. His sense of manhood softened the insult cast on his sexuality, but *chato* touched a raw nerve of sensitivity over a flat nose. Another time, he bashed in the head of a pimp and planted bootleg rum on suspects. But they were lowlife scum violating the law and order he swore to uphold.

Politics was supposed to be different, but the constitutional rights of the nationalist prisoners didn't concern him.

Finding Gregorio did.

And well into the T's, Gregorio Tejada's picture rewarded his diligence. It matched descriptions of a slender man on the beach the night of Howard Saunders' murder: a gold tooth and a pompadour. The same Gregorio his brother pictured. Tejada, arrested at a nationalist rally on a gun violation, boasted none other than Pedro Albizu Campos as attorney.

An older brother, Arturo Tejada, died at the Ponce massacre in '37. "That would make you a nationalist," Papo decided. He had his man. Although indulging in a few moments of satisfaction, he knew his journey was just beginning.

It occurred to him that Gregorio Tejada might have left Puerto Rico already. He decided to first check the ship terminal and airport to cover all possibilities. There he searched the records and showed Gregorio's picture to employees. The name didn't appear on passenger lists, and no one remembered the face. At Isla Verde Airport, however, Pan American employees recognized him as the man boarding Flight 353 to New York under the name Rafael Lullanda that very afternoon. Gregorio Tejada didn't appear on the manifest. Papo missed him by just hours.

Combing newer arrest records and the civil registry, Papo found Tejada's birth certificate, driver's license, and marriage records. Scouring the addresses, he tracked down the parents of Tejada's estranged wife, Consuelo Loma de Tejada. The mother, a middle-aged woman with green eyes, opened the door and bit her nails as she called her husband after closing it.

"What do you want?" he asked, opening the door slightly.

"I'm a friend of Gregorio. Wanted to look him up."

"We don't know."

"And Consuelo?"

"She's in New York. We haven't seen her in a while."

"Do you have an address?"

"No. Get out." He shut the door.

After speaking to neighbors, he discovered she'd worked as a seamstress in Rio Piedras. Papo visited her last employer, using his police badge this time. Her old boss, in an apron and glasses, provided a Manhattan forwarding address in East Harlem. Her boss and co-workers described a beautiful woman, with green eyes and copper skin, who had gone to New York with her daughter to flee an abusive husband.

Back in the Vice Squad office, he finished the report, including his hunch that Gregorio Tejada was the killer. He didn't mention his brother, citing only unnamed confidential sources.

He avoided Pietri, quietly turning in the report, without fanfare, to an assistant in homicide. From a contact in the political section, he got an address for nationalist party headquarters in New York and the names of party activists: Manuel Landia, a lawyer debarred for noncompliance with Selective Service registration; Luis Blanco, who owned a factory; and Osvaldo Cotto, metal polisher.

In the bank he cashed his check and withdrew five hundred dollars to see him over for a month or so. He'd go on a holiday—a working holiday—and booked a flight to New York leaving the next morning.

There he'd find Goyo Tejada.

CHAPTER 19

Pan American Flight 353 from San Juan landed at Idlewild Airport in New York City after eight hours in the air. Goyo got off without incident, and flowed through the gates with waves of passengers, his countrymen, who came in search of improvement. No one stopped him. No customs. No immigration. *It's easy*, he thought, remembering the difficulties of customs in Cuba—and the required bribery and complexity of doing business there.

It occurred to him this easy ride would end with Puerto Rico's independence. But he didn't dwell on the niceties of his politics. He needed instead to find a green Chevy in Section G of the parking lot.

First, he retrieved from the baggage claim area two suitcases with tags in the name of Rafael Lullanda and a false address in Brooklyn. The travel agency in the Marina outside Old San Juan gave him his new identity and a plane ticket. His sturdy luggage stood out among the other cardboard suitcases and boxes carrying the meager possession of his fellow travelers come to try their luck in the great metropolis. He headed for the exits, walking casually so he would not attract attention, especially from three policemen outside the luggage claim area. They took no notice him, and Goyo avoided studying them. He lost himself in the giant lobby of the terminal, tuning out its din and bustle and the mass of passengers speaking a polyglot of languages, like Babel after the tower fell, in the great din of International Arrivals.

He stopped to study his countrymen, unmistakable among the other arrivals with their plantain stained faces. Ill clothed against the New York weather, they were mostly *jíbaros* not long removed from the hills, their straw hats and country dress hastily exchanged for city garb, their machetes left behind. After a brief sojourn in the sprawling shantytowns of San Juan, they'd exchanged their horses and donkeys for the propeller planes that took them on this mass exodus from the sugar cane fields of Puerto Rico across miles and centuries to this big city.

Their plight saddened him and he took pity on them. And it occurred to him that for their sake he too had come on his mission for the party.

In the parking lot, the green Chevy waited . Goyo approached the passenger side.

"Does this car go to Green Point?"

"No sir, this car goes to Red Point."

"Then take me to Yellow Point."

The driver got out and placed the suitcases in the trunk, and then they got in the car. "Gregorio, I'm Osvaldo Cotto." Goyo sized up this balding man with large spinnaker ears, rimless glasses and a conservative gray suit. After shaking hands, Osvaldo started the car and they drove out of the airport.

"What's happening down there?"

"It's going to break soon."

"How's Don Pedro?"

"Not well. Gaunt and pale."

"And Arcadio?"

"Fine. Gave me instructions for you and Landia. Made it clear you're not to go to Puerto Rico. Put Operation *Huracan* into effect when you hear of the first attack. Liquidate *El Hombre Verdadero*.

Osvaldo's eyes widened and he breathed hard. "Operation *Huracan*?" he repeated. Goyo studied him. Cotto reined in his emotions and concentrated on the traffic out of the airport as they drove in silence. The roar of planes flying eerily low over Idlewild Airport broke that silence as they landed and took off.

"What's *Huracan?*" Goyo asked when traffic eased.

Osvaldo seemed absorbed in his own world.

"What's *Huracan?*" Goyo repeated, probing him.

"El Hombre Verdadero?"

"Patience, Gregorio." His eye left the road long enough to look him in the eye. "You're hot." His eyes again tended to traffic. "If you're picked up, it's not good you know. We'll explain it all to you in a couple of days. Right now, I'll get you to the Bronx—to a house there. Instructions will come soon."

They rode in silence all the way to the end of Queens County. The bright lights of the TriBorough Bridge appeared, and the skyline of Manhattan ablaze with life. Many cars, points of light in the night, drove across to Manhattan, the Bronx, and Queens.

"Look at this bridge, Gregorio," Osvaldo broke the silence when they, too, crossed. "Isn't it wondrous, this marvel of American technology and engineering? But vulnerable. A few men with bombs and a cause can destroy in minutes what ages built."

Goyo mulled over these words. "And "El Hombre Verdadero'?"

"An important man."

They crossed the bridge into the Bronx and cruised north up Bruckner Boulevard. At Hunts Point, Osvaldo made a right and drove up the peninsula toward Point Morris, stopping the car in front of a lone cabin. Far from other houses, it faced the East River.

"It belongs to a party member," Osvaldo explained. "Rents it in the summer." Osvaldo showed him in and gave him keys, telling him that if anyone asked, he was Rafael Lullanda, the caretaker. It had reasonable comforts, including a radio and a small refrigerator stocked with cold cuts, milk, and Coca-Cola. Two cots for sleeping looked inviting after his journey.

"Make due," Cotto said." I'll be back tomorrow around five to pick you up."

"I need a favor," Goyo asked. "I'm looking for my wife, Consuelo Loma de Tejada. She left me. Came here. You know a lot of people. Maybe you can help me." Goyo gave him the briefest of details.

Osvaldo considered his request. "We'll see what we can do."

CHAPTER 20

They buried Martin in the cemetery in Old San Juan. Papo felt uncomfortable in his police uniform never worn undercover and too tight after his weight gain. The priest read the last rites and a twenty-one-gun salute followed. The gray line of policemen in the honor guard lifted the casket. The skies above matched the somber gray of the uniforms. Taps sounded. The widow sobbed. The younger children watched bewildered, the youngest daughter skipping and frolicking. The son sucked his thumbed. Only the older daughter cried with her mother and grandmother. They put him in the ground.

Papo, eyes dry, had exhausted all tears. They whisked the widow away in a waiting car before Papo could speak to her. Pietri snubbed him, and his fellow officers seemed indifferent. He felt alone.

At the end of this ordeal, he drove to the printing shop and told Uncle Ciro that Gregorio Tejada was Martin Lanza's murderer.

"I'm going to New York."

"You're *loco*. Don't do this. Your place is here with the family."

"I must avenge my friend and *compadre*." He asked about nationalist leaders in New York.

Ciro didn't know Osvaldo Cotto. Of Manuel Landia, the president of the New York chapter, he knew only he'd been arrested during the war for refusing military duty and disbarred from his law practice. He knew a lot about Jose Cabranes, secretary and treasurer of the party in New York, for whom he'd once printed materials.

"*Maricon*," Ciro said. "Goes by the name Chucho. Although Cabranes kept his homosexuality under wraps, the rumors didn't. "Saw him once leaving the Azul Bar with another man."

Papo knew the Azul Bar, near the family's old shop in the commercial district and once raided it with the Vice Squad. Papo remembered El Negro, the black bartender who'd served him a drink before the raid. Papo found this information most interesting.

Ciro told him to be careful and to look up his son Guillermo in the Bronx. Papo asked that he keep the trip a secret, but he took Guillermo's phone. Ciro blessed him and promised to light a candle.

He got in his car and drove home. In the rearview mirror San Juan receded on the coastal road to Toa Alto. Tomorrow, he'd fly to New York. There, he'd find Gregorio Tejada. Goyo. He'd avenge his friend and prove his worth to his superiors.

In twenty-four hours he'd be in the South Bronx, the roots of his childhood. His mother had migrated to East Harlem, then the South Bronx, and at age twelve, she'd uprooted him again. Then Dona Inez married his stepfather, Santiago Maldonado, a childless widower who'd labored in various factories. His frugal stepfather labored and saved and returned to Puerto Rico. Papo never called him father, but Chago. The patient Chago never had a cross word for him, despite Papo's resentments and jealousy. Papo grew to love the always understanding Chago, who ran a *bodega* in Santurce for years with his mother, Inez, until their retirement.

Back home, he inspected the day's laundry on the clothesline. His daughters' regulation blue school skirts and white blouses hung there next to his boxer shorts and T-shirts, stains scrubbed and bleached away. It pleased him, as he was in a hurry to pack. Inside, the girls asked for the customary *bendicion*, and so he blessed them, invoking on their behalf the protection of not only God and his mother Maria, but also all the saints.

Getting a beer in the kitchen, he inspected the red kidney beans set to soften in a dish of water and watched Marisol prepare dinner. The salt pork frying in the pot melted slowly, its soft aroma filling the kitchen. The rind turned a succulent dark brown. "I've got something to tell you." The grease had melted in the pot and she put in the *sofrito*, stirring the grounded condiments until they'd soaked up the fat.

"I'm going to New York."

She showed no emotion and instead took out the shriveled pieces of salt pork and put them aside to cook. "Got to look for a suspect there." Mixing the simmering mixture in the pot, she said nothing, and added a can of tomato sauce and olives. "I'm leaving tomorrow." She added the rice and poured water, along with a large helping of lard.

"For how long?" she broke the silence.

"Don't know. A week, maybe two. Depends how fast we catch him."

"Who's sending you?"

"Pietri from Homicide," he lied.

"Carla! Natalia!" she shouted.

"What!" Carla shouted.

"Come, find out!" the mother shouted. "You going alone?"

"No, with two detectives," he lied again. "We're working with the New York police. Are you upset?"

"Upset? Why? You're never here. Go to the moon."

"You're upset." He took her hand.

"Get away."

"Come here, Marisol." He pulled her to him and forced a kiss. It was not refused.

The girls came and giggled at the oddity of their parents' embrace.

"There," Marisol pointed to pieces of toasted pork fat on a plate, "*tocino*." The girls took them and left.

After dinner, she packed his suitcase, as he washed and went to bed. After packing and tucking in the girls, she came into the bedroom and removed her blouse. Her breasts, large and still firm after many breast feedings, aroused him. He took her hand and pulled her to him. She kissed and embraced him, sitting on his lap. He kissed her breasts, sucking gently the nipples.

"I still appeal to you?"

"Yes, more than the first time."

"It's hard competing with twenty-year-olds."

"That was madness. I succumbed. But I love you, the mother of my daughters." He laid her gently on the bed and made love to her.

She fell asleep. He tried but couldn't, as Gregorio Tejada's mug appeared to him. When he finally slept, Martin appeared to him and the South Bronx. Back in P.S.35, he saw his teacher Ms. Murphy and an American flag. Howard Saunders body floated in and out of his dream.

From the airport the next afternoon, he called Pietri. "I'm going to New York."

"What for?"

Papo told him.

"You're crazy," he yelled and reminded him he was no longer on the case. "Don't get on that plane or I'll file insubordination charges."

"I'm on vacation. Instead of the mountains of Puerto Rico, it'll be New York, that's all. If I brush against Gregorio Tejada on a subway, or somewhere, I'll hold him."

"You're crazy!"

Papo told him Tejada was a nationalist assassin and said the fanatics would make a move.

"This is wild. The brass will have your balls and squeeze them hard. I heard you went farting around in the political section. Some people are pissed. Be careful."

Papo now realized his grandfather was right. The higher-ups knew of the nationalist connection but covered it up because it was bad for American investment.

"Tejada has a wife in New York. I checked on her, talked to relatives. Got an address for her in New York. I'll find her—and him. Read my report. Just one favor: if you can hear me out. My plane leaves in a few minutes."

"My patience's about to fly off."

"I'll give you a phone number in New York. Call me if you need me. You'll need me."

"You got balls."

"You got the number?"

"You have your warning."

Papo boarded his flight.

CHAPTER 21

Goyo hid for two days in the safe house on the Hunts Point peninsula. A car picked him up on the second night and took him to a brownstone on Bruckner Boulevard. Osvaldo Cotto answered and led him through a long hallway lined with pictures of Puerto Rican rural landscapes. Goyo stopped to study one of a typical *bohio*, with *jibaros* in straw hats outside this hut. Another of a flaming red famboyan tree, typical of his native Ponce, also caught his attention.

Inside, a spacious living room elegantly furnished waited. A yellow sofa with a matching sofa and loveseat with adjoining living room tables rested on a brown rug with intricate geometric shapes. A brown coffee table with ashtrays and expensive bric-a-brac sat in the middle. A small bar amply stocked and a large radio playing fast rhythms of Cuban music completed the décor. Large picture windows looked out on the tree-lined boulevard outside.

The men sitting on the loveseat, unshaven and unkempt, seemed out of place. He finished a high ball and took a last puff on a Chesterfield, crushing the butt against an ashtray. Getting up, he poured himself a refill at the bar and took a long sip. His bronze skin blended well with the filthy red plaid jacket he wore. Lighting another Chesterfield, he took a long puff of the filterless cigarette, savoring it long in his lungs before releasing the smoke.

"Goyo, Jose Robles," Cotto introduced them. "We call him Indio."

They shook hands. A strong odor of sweat that Goyo found offensive emanated from Indio. Another man appeared, their host, well dressed in a gray business suit. Cotto introduced him as Manuel Landia, president of the New York nationalist chapter.

"Happy to meet you, Tejada," Landia shook his hand. "We've heard about your abilities, Goyo," Landia said in an elegant, well-enunciated voice. "Want a drink?" Goyo nodded and Landia poured him a shot of Chivas Regal.

Absorbed in their discussion, no one heard at first the radio whose music faded, replaced by a jingle and a soft voice in flawless Spanish. Goyo listened to the commentator's opening lines. "Shultz Jewelers, the friend of New York's Latin community, presents the *Six-Twenty Report*."

"Shut up!" Goyo screamed. It's news from home!"

"San Juan, Puerto Rico," the commentator continued after the commercial. "The extraordinary series of events rocking this peaceful Caribbean island spread today as the wave of nationalist terrorism continues unabated. The fanatical followers of Pedro Albizu Campos attacked and burned several police precincts on the island. In the town of Jayuya, one policeman, identified as Virgilio Camacho, was killed, and one nationalist, Carlos Irizarry, was wounded and later died in Utuado Hospital. Three more nationalists were arrested, including a woman identified as Blanca Canales. By all accounts, a fierce battle now rages for control of the mountain towns of Jayuya and neighboring Utuado.

"Governor Luis Munoz Marin appealed for calm on the island, expressing confidence the police would bring the situation under control. The governor claimed the nationalists sought to disrupt the coming election for members to the proposed constitutional convention. 'They will not stop our march toward democratic government,' he added. Stay tune to this station for further updates … Trujillo City, Dominican Republic. President Rafael Trujillo announced today …'"

"This is it!" Osvaldo exclaimed, his fist crushing down on the radio. "And I'm stuck here!"

"We've crossed our tropical Rubicon," Landia said, "but I fear we've crossed too soon."

"Jayuya is the birth place of the republic," Osvaldo lamented. "And I'm in the Bronx."

"This struggle will be long, Cotto," Landia assured him. "And fought over this hemisphere. There's work here. We had better start. Gregorio, you have a message for us?"

"For you and Cotto." He eyed El Indio. "I was told to tell nobody else."

"It's all right. Indio is part of the family, with useful talents like you. You may speak."

"Don Pedro says put *Huracan* into effect when you hear of the first precinct bombing. Don't go to Puerto Rico—the police will pick you up if you do. Your job's here, launching *Huracan*. Liquidate El Hombre *Verdadero*. Put me to use. You know what I do."

"We do, Goyo, we do," Landia assured him. He explained they were already under a microscope and that the police and FBI would be watching even closer. They'd break into cells working independently without contact with the rest of the movement. The party would organize protests throughout the city and handle legal needs. Two cells were working already on parts of *Huracan*. Two more would emerge from their meeting tonight. Indio would lead one and Cotto and Goyo the other. Landia would work in the open, and give them money until *Huracan* began, and then he too would go underground.

Goyo poured another drink and took a hard gulp, looking long and hard in Landia's eyes. "Fine. And what *is Huracan*? And *El Hombre Verdadero*?"

"Osvaldo," Landia said.

"I gave you a hint in the car that night. Remember the expressway and the bridges? We're putting bombs on those bridges and in the airports, the docks, and the train stations. We're at war, Gregorio, with America. We'll hit the *Yanquis* where it hurts. They won't feel a riot in Puerto Rico—but they'll feel a bomb in Grand Central Station, or Idlewild Airport, especially if there's killing and wounding. They'll feel vulnerable if we tie up traffic, close the airports, and the trains don't run. They don't know where Puerto Rico is, let alone that it's an American colony. We're not part of the American conscience. They're ignorant of our plight. That's one phase of *Huracan*."

Goyo took another sip and listened. Osvaldo explained they were soldiers, like in commando movies where British agents jump behind enemy lines. "We're already behind enemy lines. We come in through the front door. America's openness makes it vulnerable."

Cotto had discussed it with Don Pedro who stayed in his house in 1946 after his release from his Atlanta prison.

They'd discussed Ireland and India and Israel—and other independent movements. Don Pedro felt Gandhi's approach in India wouldn't work in Puerto Rico without the masses needed to resist peacefully. "The Irgun's approach in Israel and that of the Irish Republican Army he'd deemed suitable for us. There are more Puerto Ricans than Israelis."

"But more Jews than Puerto Ricans—and more Irishmen. Jews are rich. And smart. They have scientists that know about bombs—and the Rothschilds to bankroll them. Those Jews Einstein and Oppenheimer put the big bomb together. That's a skill our people lack—the ones on our side, anyway. It's expensive, too. Assuming you get the materials, and they don't come cheap, where do we get the people?"

"It's doable," Indio said, lighting another Chesterfield. "We don't have Einstein, but we don't need atom bombs. I have a group of like-minded men who believe in the cause, men unafraid to die. I alone know their identities. Materials are no problem. We need pipes from hardware stores. The black powder we get in gun shops, but upstate, not here in the city. Or, potassium or sodium nitrate mixed with charcoal and sulfur. We drill holes in the pipes, place fuses in them, and seal their ends with caps."

"Then you light the fuse and run?" Goyo frowned.

"No. We make timers. It takes batteries, blasting caps, watches, and electric circuits. Crude but effective. We can't give the *Yanquis* a big bang, but we can give them a jolt, although I'm no Einstein. And I'm no Rothschild." He looked at Landia.

"You'll have money," Landia said. "Don't have your stuff traced to us."

"And the other part, Cotto?"

Cotto explained they'd liquidate enemies of the Puerto Rican republic. The Resident Commissioner for Puerto Rican Affairs in Washington and the head of the Puerto Rican Migration Office in New York, for starters.

"But they're Puerto Ricans, for better or worse, and Americans wouldn't care, except that it happened on American soil. They'll notice dead Americans, important Americans." Cotto explained they needed exposure so the media would investigate their people's plight, which Americans wouldn't see until Puerto Rico affected them deeply. The world would see their colonial status and pressure the United States as it pressured the Soviets over their colonies. Bombings and assassinations would ratchet up the pressure. "Whose death would they feel the most?" Cotto asked.

"*El Hombre Verdadero*," Goyo answered. "Who is ...?"

"How's your English, Gregorio?"

"Good. I was forced fed the language in grade school."

"What's *hombre verdadero* in English?"

"Man real? No, Real man," Goyo thought aloud. "Man true. True man. True man?"

"We're going to shoot Truman. Harry S. Truman."

"Truman? President Truman?"

"Yes."

"I need another drink." At the bar, he poured one himself, taking a long sip, and then digested the words. "We're going to shoot the President of the United States?"

"Shooting a few political hacks from Puerto Rico won't faze the *Yanquis*, but killing the President of the United States will focus America's conscience on Puerto Rico and the conscience of the world. Our people will take heart and join the struggle. The death of a president will create chaos in this country and bombings and acts of sabotage will add to the confusion. And along with the mess in Korea, the right climate will appear for Puerto Rico to slip away."

"Your political reasoning is sound. But how do we get to him? He must have a hundred guards surrounding him in the White House—Munoz Marin must have that many."

"Munoz doesn't take morning walks around Old San Juan as President Truman does around the capital. He gets up early and strolls around like any citizen. We go to Washington, walk around the White House like any tourists, and when he goes for his walk, we blow him away."

"How do we get away?"

"We don't."

"I see." He took another gulp. "Who are we?"

"You, me, and three more men who'll join us."

"Don Pedro himself ordered this hit, Goyo," Landia said. "He chose you for your aim."

"And your *cojones*," Osvaldo added. "You got balls. We all know it."

"I never turn down an order from Don Pedro—or the party. I need to see my wife and daughter first."

"You will," said Osvaldo. "I've asked around. I found people who know her."

"Where is she?"

"Don't know yet. I'm working on it."

"I want to see her."

"You will, be patient. It's a delicate matter. Right now we're going to need a couple of guns and ammunition. The other colleagues are provided for."

"We have a contact for you, a Spanish gentleman, a Falangist," Landia said. "Mirabal's his name. He's got connections in the Spanish government. Get in touch with him. We'll provide the money."

"You'll have use of my car and money for the expenses in Washington and hotel rooms. The guns can't be traced to Mirabal. He mustn't know what they're for."

"Fine."

"I'll be in touch," Osvaldo said. "We'll meet the others and plan this. You'll have the guns when we meet again in two days—and I'll have information about your wife."

"To Harry S. Truman," Goyo raised his drink in a toast and gulped it down. He'd often thought of dying in a blaze of glory, and the scenario of falling in the enemy's capital appealed to him. But though he'd always answered the party's call, this was suicide. He didn't want to die yet. He'd find his wife and daughter and start again. These plans he kept to himself.

CHAPTER 22

Chief Howland studied his hand casually and the latest pot piled on the table. The other players sipped their drinks, puffed cigars and cigarettes, and studied theirs. He learned to play poker in the minor leagues in his baseball years, on the team bus and in cheap road hotels between cities and games. The smell of tobacco and alcohol filling the conference room of Blair House began to bother him. He disliked smoke-filled rooms. For poker, he never developed a passion and knew gambling and its companion sins could ruin a man.

The Chief played out of courtesy to the President, whose occasional invitation couldn't be refused.

"See you a quarter and raise you two," Mr. Truman proclaimed, touching off a chorus of *oohs* and *ahs*.

Admiral William Leahy studied the cards and peeked at his hole card, the taut, leathery face, tanned and beaten by the sea's elements, stretched in concentration. "I'll see you three, Mr. President." The Admiral added three quarters to the ante. With the nine of diamonds and the ten of hearts showing, he harbored hopes of a straight.

The Chief saw the bet, adding his share to the ante. Although he'd unfastened the tie and rolled up his sleeves, he began to sweat.

The dealer, General Bret Halleck of the army, lay three more quarters on the table to make an impressive pile. "And now, the honorable gentleman from the state of Missouri."

"The Congress adjourns for the rest of this deal," Congressman Stuart Symington announced, then mumbled something about gambling with soldiers and sailors.

General Halleck blew smoke before resting his cigar on a central ashtray, already host to a handful of cigarette butts. He picked up the deck, and as his deft fingers slipped out each card, he offered commentary. "A Jack for the President. Watch for a straight. Another Jack for the navy. Possible straight, boys. A king for the Chief. My, all this royalty. A six for me. The army retreats."

"Don't say retreat in front of your Commander-in-Chief, Bret. But if you're out, four more bits says I have a straight here." He slipped in the coins and admired the growing pot.

"Two more bits say I have it, Mr. President," the Admiral offered. And with a Jack to add to his ten, seven, and eight, it was not an empty boast.

"The secret service rests," the Chief said.

"The secret service never rests," the President sallied.

The Chief smiled, reading in Mr. Truman's retort the ever present, though always gentle, plead for less intrusive protection.

"But if you and the General are out, it's between the navy and this old army captain. Four more bits say I've got the straight."

"You're on, Mr. President," came the Admiral. Four more quarters went into the pot.

The General dealt. "A deuce for the President, another six for the Admiral."

"There it is," said the President laying down his cards and raking in the wins. A straight. What's the probability?

"Slim," said the General.

The Congressman next dealt and went with five card studs. The President felt lucky with five card studs, but not the Chinese. General MacArthur, he

114

confided, swore at their meeting in Wake Island that the Chinese wouldn't cross the Yalu. "But I wonder a lot these days about that son of a bitch, his Majesty the General."

The Chief recalled the conversation he'd overhead on Wake Island. The pompous MacArthur, after apparently ordering his pilot to circle the air field, forced the President's plane to land first so Mr. Truman would greet the General and not vice versa, as protocol dictated. "I don't give a good goddamn what you think of Harry Truman," the President dressed down the General. "But don't you ever keep your Commander-in-Chief waiting again." The embarrassed General swallowed hard.

They took a break when Hayes, the Negro butler, rolled in a cart with snacks. The Chief ate a roast beef sandwich, as did the General, invoking the cliché that an army marches on its stomach. The Navy had a Scotch and soda refill, and the Congress passed. Hayes served the President more water and bourbon.

"Let's strike a blow for freedom," he toasted and downed his liquor in one gulp.

The Chief toasted with a Coke and munched on his roast beef sandwich. The smoke bothered Chief Howland, who didn't drink or smoke. Intuition told him inhaling smoke did damage, and he thought science would one day prove it.

In life, he'd known good men ruined by drink. In his hometown of Battle Creek, Michigan he saw early the perils of alcohol, confirmed by abounding examples. He remembered the days of President Warren G. Harding spent in the White House and remembered wild poker games and heavy drinking—during the era of Prohibition, when alcohol consumption was supposed to be illegal. And like the rest of America, A. B. Howland also knew of other scandals and improper land speculations that sent some of his poker cronies to jail after Mr. Harding's untimely death while on a trip to San Francisco. No, it'd been an assassination. No one spoke about this theory in his early days in the secret service.

Everybody spoke back then about the lemonade served by Mr. Harding's teetotaling successor, Mr. Coolidge. The Chief, too, tasted some.

Coffee, his vice, he consumed in large quantities. Perhaps it also did harm.

Smoke never bothered Harry S. Truman, who, though not a smoker, the Chief knew to be a veteran of many poker games and many smoke-filled rooms.

Mr. Truman asked about the Chinese troops captured south of the Yalu.

The Admiral thought them advisers to the North Koreans but cautioned our troops be kept far from the Yalu bridges. "We can bomb them later if need be. Macarthur needs to shut up and stop calling the Chinese cowards in the press."

"Made it clear to him on Wake Island. Not sure he listened."

General Halleck took a long puff on the cigar, held the smoke in for an eternity, and then released it slowly. He agreed there was nothing's worse than a commander thinking himself above the Commander-in-Chief and added everybody learns that at West Point. "Commies do cross the Yalu, bomb them. Talk straight to Stalin. Any funny business, World War Three starts right there. First sign of Russkies anywhere, we say move or we sink two of your cities into the earth. You've got that ace showing, Mr. President. Japs called your bluff. Stalin's knows it."

The President thought. "I'll play that hand when it comes."

Silence followed.

The Congressman broke it. "Speaking of deals, time for another." They anted up again for five card studs with one-eyed jacks in the hole wild. The President got his one-eye jack and two kings, good enough for three of a kind to beat the Chief's two of a kind.

"Yes sir, I feel lucky," he said, pulling in the pot. "Feel a string of luck running my way. My deal."

The General heard nature's call and called a halt to the deal to answer it.

The Congressman asked about Puerto Rico while the President pulled in the cards and shuffled them.

"Just a few nationalist fanatics raising hell again."

"The Russians might raise a stink," the Congressman feared.

Mr. Truman defended his record, reminding them he told Congress in '45 the United States would abide by the wishes of the Puerto Rican people, telling the Puerto Ricans themselves in '48 he'd fight for whatever status they chose. He boasted he appointed Jesus Pinero governor—the first native ever under Americans or the Spaniards. They'd get statehood, independence—or Governor Munoz' plan, at the ballot box, not on the battlefield. "That clown Pedro Albizu Campos couldn't win a race for dog catcher of San Juan in a free election."

Admiral Leahy, whom the Chief remembered served as military governor there in '39, mentioned Joe Stalin brought up Puerto Rico at the Potsdam Conference five years back, in '45. "He wanted to swap Latin America for Eastern Europe."

The President laughed, recalling talks with the Russian leader over the UN Charter. "Stalin asked why we objected to the admission of Albania and Rumania as free states when our colonies Puerto Rico, Honduras, and Nicaragua would also have votes.

"An even trade." The Congressman laughed.

The President added Stalin promised not to protest our special relationship with Latin America if we didn't make a stink over Eastern Europe. "The bastard was grabbing everything in sight and threw us a bone."

It all reminded the President of a Missouri farmer down South who couldn't find a bathroom and peed on Robert E. Lee's statue. Arrested, he pleads guilty, gets fined three dollars, gives the clerk a five, and walks out. The clerk calls him back for his change. The farmer stops and turns. "Keep it," Mr. Truman threw in the punch line. "I farted, too."

It caused uproar. The Chief stifled a blush. Harry Truman's earthy jokes made his men laugh. Chicago's mayor, Anton Cermak, also made them laugh with the one about the Slovak cow and the Czech farmer and took them off guard before he took the bullet fired by Giuseppe Zangara meant for Mr. Roosevelt that fateful night in Miami's Bay Front Park. "Too many are hungry."

But Puerto Rico was no laughing matter. Protective Research Bureau memos kept him abreast of growing nationalist activity in New York. And the new violence on the island itself had created cause for concern for the

President's safety. He again remembered the violence there in the thirties, when threats and scorn were heaped on Mr. Roosevelt.

The President stretched while the laughter subsided, got up, and took a bathroom break, as did the Chief. Upstairs, he saw the President stick his head out of the library window for a whiff of air. The Chief hated when the President stuck his head out of windows.

Everybody returned.

"Five card studs, boys," the President picked up the deal. "I feel lucky."

CHAPTER 23

Papo took a cab from Idlewild Airport to the Carlyle Hotel in Times Square after a long, grueling flight. Engine trouble forced an unscheduled stop of several hours in Atlanta, Georgia. He slept several hours after dropping on the hotel's soft bed, for his mind and body ran were running on fast-forward and needed to pause. He woke around dinnertime and ordered a newspaper and breakfast from room service. The busboy, in a bellhop's blue uniform with two rows of shiny buttons and cap, studied the dollar tip and gave him a long smile.

"Thank you senor," he said, eyes bright. The youngster treated him regally after that. He ate four fried eggs, sunny side up, with sausages, home fries, toast, a pitcher of orange juice, and two cups of coffee.

An article buried deep on page twenty-three of *The Daily News* reported that members of the Puerto Rican Nationalist Party controlled the interior towns of Jayuya and Utuado, high up in the mountains. In Utuado, they'd destroyed the fire station and battled police reinforcements from other cities. The article said only that violence was spreading fast on the island, giving few details.

Papo worried less his family be caught up in the violence, picturing Marisol and the girls and bullets flying in the air. And he felt guilty with the selfishness of leaving them on a whim to avenge a friend dawned on him. His job was there with them—and his comrades in harm's way in Jayuya and Utuado. He agonized in his hotel room, depressed and alone. But his hunch of an imminent nationalist uprising came to pass—a hunch communicated to the pig headed Pietri. He'd call his cousin Guillermo in the Bronx. Perhaps Pietri had already called and left a message. And he knew the sensible Marisol would care well for their daughters. Deep down, Papo knew the nationalists lacked wide support. The fire they'd lit would be quickly extinguished.

He'd traveled far these last two days with a purpose. Tomorrow, he'd begin his search for Gregorio Tejada among the nationalists here. Deciding to pose as a sympathizer recently arrived in New York, he'd drop in on the nationalist office in the Bronx and say he wanted to help. And he'd look for Tejada's wife at the East Harlem address Papo managed to get from her last employer, posing as a family friend with a letter from Puerto Rico.

Needing fresh air, he dressed and took in the sights.

The glitter and excitement of Broadway and the bright lights of the Manhattan skyline revived his spirits. It all felt like a dream. His tropical poplar suit proved inadequate against the cold. More people strolled through these streets than lived in all San Juan. And he marveled at the variety of humanity—black, white, oriental, and Latinos, and especially the exotic Jewish orthodox Hasidim in yarmulkes, long beards and flowing locks, along with Indian Sikhs in turbans.

At the very heart of Times Square, he stopped to read the electronic news flashes circling around the Western Gulf Building. General MacArthur neared the Yalu River and the Chinese border. Senator McCarthy made fresh allegations of Communist sympathies among government officials. And in Europe, Russian dictator Joseph Stalin again menaced West Berlin.

More marvelous still he found the cinema marquees and he toyed with the idea of a movie. From one, *Cyrano de Bergerac* beckoned, featuring his fellow *Boricua*, Jose Ferrer, duded up in seventeenth-century garb. He wore the large hat and cape of the French courtiers of Versailles and brandished a sword as long as his nose.

He walked instead up to Columbus Circle around Central Park. The people of the Manhattan night entertained him more than a movie. The *gringa* hookers cast furtive glances. One, a pretty red head in a tight revealing dress, twirled her pocketbook and called to him, "Wanna go out, honey?"

He kept walking, his interest purely professional, relived he was not obligated to bust them.

"Where you from handsome? Sure look exotic."

"A faraway land called the Bronx."

"Well, you're far from home."

He lingered for a while and looked at her. Then he thought about Marisol. "Eyes that don't see, hearts that don't feel," he remembered an old adage. There were no evil tongues here to tell on him. But he kept walking.

Back in the hotel, he called his cousin Guillermo, who scolded him for not calling earlier. The eldest son of Uncle Ciro, Guillermo had come to New York on a ship of the *Marine Tiger* line before the war, in the late thirties and now lived with his wife and two boys in the South Bronx. He rarely visited Puerto Rico. His cousin invited him over to the Bronx, offering to put him up and promising him a good meal.

That Guillermo had no messages from his superiors in Puerto Rico disappointed Papo. Of his business in New York, he told Guillermo only that the Puerto Rican police wanted a killer believed hiding in New York. His own assignment involved tracking the killer's family, including a nationalist sympathizer. Intrigued, Guillermo probed, but Papo gave only the sketchiest details, mentioning neither Howard Saunders nor Gregorio Tejada.

Of Julito's problem he said nothing. Papo asked that his cousin speak to no one about it, calling his work top secret. Papo asked about nationalist activities in New York.

A Popular Democrat, Guillermo praised Governor Munoz Marin and dismissed Pedro Albizu Campos. "That crazy mulatto comes to power. We'll all return to the cane fields. Let his black mother cut sugar cane in that sun."

He avoided his own statehood views, knowing his cousin's opinionated ways, and asked where the nationalists met. Guillermo explained the Puerto Rican Nationalist Party met in a hall on East 138th Street, near his cousin's Saks Fifth Avenue warehouse. He also mentioned a heavily publicized meeting for the following night, with the President of the New York chapter, Manuel Landia, slated to speak. Papo also learned of a heavy turnout at meetings since the outbreak of violence in Puerto Rico.

Papo thanked him and promised to visit.

The next afternoon, after browsing all morning through the shops in the theater district, Papo took the Third Avenue El Uptown to East Harlem in search of Consuelo Loma de Tejada. He was shocked to see that the token fare had risen from a nickel to a dime. *Exorbitant*, he thought.

The ride proved nostalgic and exciting. He remembered riding the El with his mother to visit friends in East Harlem, where they'd first lived with relatives, on the edge of Little Italy. But after his mother married his stepfather Chago, they'd moved to the largely Jewish and Irish neighborhood in the South Bronx. Chago, light skinned and Italian looking, got the apartment, then brought the dark skinned Ines and Papo, raising eyebrows in this all white neighborhood near the Willis Avenue Bridge, where Irish cops routinely stopped Negroes and Puerto Ricans sent back to East Harlem across the East River.

He got off on East 110th Street to look up Consuelo Tejada's uncle, Felix Norat. East Harlem's sounds grew familiar, as did its dirt and perennial shadows below the El tracks where little sunlight fell. It teemed with people packed into tenements. On the streets, everyone hurried. He heard less Italian and more Spanish, its lexicon grown with English words Hispanicized, their harsher Germanic endings rounded into softer vowels. The sounds of a *bolero* coming from a music store sounded familiar. A train thundered above the tracks raining down sparks. He felt at home here.

He found the address, an old tenement on 110th Street beneath the El. An old woman in an apron and in a daze answered his knock on the first-floor apartment.

"Good evening, mother. Does Don Felix Norat live here?"

"No, they no longer do, *mijo*." Her puzzled eyed looked him up and down.

"Do you know where they live? I have a letter from mutual friends in Puerto Rico."

She said they went back to Puerto Rico, though the niece, who worked as a as seamstress somewhere in the Bronx moved out and she suggested a baby sitter, a Pura Maldonad might know.

"She lives on 112th and Second. Don't know the address, but ask on the block. Somebody will."

"*Gracias. Muchas gracias.*"

Papo thanked her profusely and walked two blocks to a *bodega*, where he was told to go a few doors down. A large woman in rollers and a bathrobe answered, an annoyed look on her face. He heard the sound of children in the background.

"Yes, Consuelo." She sighed. "Haven't seen her in a while. I used to care for her little girl, but we had a problem. She came late." Her eyes grew firm. "I'm strict about that. By seven all the children must leave. I have a husband and children of my own. Told her to get somebody else."

"Would you know where she lives?"

She didn't, but said she worked as a seamstress somewhere on Intervale Avenue and Westchester Avenue, near East 163rd Street in the Bronx. She said a girl named Fita, a baby-sitter, might know and directed him to Lexington Avenue and the corner of 104th. "The building next to the laundry."

"Thank you very much, Dona Pura. You've been very helpful."

Fita, sipping a can of beer, answered the door, eyeing him suspiciously. Though light of skin color, her hair, overheated by hot electric combs, could not subdue the Negroid features she tried to hide. It upset him people tried to play down their racial roots.

"Who sent you?" she sneered.

"Her uncle's neighbor," Papo answered.

Claiming no recent knowledge of Consuelo, she seemed anxious to be rid of him.

Papo thanked her, and she seemed relieved when he took leave. He walked slowly under the El. In front of a *cuchifrito* restaurant, he studied the dumplings, roasted pork and fried plantain displayed appetizingly behind the eatery's window. The strong aroma of *criollo* cooking set his gastric juices swimming in a cultural reflex. The *alcapurias* filled with crabmeat in crushed plantain enticed him, as did the *bacalaitos* stuffed with codfish.

He entered and sat on an empty stool in front of the counter. The other customers took no notice of him. In Puerto Rico, he would've elicited token nods from fellow diners, but here, the impersonal anonymity struck him. He ordered blood sausages, pig's ear and boiled green bananas swimming in a rich sauce. He asked for a large coconut drink, with a glass of water.

The young girl Fita knew something. Consuelo Tejada lived somewhere in this neighborhood. Tomorrow early, he'd visit the shop on Intervale Avenue and Westchester. Having eaten, he walked back to the el after his meal and headed for the Bronx.

A cool October breeze greeted him outside the East 138th Street Station— and shock, for the place was transformed. He saw old and new sights. A largely Puerto Rican throng milled about 138th. It all smelled different, for though the kosher Deli still catered, the *cuchifrito* restaurant did most of the business. In the Irish pub, he saw a handful of old men drinking unobtrusively behind the grimy window. But in the bar across the street Cuban music merged with jazz rhythms. And on every corner stood the ubiquitous bodega.

He found the Catholic church unchanged. But a crosshead replaced Hebrew inscriptions on the Jewish synagogue's facade, now a Pentecostal church. His mother raised him a Catholic; however, his grandmother Dona Alba attended Pentecostal services and took him to service. As a boy, he'd played stickball in front of the synagogue Saturday mornings, often turning on the lights for the old Jews. Puzzled by their strange ways, he later learned of the strict Jewish injunctions against work on the Sabbath, including flicking on a switch.

Singing and loud "hallelujahs" came from the old Jewish holy place, not the mournful Hebrew chants nor the stately choir music of German and Irish working class Catholics. This was *jibaro* music: *guarachas* from the hills and *plenas* and *bombas* from the coast. These forms, he'd once learned, fused the Spanish guitar and tambourine with African drums and Taino guiros and maracas.

Familiar too were the voices. Spanish was now spoken here.

At the Forum Theater he'd watched Gene Autry, Hopalong Cassidy, the Cagney movies, and Flash Gordon. On Sundays, his mother gave him a quarter, and after paying a dime admission, he spent the rest on candy and soda. But in place of the Forum stood the *Teatro* Puerto Rico. On the Spanish language posters, Mexican *bandidos* and Argentine singers replaced the gringo cowboys of old.

Immigration had transformed the Bronx of his boyhood, an immigration he'd heard about but whose dimensions he'd never comprehended. These turn of the century tenements bulged with people, his people, *jíbaros* one step out of the hills. And he wondered how they'd spread so fast.

A regular procession of propeller planes droned overhead now. Papo watched them fly low over the South Bronx on their approach to LaGuardia Airport. Fuselages and wings flashed by steadily, guided by the searchlights in the distance.

Even the skies here were alive.

After walking two blocks, he found the offices of the Puerto Rican Nationalist party, a large meeting hall above a row of stores.

CHAPTER 24

Upstairs, the large hall packed with people seethed with excitement. Puerto Rican expatriates filled every row of folding chairs and many more stood in the back. Anticipation lined their faces and the place buzzed with talk of violence and of expectations of things to come.

The large flag of Lares with its white cross against a blue and red background spread out on the stage. To its right hung a portrait of the man who raised it, Dr. Emeterio Betances, whom Papo remembered was the leader of the 1868 uprising against the Spaniards, who silenced the "Scream of Lares."

On a podium, two guitarists strung their instruments and harmonized "La Borinquena," Puerto Rico's national anthem. Some party dignitaries talked next to them. And behind the podium loomed a larger than life portrait of Don Pedro Albizu Campos, the large black eyes of the party leader gazing hypnotically at the audience.

Papo studied the crowd from the back and Albizu's portrait. He remembered a line from a nationalist poster: "Before they take our land, they will first have to take our lives." Anxious less he looked too much like a cop, he feared he was too quiet. Two men in the next row in front talked. Papo waited for a good moment to jump in. One, a fat man with a mole next to his nose, complained about the lack of coverage of Puerto Rican affairs in the American press. Another, a skinny man with an ill-fitting toupee, agreed.

"I tell you, *companero*, the Russians fart in East Berlin and it makes the front page of *The New York Times*," the fat man lamented. "But dead Puerto Ricans they bury on page thirty-nine of the *Daily News*."

"That's why we're demonstrating, brother," the skinny man said." You signing up?"

"*Si*. To picket the UN"

"Me too."

"What good will it do?" Papo interjected.

"It helps," the fat man said.

"Waste of waste of time, *companero*. Let's plant a few bombs here in New York. Why march up and down like a bunch of *faggots*." Papo warmed to his role. A nationalist meeting once attended with his brother Julito felt strangely enough like the Pentecostal church services attended with his grandmother as a child. Most convincing was the fervor of a Pentecostal convert, he thought.

"Never seen you here," the fat man said.

"Just got to New York. Come from Bayamon, here, to try my luck. I've always believed in the cause. Want to help the party here. My grandfather told me to look up some people. Which one's Landia?"

The skinny man pointed out a white man in a black suit talking to people on the podium. He explained Landia, president of the New York chapter of the Puerto Rican Nationalist Party, wanted volunteers to march and write letters. He pointed out an American near the podium in a suit. "That's Earl Browder, former head of the American Communist Party."

"They say Marcoantonio's coming, too," added the fat man.

"Who's he? " Papo asked.

"An Italian socialist," the skinny man said. "He's the congressman from East Harlem. Lawyer. This Italian defended Albizu in court. He speaks on our behalf in the Congress."

"Marcoantonio makes me nervous, too," the fat man came back. "He's a fascist. Used to kiss Mussolini's ass before he started kissing Stalin's.

We shouldn't be associated with those people. Senator McCarthy might be watching."

"Who's McCarthy?" Papo asked.

"A paranoid Senator from Wisconsin who cries hysterically the communists are taking over America," the fat man explained.

"McCarthy's crazy," the skinny man added. "He'd call his own wife a communist if she climbed into bed from the left side."

"Yeah, but there's too much hysteria over the Russians. We don't want the gringos thinking they're bankrolling us."

"Well we can't just throw them out," Papo butted in again. "And if Stalin shows up with money bags—or Mussolini, for that matter—let's welcome them. We need help from whoever's willing to give it. Can't be but so choosey. "

"Me, I like to guess who the police informers are," added the skinny man.

"Do they bother us?" Papo asked nonchalantly, looking the man in the eye.

"They're here," the fat man said.

The guitarists came to the podium and the audience quieted after a few *shhss* and stood for "La Borinquena." *"La tierra de Borinquen donde he nacido yo ..."* Ignorant of the words, Papo faked it well. At P.S.35 he sang "God Bless America" and "The Star Spangled Banner," the only songs he knew. He deemed "La Borinquena" a pretty song, one he should know. When the music stopped, Manuel Landia came to the podium.

"Companeros," he began, unbuttoning his black double-breasted suit, as it had grown perceptively warmer. "The hour of decision is upon us." He spoke in a precise and elegant manner, sweeping the air with one hand and clasping his waist with the other. "In two weeks there will be an election in Puerto Rico and delegates will be chosen for a constitutional convention. The President of the United States and the American press hail it as a great and true test of democracy under the American flag and they point to the Soviet satellites and dare Stalin to hold elections in those countries. Let us take a close look at our elections.

"*Companeros*, as you all should know, in July of this year, the *Yanqui* congress passed a law permitting Puerto Rico to write its own constitution. We may choose independence, we may choose to be the forty-ninth state of the union, or we may continue as a territory like Hawaii and Alaska, a colony, really, although they package it under another name, an *estado libre asociado*, a Commonwealth, they call it euphemistically in English—a freely associated state which will be neither state nor associated nor free."

These words drew a strong applause.

Landia then made the case that the Congress of the United States lacked the right to tell Puerto Rico what to do as it lacked legal jurisdiction over Puerto Rico. He condemned the Sepoy army of police who bloodied the heads of their own brothers at home in carrying out the will of the invaders, and the army of *jibaros* whose blood it spilled fighting in far off Korea for a freedom they didn't enjoy at home.

Papo knew now Sepoys to be native troops used by England in the nineteenth century to police their colony in India. When he heard the term applied to the Puerto Rican police, he cringed.

Landia then evoked the name of Don Pedro Albizu Campos and the crowd broke into a loud applause and shouts of "Don Pedro! Don Pedro!"

Landia explained Don Pedro's position, which held Puerto Rico, by international law, to be an autonomous state under Spanish law, voiding the provision of the Treaty of Paris ending the Spanish American War, which made Puerto Rico American property. "Spain couldn't just cede us away like some whore it'd grown tired of," Landia declared. "Can you sell a house you have no deed to?" he asked rhetorically. "They cannot repress the national will."

Papo thought this argument weak. It made about as much sense as the American Indians claiming to be the true proprietors of the United States. Both held some truth. But Indians would be as naïve as the nationalists to deny the historical fact of the American conquest. He found the speaker pompous and full of himself, a self-proclaimed intellectual, a *"perfumado,"* like the ones his stepfather Chago derided.

Landia continued, "Ostensibly, this constitution would reflect the wishes of the Puerto Rican people, but we will not ask who will control the Constitutional Convention. Maria? Pedro? Jose? Juan? No. You know who'll pull the strings.

They read like quotes from the stock market: Gulf, Standard Oil, General Motors, Ford. Yes, American business will pull the strings—through their proxy, Luis Munoz Marin."

Loud, contagious boos followed the mention of the Governor's name. Papo booed as well, although for reasons different from the nationalists boos. A statehooder, he opposed the Governor's middle course between statehood and independence.

"Now we will ask who is Luis Munoz Marin? We'll forget his past, his womanizing, Bohemian, marijuana-smoking past, forget that he's not morally fit to lead our nation. We'll forget he's a poet, a very bad poet," he added, emphasizing the *bad* and drawing a few chuckles from the audience, as well as some *ooh* and *ahs* for his personal jabs.

Papo knew of the Governor's Bohemian past in Greenwich Village and heard the whispers about vices and youthful indiscretions. But past personal failings Papo thought invalid issues.

"We'll forget all this and see who Senor Munoz Marin really is," Landia continued. "We can't forget he's the son of Don Luis Munoz Rivera. Yes, Don Luis the father," he sighed. "Don Luis the father believed in independence *manana*—tomorrow. You know the word. That's what the Americans think we're always saying, *manana, manana, manana*. Know where they got the stereotype? From Don Luis the father who as Resident Commissioner for Puerto Rico in Washington early this century wanted independence, but always *manana*.

"It was independence after our trade developed, independence after our internal communication and transportation systems improved, independence after our civil service functioned more efficiently. *Manana, manana, manana*." The crowd picked up the mocking chant and Landia availed himself of the long period of jeering to swallow a glass of water and wipe perspiration from his brow.

Papo studied the man. Landia could stir a crowd.

"And now, like father, like son, for the sins of the father are now committed by the son. *Manana* says the father, *manana* says the son. If Governor Munoz gets his way, we'll first build our economy and then address our political status, which the Governor thinks irrelevant now. Yes, irrelevant to him, irrelevant to the *Yanqui* businessmen. More relevant are huge profits. And when they've sunk

131

their tentacles deeper into our economy and homeland, when our economy is "better," twenty-five, fifty, a hundred years from now, we'll still be "unready," *companeros*.

"But we're ready, now, Mr. Truman, we're ready now, Mr. Munoz Marin. We are ready now, Mr. Speaker of the House Rayburn. The will of the Puerto Rican people cries out to you. We're telling the son, stop writing those terrible verses! We're telling the *Yanquis, independencia! Manana*, no! Now! Now! Now!" he shouted, his clenched fist dealing the podium terrible blows with each 'now.'

The crowd went insane, clapping wildly, and beginning to chant. *"Jibaro, si, Yanqui, no! Jibaro, si, Yanqui, no! Jibaro, si, Yanqui, no! Jibaro, si, Yanqui, no!"*

Papo, too, clapped. He yelled. But secretly, he distanced himself from the mindlessness that come over this crowd, whipped into frenzy by Manuel Landia, as Pentecostal converts overcome by the Holy Ghost.

When the shouting subsided, Landia exhorted the crowd to reject the invader from the north and his deceptive promise of superior technology. He warned of the great peril of sacrificing Hispanic honor and personal dignity for Nordic materialism, and Latin idealism and belief in family for Anglo-Saxon individualism. He spoke over and over of the will of the Puerto Rican people. Papo wearied of the rhetoric.

Finally Landia called for volunteers to picket the United Nations, the United States Congress, and the White House in support of the patriots who had risen for the homeland Puerto Rico. Others were needed to leaflet and help with a mailing appealing for money and manpower.

The shouting over, Papo mingled. He heard someone call Jose Cabranes, the party secretary. Cabranes spoke with some people and took them into an office behind the stage. The men came out with some material Cabranes had given them. Papo observed him from afar for a few minutes. Uncle Ciro said "Chucho" Cabranes was a homosexual. But far from effeminate, Cabranes appeared masculine, with a large, well-kept mustache and a long, prominent nose, smartly dressed in a blue business suit. When the right time came, Papo too approached him.

"*Senor* Cabranes," Papo approached him. "Fulgensio Obregon," Papo extended his hand.

"Jose Cabranes." The party secretary shook it.

"I want to join."

"Sure. Come into my office."

They went behind the stage into a small, dingy office cluttered with papers and file cabinets. "How many members do you have here in New York?" Papo asked. He stared at the files that perhaps held an address for Gregorio Tejada—or for Rafael Lullanda, the name he was using.

"A few hundred active members just in the Bronx," the party secretary said.

"About two thousand members in the Greater New York Metropolitan area. Don't all show up the same nights, but we've pulled in a lot lately. Events on the island packed them in. And you? What's your background?"

"I've been here a month. Work in a *bodega* and rent a room here in the Bronx, hoping for something better. I'm working on my English. My grandfather told me to look up some of his friends." He mentioned Landia and Osvaldo Cotto.

"Osvaldo Cotto's away. Landia's busy. Maybe I can help you. What did you do back on the island?"

"Worked in a travel agency in the Condado back home. I type and do accounting. But here the English keeps me down." Papo paused for a few seconds. "Say, I knew you back home."

"I don't remember."

"Yes you do, Chucho," he used the name his uncle Ciro said he went by back home. "The Azul Bar. I've seen you there."

Chucho's eyes sprung up, and looked around cautiously. "The Azul Bar? Never heard of it."

"Yes you have, Chucho. Once, while I spoke to El Negro, you came over and bought me a drink. We all laughed at Roberto's jokes—you, me, and some friends of mine, Roberto and Jaime." El Negro Papo remembered had been the bartender when he'd once raided the bar. Roberto was Papo's homosexual brother-in-law and Jaime Papo's cousin.

Chucho twirled his mustache a little, then wet his lips with his tongue. He looked around again. "Don't talk about that here," he whispered.

"Then help me, Chucho. I'm down on my luck."

"Come around more often. Become active in the cause." He stood, came closer, and put his hand on his shoulder. "Cooperate with me and I'll be useful. I'll lift you. You worked in a travel agency. You sail?"

Papo worked vice long enough—and lived long enough to understand the pitch. He softened his own voice slightly and bent his wrist alluringly. The job of infiltrating criminals had made him a good actor. "I like to fly."

Cabranes' eyebrows rose. "Good. We'll fly together. Follow me and you'll soar high. Come more often. But let's be careful. Don't talk here."

"Then where, Chucho?"

"Call me at my business. I run a realty firm on Southern Boulevard." He gave Papo his card and told him to call on him.

Papo thanked him and the two men shook hands, Cabranes rubbing Papo's hand gently with his fingers. Papo volunteered to help with a mailing to inactive party members. Chucho explained he was leaving for a few days on party business and asked that Papo call him in a few days. He told him to look up a woman named Maria tomorrow.

Papo thanked him and promised to call. He walked out in front of the stage and continued to mingle. Looking into every face, he didn't see that of Gregorio Tejada.

But he'd found a foothold inside the party.

CHAPTER 25

The next morning, Papo shopped for clothes. In his tropical suit far from home and far from fashion, he felt like a *jibaro* fresh from the mountains. He walked to the East Side and found prices cheaper at Greenberg's.

"Vat can I do for you, young man," Mr. Greenberg asked, rubbing his hands in anticipation.

"Some suits."

"Dese are real nice." The owner showed him two fall suits, a basic black and a gray pinstripe, double-breast. "Dey are in fashion." Papo tried them on and took them. "Handsome. Very, very handsome," Mr. Greene beamed. "And some shirts?"

Papo picked up four with matching ties. A tan double-breasted belted trench coat and white hat completed his purchases.

He took a cab to the hotel and dialed Chucho Cabranes. Uncle Ciro was right—Chucho flicked a bent wrist. Evil tongues would call him a *maricon*. Papo had arrested some in vice raids on clubs where they consorted. Like female whores, the authorities left *maricones* alone, except when their establishments became public nuisances. Only for drunkenness and fighting were they shut down—like the Azul Bar. His uncle saw Chucho Cabranes around there one night. Conventional wisdom pegged *maricones* as sociopaths without shame, getting back at parents or society for slights, real or imagined. But Papo believed loose wiring in the body mechanism determined one's sexuality. A healthy, well-constructed male loved women by instinct. Sexuality sprang not from a conscious will but biological forces beyond one's control.

Though he found it repugnant, he understood homosexuality to be natural for some, like Roberto, Marisol's brother, and his own cousin Jaime. Should Consuelo Tejada not appear, Chucho Cabranes presented the best chance to penetrate the nationalists' inner sanctum and find Gregorio Tejada. Chucho wanted his homosexuality kept secret. That fact would play in Papo's favor.

A female receptionist told him to hold. Then Chucho picked up, saying he'd asked around about jobs, had nothing, but would keep trying. Again urging him to become active in the party, Chucho stressed Papo not use his name. Nor must they be seen together. Chucho lamented not helping but offered on his return from his trip to take him out for a drink and discuss old times.

"That'd be nice," Papo said. "I have friends in the party I've lost touch with. I'd like to find them."

"I have a master list at home. We can sit down in my apartment and study it."

"Sounds really nice," Papo feminized his voice.

"Call, Obregon." Excited, Cabranes told him to ask for Maria, who was in charge of mailing inactive members, at party headquarters. Chucho instructed him to say Israel Pedraza from Brooklyn sent him. When Papo probed, Chucho said Pedraza recruited volunteers during street campaigns. Chucho stressed that he not use his name.

Papo showered and put on the black suit—but not the trench coat or hat—then he took the El back uptown to nationalist headquarters and walked up one flight. At the door, an odd human being asked what he wanted. With no neck, his large, baldhead seemed to roll on the chest. A white turtleneck and baggy pants made him appear more absurd still.

"Maria?" Papo asked, not staring.

"Over there," the man pointed out a plump, dark woman.

"*Gracias.*"

No Neck studied him with interest.

The hall buzzed with activity, even with fewer people. The folding chairs that filled it last night now lay stacked on the side, and the hall seemed larger. On one side of the dais, party members wrote slogans on posters for demonstrations. On the other, more of the faithful printed leaflets on an old rexograph machine. And from his portrait on the stage, the omnipresent Pedro Albizu Campos seemed to direct them.

Papo found Maria's large black eyes purposeful and, even with a long, pointed nose bent in contempt, pretty. As Chucho instructed, he told her his purpose and she asked no questions. After giving him a list, she directed him to a table stacked with envelopes. But first, she told him to fill one out. Finding his handwriting tolerable, she asked he finish the rest, explaining the party solicited contributions of time and money from active and inactive members.

At the table, a man named Mario finished a set of envelopes. Mario gave him a smile less nod, rose, and took the finished batch to another table to stuff. He was thin and sickly, surrounded by an aura of suffering. A second man, fat to absurdity, they called Lorenzo. A flicker of an eyelash went for acknowledgement. Pablo was the third man, with that hard, tough sort of look short bitter men take on. He was rude and refused Papo's hand. Although attractive, Maria, he thought, took herself too seriously.

Papo worked on the D and E list. He glanced around the table, furtively searching for the letters T and L. Although doubting either Gregorio Tejada or Rafael Lullanda would be there, he deemed it worth a look. Lorenzo, the fat one, worked on the T's, while Pablo, the small, mean one, took the L's. After addressing a few envelopes, he sensed someone watching him. At first, he took no notice of another man, also short, with large ears and a monkey-like upper lip. But looking up suddenly, they locked eyes. He caught monkey face studying him with familiarity two tables down. They averted their eyes and Papo continued addressing his envelopes. He tried to make small talk but found the others stingy with words.

Finishing his lists, his hand felt sore and he took a break. The fat Lorenzo finished addressing the T's and Papo went over and picked up the list. Lorenzo's obese face registered a quizzical look. "I'm looking for friends," he explained. "The Torres brothers from Bayamon, who live here in New York now." He glanced at the list but found no entries for Tejadas. "They're not here," Papo said, handing back the list. "They were very committed back home."

The fat man stared.

"Had another good friend, Jose Llanos," Papo continued. "He's here in New York, too." He went over to the little man and borrowed the L's, perusing the list but not finding Rafael Lullanda.

"What are you doing?" Maria came over, the stern eyes filled with rebuke. He repeated his desire to find friends, but she ignored his attempts at conversation. "These lists are confidential." She was cold and distant, never smiling. With no marriage band or engagement ring, Maria appeared like one submerging past disappointments and present disillusions for the cause.

Misfits, Papo thought. *Misfits with a common grudge against the world.* And he pegged their leader, Pedro Albizu Campos, staring down from the portrait on the stage, the biggest misfit of all. They shared a collective dissatisfaction with life and a disillusionment that nationalism fed on.

The content didn't rebel.

Monkey face still stared. A pronounced upper lip made him simian in appearance. A clubfoot and limp gave him a gate not unlike an ape. Then a picture focused in his memory. This man he'd once arrested. Burglary. Santurce. Years ago. The name escaped him. Monkey face approached No Neck and whispered in his ear. They stared, then disappeared behind the dais.

Ortiz. Santo Ortiz. Papo now recalled a warehouse on the docks outside old San Juan, where he'd been assigned to safe guard against robbers preying on export companies. There he'd cornered him like a rat. Ortiz resisted, lunging at him with an iron bar. Papo turned in time to avoid the blow, kicking and beating the un-saintly Santo over the head with his club for his disrespect of the law. Ortiz muttered curses and threats before hauled away handcuffed. Papo needed to haul himself out of here now.

Bidding everyone good night, Papo handed the lists to Maria, who didn't return the courtesy. He walked briskly to the El, feeling someone following. Turning, he saw two men walking in his direction. On East 138th Street, he turned down a side street and walked three blocks, looking over his shoulder.

Near the bridge, at the deserted red brick school building on Brown Place and East 135th Street, he stopped.

He thought he'd eluded his pursuers.

P.S.35 had loomed large in his memory. The front stairs had seemed a long climb, and the main entrance on top like the portals of Mount Olympus. How small and insignificant they seemed now. Wondering if Miss Murphy, his first grade teacher, still taught there, he concluded she must be dead or now retired. A flaming redhead with nipper glasses worn on a string, she was already old then.

She taught him to properly pledge allegiance to the American flag. One day at an assembly, Miss Murphy clamped her nippers over her nose and inspected her charges, making sure their backs were straight and their hands properly placed over their hearts. Seeing he slouched, she marched up the aisle, barged down his row, shoving aside the puny children until she got to him. She yanked his left hand off his chest, replacing it with his right, pounding it against his heart. Papo felt humiliated. But rebellion or back talk was unthinkable. His mother told him about the infallibility of teachers and warned about the consequences of disrespect.

Yet now he realized now how terrible it'd been. Although he loved Miss Murphy, he'd never forgotten the incident.

The playground next to the school lay quiet and deserted. A solitary streetlight lit the Brown Street entrance, but the rest lay ominously dark. He went in. A chain link fence atop the stone wall surrounded the playground, just as he'd remembered. Where stones had fallen out, gaps in the wall now appeared.

Suddenly it was recess again, and he heard laughing children playing. He saw himself climbing the wall and slipping through the holes in the chain link fence to chase after balls hit over and onto into the street. But in once open spaces surrounding the playground, he saw factory warehouses now sprung near the bridge. It grew quiet and deserted again.

Having indulged his nostalgia, he walked toward a second entrance he remembered on the East 135th Street side of the playground. He'd walk toward the Grand Concourse and the subway downtown, avoiding Third Avenue, where his pursuers might be lurking.

A shadow moved across and stopped. It lingered. Unfriendly, he thought. He turned, walking back to the other entrance. There, another blur appeared and gradually grew visible. Papo made out an apelike gait. The simian Ortiz, in grotesque silhouette, dragged his deformed foot.

Papo turned cautiously to his left, then right, and saw Ortiz approach. Ortiz was dangerous, no doubt still angry with the justice Papo meted out.

"Stop right there, Ortiz. I kicked your ass once and I'll kick it again."

"No you won't, policeman. I meant to kill you then. Going to kill you now." Papo made out an object in his hand. A knife sharpened into view.

"With what? That toothpick in your hand? I'll shove it up your ass. Make a *maricon* out you. I'll give you a swollen ass to match your swollen foot."

"You abused me once. You won't again. I was hungry then. My whole family was. But you didn't defend us. You guarded the food *gringos* steal from us. You're worse than a traitor, policeman. You, Sepoy, carry out the will of the *Yanqui* invaders. You help them keep our land and people in bondage. You walked into our sanctuary and defiled it. For that alone, you'll die." Ortiz continued coming.

He'd beat this monkey in a horse race, but at the Brown Street entrance not one, but two shadows appeared and came into focus. One had a gun. He made out a tear in the fence above the wall, a few yards down. He ran, jumped, and grabbed on to the fence. His fingers grasped the metal links. Pulling on them, he lifted himself up, his feet pushing up against the stone wall. It was easier hoisting himself up atop the wall, taller now, and stronger.

He heard his pursuers' footsteps and began to push his body through the hole in the chain link fence. He was ten and skinny once, but now his greater height and girth made getting through the hole more difficult. Pressing harder through the opening, he felt the sharp loose metal links tearing his new suit. Sharp, jagged edges pierced his skin. Papo heard a gunshot and the bullet ring against the metal fence a few feet away. A second came closer. He pushed frantically through the hole, further ripping his new suit.

Squeezing through the fence at last, he jumped to the sidewalk below in time to avoid more bullets. Running across the street, he stopped, hid behind a dark lamppost, and pulled out his gun. A shadow appeared atop the playground wall. Papo aimed and fired two shots, heard a groan, then a thud. The shadow disappeared.

He ran, not stopping to watch for the steps he heard. A shot rang out. The bullet ricocheted against an empty warehouse. He reached the bridge and crossed on the pedestrian walk over the dark, murky waters of the East River. Several cars drove over it. He stopped to catch his breath, then walked briskly, turning to look behind him, sure now he'd eluded them.

Though cold, he took off his tattered suit jacket and folded it over his arm. Reaching Lexington Avenue on the other side, he walked two blocks before hailing a taxi. On Eighty-Sixth Street, he got off, walked a block to Eighty-Fifth, and hailed another cab. It occurred to him he might have killed a man and couldn't have his ride traced by the New York police.

In his hotel, he found a first aid kit in the bathroom. With hydrogen peroxide that stung, he washed his cuts, and then bandaged them.

His fateful reunion with the deformed Santo Ortiz played over and over in his mind. But for this chance encounter, the nationalist's office might still be open to him, making things easier. But such was destiny, much as one talked of free will. Now, it would be harder. And he wondered how long it be before Chucho Cabranes learned of all this. But Chucho was away. And Papo again hoped his insistence they not be seen together would work in his favor.

Nationalist bullets missed him, but Santo Ortiz' words had not. They'd left deep wounds, as had the same accusations his own brother had fired at him. Was his job then protecting gringo interests against his own, hungry people? Was he a traitor?

No. He was no traitor, or Sepoy carrying out the will of the *Yanqui* invaders. He was a policeman upholding law. Still, the words stung.

He'd not back down. In the Bronx he'd follow up on the baby sitter's tip Consuelo Tejada worked in a factory there. If he found her, he might find Gregorio Tejada.

Sleep proved fitful. In a dream, Santo Ortiz dropped out of a chain link fence like an acrobatic monkey from a tree and slashed him with a knife. Martin Lanza also appeared at the playground. And Miss Murphy came out of the schoolhouse waving her flag. This jaunt down memory lane had become a nightmare.

CHAPTER 26

Goyo's cabin facing the dark, murky waters of the East River offered safety, if few comforts. It seemed to guard the entrance to the Hunts Point Peninsula. For two days, he gazed with wonder at the three bridges connecting the Bronx mainland to the island boroughs, and the traffic across it. Yet when he tuned out the bridges, it all seemed strangely rustic, the nearest house half a mile away. Goyo didn't venture far at first. Julito or El Loco or both might be in custody. They may have talked to police, who were perhaps looking for him by now—even here in New York.

Neither Manuel Landia nor Osvaldo Cotto came for three days. Goyo spent his hours watching, besides the bridges, the barges float on the river and the planes land and take off from the airport across it. The third night he walked the mile or so to the plaza around the Hunts Point subway station.

Memories and ghosts haunted his solitude, in the shape of his father. Naive in business, Hortencio Tejada gave away the family plot to run a bodega in San Juan. More dreamer than merchant, he loved alcohol, music, and women. And he wrote verse. Dying prematurely, he left his wife Altagracia and the children the little not squandered. The frugal Altagracia supplemented it with her needle skills and the help of Uncle Justo and his brother Arturo. They lived comfortably until the police gunned down Arturo in the Ponce massacre.

Against their mother's wishes, Arturo attended a march, and later Goyo remembered the blood staining his mother Altagracia's white dress as she held her son Arturo and wept. Arturo's face writhed in pain and died in their mother's arms. Goyo cried for the last time that night and he'd lost respect for pain and death.

Life grew harder still when his father's inheritance ran out. Uncle Justo's import export business suffered when German submarines prowled the sea-lanes near Puerto Rico. America, absorbed with the war in Europe, rarely sent ships to Puerto Rico. He remembered their meager diet of corn meal and red beans Goyo hated his poverty, his father Hortensio for selling the land and the pittance land dealers in the pocket of the sugar company paid.

Two cars drove up on the fourth day. Landia drove one, another man the second. The second driver waited outside. Inside, Landia, decked in a suit as always, said the barber Arcadio Diaz relayed a message from a nationalist sympathizer at Isla Verde Airport. The *companero* described a heavyset policeman with large eyes and thick mustache. The policeman was tailing Gregorio and knew he'd left San Juan under the name Rafael Lullanda. Party members in the Bronx spotted another policeman fitting this description and Landia suspected the same man tried to infiltrate party headquarters in the Bronx.

"A passionate *companero* with a personal grudge tried to kill him." Landia paused and sighed. "He got away. Wounded another *companero*. We're looking for him. If he threatens *Huracan*, we'll kill him."

Landia paused while he digested it all. "Nevertheless, we'll proceed," he continued. A Spaniard named Mirabal, already provided for, would procure guns. Landia left newspapers, groceries, and sundries.

He left also a '46 Chevy before driving away in the second car.

Landia only confirmed Goyo's suspicions. Somebody talked—because he'd not acted alone, knowing he could trust only himself. He felt naked without a gun.

The newspapers also bore bad news. Police cornered and killed a nationalist named Carlos Miranda in an old coffee mill. Unnamed, reliable sources called

Miranda a suspect in the murder of three policemen outside Santa Isabel. He studied the dead man's picture sprawled on page one. El Loco. More troubling, an eyewitness reported two suspicious cars unload crates the night of the killings. The eyewitness gave a description not only of El Loco, but of Julito as well. But not of Goyo, who drove that night. The paper made no mention of the driver.

Maybe he slept with Lady Luck. Maybe Julito got away. Perhaps not. The college boy would talk if taken.

Goyo drove to East Harlem and found Mirabal in the candy store the old Falangist operated in the Italian section. Osvaldo Cotto had hinted at Mirabal's Mafia ties and said he worked as an agent of the Spanish government, which had no diplomatic relations with the United States since its Nazi alliance during the war. Mirabal ran an illegal numbers racket out of the candy store, and rumor had it dealt in narcotics. Short, with white wavy hair, the old Falangist smelled of the garlic and fish Spaniards love. Goyo found his thick Castilian accent annoying.

"Who sent you?" Mirabal asked suspiciously. He pronounced his S's with a *th* sound, like the Spanish priests Goyo had hated.

"Manuel Landia. Said you're a friend of our cause and would help."

"I'm Landia's friend. How do I know you are, too?" The Spaniard studied him curiously.

"Check with Landia."

"I will. Where you from?"

When Goyo said Ponce, Mirabal recalled his time there. He'd met Don Pedro.

The Spaniard asked why he'd come. Goyo needed three Walther automatics with nine round clips. Mirabal thought for a few seconds, still studying him curiously. He asked no more questions, saying he'd get them for him.

Goyo examined the candy and sundries Mirabal carried in the store. He picked up a can of Coca-Cola, candy, and some gum. He took a copy of the *El Diario* newspaper and another of *La Prensa* and took out some change to pay for his purchases.

"It's on the house," Mirabal told him.

"Gracias." Goyo raised his right arm stiffly in a Falangist salute. "Long live mother Spain and its glorious leader, Francisco Franco."

Mirabal returned the raised salute. "Long live a free Puerto Rico."

Later that night, Osvaldo Cotto drove up. Big Ears, Goyo dubbed him, for he was a short man with large ears and glasses. Cotto impressed Goyo as a serious, responsible person, well dressed at the airport and at their second meeting, when he'd explained their task. Like Julito, he seemed scholarly but older, less abrasive, and more reserved.

Cotto first mentioned the policeman, then told him to be careful, but assured him the party would take care of it. About his wife, Consuelo, Cotto had no news. "I've asked around," he said.

They took a walk by the river. Cotto revealed he came from Jayuya on a ship of the Marine Tiger line in 1937 and had lived in New York these thirteen years. He worked for a Jew named Rifkin polishing handles for women's pocketbooks, but he had given notice.

"My wife's from Jayuya," Goyo said. "I lived there. I went on a mission for the party and when I returned, she was gone. I need to find them." Goyo gave him details about her family.

"I'm working on helping you track her down. Be patient. It's a big city, but our community's small."

They sat on rocks, their backs to the river. The last flickering rays of the afternoon sun sifted the branches. A wind blew across the peninsula, causing the bushes and branches to sway.

It reminded Osvaldo of harvest time on his father's land and he described a vision of *jíbaros* in wide brimmed straw hats, their machetes glistening in the sun as they cut sugar cane. The oxcarts drew the harvest to the sugar mills. Big Ears even smelled the aroma of burning sugar cane rising from the mill.

Osvaldo's father appeared in his visions, young and prosperous.

Goyo marveled at his imagination, for although pleasant enough, this was not Puerto Rico and didn't compare in beauty to their native land. He listened silently to Cotto indulge in yesterday. Goyo himself retained less idyllic memories of the land. It did provide his father a living before Hortencio lost it all. But he remembered also the toil on the land, the backbreaking task of cutting sugar cane on a hot day. He remembered hurricanes, bad crops, and low prices.

"Let's talk about Truman."

Osvaldo though a few minutes. "The President's a decent man, Gregorio," Cotto finally said. "He's a son of the land like us." President Truman came from Midwestern country stock, Missouri pioneers who'd tilled the western soil. A common man. Family man. "But he must die," Cotto said without emotion.

Two others would join them. A third man, with children and a wife, had bowed out. Cotto would reveal only that one man came from Ponce and the other from Mayaguez. When they got the guns, they'd take target practice here by the river. Goyo would show Osvaldo and the Ponceno the finer points of the guns. The man from Mayaguez, an army veteran who'd served with the *Yanqui* army in Panama, knew automatics. The Ponceno owned a car and would drive them to Washington.

They'd get hotel rooms and pose as tourists, and perhaps they would chance on the President on his morning walk. They'd study the newspapers for the President's activities. An opportunity would arise. They'd coordinate their attack with the bombs exploding in New York City.

"It's a fine plan," Goyo said. "Except for the guards. Those *Yanqui* G-men are good. Anybody who tries it dies. But will Truman?"

"He's a man of the people," Osvaldo countered, "open and relaxed. The papers say he walks through Washington, stops, and talks to people. He's not Joseph Stalin, or Chiang Kai Chek of Nationalist China. He's Harry Truman. We can get him. You get the guns. Teach us how to use them. We'll hold target practice here where neighbors can't hear. I will die if I have to for this cause. I'm not asking you to. Follow your conscience." Cotto told him he'd be in touch and left.

Goyo thought it out.

He'd like to find Consuelo and Ivelisse and go home to a normal life.

But he knew it might be for naught. Assuming he could convince Consuelo of his love, and assuming she'd forget the past, other obstacles impeded reconciliation. Sooner or later, Julito would talk. It was only a matter of time until the police would come for him. It was one thing to kill a gringo lawyer; killing a policeman was another.

He'd get the guns from the Spaniard and train Cotto and the others. Then maybe he'd disappear. He'd served the party well and now felt his debts to don Pedro had been paid.

CHAPTER 27

Papo called his cousin Guillermo every day and checked for messages. Pietri of Homicide had Guillermo's number and Papo expected not only confirmation but praise for his hunch about Howard Saunders' death. He hoped for authorization to find Gregorio Tejada and contact the New York Police Department. Calling Puerto Rico twice, he failed to reach Pietri, and no one returned his calls. Each night, he waited for a message. None came.

Guillermo complained that he'd spurned them. Papo offered his busy schedule as an excuse, but he promised to visit soon.

He spoke to Marisol through Uncle Simon, her only relative with a phone. At first, fearing nationalist violence, she'd not left the house and kept the girls home. With no visible signs of trouble, she took the girls to school and picked them up. When she asked about his own welfare, he said all was well, but he would need extra days in New York.

"I love you, Marisol, and I miss you terribly. I'm sorry I had to leave you."

"I love you, too. Do your job. Be careful. Don't worry; the girls are fine."

Her words failed to set him at ease, and he shed tears. "You're sure? I'm worried. Maybe you can stay with your family a few days until this is over."

"No, we're fine. Don't worry."

"You're sure?"

"Yes."

Still not at ease, he also called his Uncle Ciro and learned that Julito still hid in the mountains with Cousin Nicolas, riding out the troubles.

Then he set out to look for Consuelo Tejada.

Mornings and afternoons, he frequented for two days the coffee house across from the needlepoint factory in the Bronx where she worked. There, he drank coffee and had lunch, mingling with the seamstresses and pressers. He posed as a machinist in a tool works nearby and kept a patient vigil.

On the third day, he overheard someone call out Consuelo, and an attractive green-eyed woman responded. She answered to the name and description of a copper skinned beauty with black hair and green eyes. He'd found Consuelo Tejada, indeed beautiful, appearing as if out of a Tahitian landscape in a Paul Gauguin painting he'd once seen in a book.

Having eaten, she spoke briefly with two other women. Papo watched her pay the check. Then, finishing his lunch, he secretly watched her return to the factory. At five, he followed her to the IRT station on Intervale Avenue, boarding the same downtown Lexington Avenue train. With her, he switched to the Pelham local at 125th Street and got off on cue when she exited on East 103.

He tailed her to the building where the hostile Fita denied being Consuelo's sitter.

She picked up the child, a pretty little girl not quite five who reminded him of his own daughters. Mother and child entered a tenement on East 104, across from a police precinct. He waited a few seconds and followed, hiding in a dark, narrow hallway at the base of the stairs.

He listened to them climb noisy wooden stairs to the second floor. A quick inspection of the mailboxes revealed no Tejadas but a C. Loma in 2B. Walking up to the apartment, he listened for sounds of a man, heard none, and walked down. His luck had held and he wouldn't push it. Leaving the tenement, he crossed the street to another building at the corner and walked up to the roof, staking out Consuelo's house for two hours.

He ate a long, leisurely dinner of rice and beans and beef stew at the corner *cuchifrito* restaurant with a view of Consuelo's building. Then he loitered for another hour. By eleven, intuition told him Gregorio wouldn't appear. He'd stake the place out, and if he didn't appear, he would question Consuelo. A premature interrogation might alert Tejada that someone was on to him.

The next morning he returned early to East Harlem and observed Consuelo leaving with the little girl. He followed her to the babysitter and the subway station where she took the train uptown to work. Papo had a breakfast of ham and eggs at the *cuchifrito*, then loitered in the neighborhood. He bought candy and soda at the *bodega*, then had coffee at the bakery, even downing three beers at the bar. At the end of three hours, he knew the neighborhood.

There was no sign of Gregorio Tejada.

One building posted a vacancy sign for furnished rooms at seventeen dollars a month. The super said he could move in with a two-month deposit. Papo considered it. There was a precinct on the block. Papo thought of approaching the police but had no authorization. In the event he took Gregorio Tejada into custody, he'd need their help. But for now, there was no sign of him. He'd try again the next day.

Papo saw two dark skinned men reading the paper in the hotel lobby. One, in a gray pinstripe suit and white hat, seemed to stir when he noticed Papo. The other one looked up. Although Arabs and Indians stayed at the Carlyle, these two seemed less exotic. Their plantain colored faces and mannerisms proclaimed them Puerto Rican—Puerto Rican nationalists. Papo eyed them discreetly while he checked at the desk for messages. They watched him. Cautious, he took the elevator up to his room, making sure they didn't.

He found his door unlocked upstairs. Someone had entered and inspected his room. He went in slowly, gun drawn, and looked around. They were gone. He took another look outside the room and thought it was time to leave. He placed his suits into traveling bags, threw clothes and sundries into his suitcase, and went down to the lobby. The two men were gone. He paid his bill and checked out.

Taking a cab to East Harlem, he spoke to the super, paid him thirty-five dollars for two months' rent, and moved into a dismal studio apartment, its walls and floor badly stained. The furnishings included a cot, a small bureau, and an old chair. It came with a private shower stall, but he needed to share the toilet out in the hall with other tenants.

But a sole window offered a view of Consuelo's building, and here he'd wait for Gregorio Tejada to show. He saw Consuelo arrive with the little girl that evening—but not Gregorio.

It wasn't clear how it'd all play out. He'd need to get Tejada off guard and somehow surprise him. Papo would pull his gun, tell him to put up his arms, and wait for the police. He thought this scenario was optimistic. If he resisted, he might have to kill him—or be killed.

The Carlyle Hotel, though not luxurious, offered amenities, and Times Square provided excitement. But he found East Harlem was quiet, except for the corner bar and the restaurant. Lonely and depressed, he thought about visiting his cousin but nixed the idea.

CHAPTER 28

Manuel Landia came to tell Gregorio the Spaniard Mirabal had the guns. Mirabal delivered them to a pre-arranged spot on Hunts Point Avenue where Goyo took possession. Goyo inspected the merchandise in the cabin: three German Lugers and several rounds of ammunition.

One pistol drew him immediately: a Welther.38 automatic. He examined its chambers, pulling on and off the safety, and fancied it'd belonged to some German officer during the war.

Landia drove out again to check on the delivery. He told him the policeman tailing him had eluded his men. When he left, Goyo clutched the German Luger, bringing it to his bosom and caressing it there a while. Smelling it assured him it had been properly oiled. He inserted a clip and rested it on his cot, feeling secure now.

Then Cotto drove out to tell him nationalist commandoes failed to assassinate Governor Luis Munoz Marin. A death squad crashed through the gate of La Fortaleza, the Governor's mansion. Munoz' bodyguards killed three and wounded two. The assassins killed two guards. The Governor declared a state of emergency. There was talk of mobilizing elements of the National Guard.

Cotto said they'd move as soon as Indio was ready, stressing the need to coordinate the assassination with bombings in New York. He located a man from back home who knew Consuelo and hoped to have an address soon. They agreed to meet downtown.

The following evening, Goyo drove to the Upper Eastside and waited outside the Achilles Metal Works where Cotto polished handles. They ordered corned beef and cabbage at a local pub.

"No rice and beans?" Goyo asked.

"No rice and beans. But it's good."

Two GIs sat three tables down. "*Puertorriquenos*," Goyo thought. The soldiers drank heavily.

Cotto told him Consuelo worked in a dress factory in the Bronx, owned by a party member. The man feared a scene and asked Goyo not show up at the factory. The man would release her address on condition Goyo not reveal the source.

Osvaldo Cotto revealed he kept company with a woman in the Bronx. If not for two teenage stepdaughters, he'd have put him up himself, but he did promise a home cooked meal.

Then Osvaldo got emotional after two drinks and lamented he'd never see Puerto Rico again. "A new day is coming," he said, tears in his eyes. Although he'd not see it, he'd help bring it about. But he dreaded most telling his common-law wife, Ana, and the girls he was leaving after eight years. He'd help Ana raise the girls from a previous marriage. After a first, unfaithful wife in Puerto Rico, Ana had stuck by him. "But something bigger than our personal happiness calls. It's the only condition I've put on the relationship."

The two soldiers got up to leave. "Where are you from, *paisanos*?" Osvaldo asked.

"Cabo Rojo," said the first one, a tall, robust fellow.

"Coamo," said the second, a short, stocky fellow with a crew cut. They had a stripe each.

"Yes, up in the hills on the road to Ponce, near the thermal baths," Osvaldo said.

"That's right," the stocky one answered.

"Long way from Coamo to Korea. It's cold there."

"I'll go where they send me."

"To fight for the *Yanquis*? You're no *Yanquis*. Your plantain stained faces proclaim you *Boricuas*. Why fight in Korea for a freedom we don't have at home? To make the world safe for Coca-Cola?"

The GIs looked at each other.

The tall one seemed offended. "No, to fight communists. You a communist? We'll start the war right here." He came toward Osvaldo.

Goyo came between them. "No, let's not fight, brother against brother. *Boricua* should not fight *Boricua*. You want to wear that uniform and kill Koreans, fine. But don't put a hand on my friend or you'll have to put it on me."

The Irish bouncers appeared. "Take it outside, mates," said the first in a colorful brogue. He wore a dirty apron. "We want no trouble."

The GIs froze.

Goyo thought it best to leave. "Excuse us," he turned to the bouncers. "My friend's had a lot to drink." He put his arm around Osvaldo and guided him out the door. They walked to the car and Goyo drove him to the Bronx, then returned up Bruckner Boulevard to the cabin.

Osvaldo Cotto proved himself a Puerto Rican patriot. His own patriotism paled in comparison. But he too had a will. He'd determine his own destiny—not Osvaldo Cotto, not Don Pedro, and not the party.

The next day, he called Cotto from a phone booth in the Hunts Point plaza and learned the man from Mayaguez had dropped out of the plan. That left three—the man from Ponce, Cotto, and himself—if Goyo agreed to join. The policeman tailing him had once again eluded Landia's men. He urged Goyo be cautious.

Cotto also had an address for Consuelo. Her boss, who believed in the cause, ran a dress factory in the Bronx, where she did needle work. Osvaldo promised Consuelo wouldn't learn the source of the information. Goyo promised not to reveal it. Consuelo lived in a tenement in East Harlem, near a police precinct.

"Be careful. Women cause trouble." Cotto asked he forgive the intrusion into his personal life and consider it merely a friendly *consejo* from an elder. Goyo assured him he took no offence. Cotto invited him to Sunday dinner the following day.

Landia had taken the car, so Goyo took the Pelham Bay Local downtown to East 138th Street, where Cotto lived. Osvaldo received him courteously.

He introduced first his pimple face fourteen-year-old stepdaughter, Rosa, decked in a long gray skirt reaching her bobby socks and a blue Morris High School sweatshirt too small for her large frame. She did homework and listened to "Chattanooga Choo Choo" on the radio. His common law wife, Ana, a large, plain woman who passed the bounds of pleasantly plump, had the daughter's round nose and oily skin. She worked in a toy factory and seemed friendly and energetic.

Goyo studied the living room while Osvaldo got him a drink. A picture of Christ hung on the wall above the radio, and next to it one of Don Pedro. In a framed photograph on top of the radio Osvaldo and Don Pedro shook hands. He asked Rosa about the couple in another faded photograph and learned they were her stepfather's dead parents. There was a desk next to the radio and a large bookcase with an assortment of histories and biographies of liberators and revolutionaries: Washington, Marti, Bolivar, Gandhi, Lenin, and Robespierre. The complete *Cyclopaedia of Universal History* filled the second shelf, and a 1946 edition of the *Werner Universal Educator* the third.

A young girl of about sixteen entered with packages and after cursory greetings, set them down. Ana introduced her other daughter Migdalia. Her smile and large black eyes struck Goyo's fancy. Unlike the mother and sister, she had a straight nose and a slender figure, no doubt inherited from her natural father.

She showed her sister, whom she called Rosie, new clothes.

"Nice, Miggy," Rosa said.

Their stepfather chided them for using those nicknames, insisting they use Migdalia and Rosa. Migdalia deemed "Rosa" old fashion and Migdalia not suited for a young girl in America. Osvaldo admonished them to be proud of their heritage.

"What's the big deal in a name, Valdie?" She didn't call him Papi, like her younger sister.

"Next, you'll stop speaking Spanish and deny your identity. Let's hold onto our heritage and remember who we are."

"Lots of people forget their identities here. It's not important."

"We're not others. We're Puerto Ricans."

The argument amused Goyo, who said nothing.

Ana ended the polemic by asking Cotto to check the rice. Osvaldo obeyed. The younger sister excused herself and carried her sister's packages into the bedroom to better admire them. The older sat next to the mother and warmed up to Goyo, explaining she was a high school junior, and asked about schools in Puerto Rico.

Goyo explained he hated school and dropped out because of the stern teachers. "I couldn't stand the 'Missies' bossing me. A beautiful girl like you doesn't need an education. You can marry rich."

Migdalia laughed.

Her mother frowned. "Here in the States, women have opportunities. It's not like back home, where a woman needs a man for support. Here a woman can stand on her own."

"But she's getting married, right?" Goyo said playfully.

"Yes, when she can work and help her husband so both can progress."

Migdalia asked what they wore in Puerto Rico, and Goyo explained that in the capital women wore the latest fashions, though in the country, they still dressed like "*jibaras*." He used the term *jibara* in its pejorative sense, meaning hick, not in the nostalgic sense of classical poets and singers who sang the virtues of the *jibaros* and country life. "Some girls in the capital wear bobby socks and tight sweaters," he said, flashing a seductive smile.

Goyo liked her and sensed it was mutual but remained careful not to telegraph his feelings. He wanted to possess Migdalia, as he did all pretty women he met. Examining her young, firm body, his mind's eyes removed her jump skirt and sweater, undressing her down to her bobby socks. Aware of the maternal eyes, he dissembled his desires, though not totally.

The mother frowned and Goyo felt his mind being read. She asked her daughter to fry the plantains. Magalia excused herself and left. Her sister Rosa and Osvaldo returned from the kitchen. Rosa turned to *The Amos and Andy Show*, but her mother told her to finish the homework, a geography lesson on India, which Rosa found boring.

"How's Gandhi's economic policy going to help me?"

Cotto explained Gandhi's wish for an economically self-sufficient India independent of English exploiters and how the English stifled Indian culture and made the Indians dependent. Gandhi called for cottage industries and land cultivation instead of modernization to serve English needs. Osvaldo noted similarities to the American presence in Puerto Rico. "And they killed him," he added.

Rosa copied furiously, omitting the parallels to American imperialism in Puerto Rico, more obvious to Osvaldo than to her. Osvaldo finished his lecture and called for Puerto Ricans to be rid of Americans as Indians were now rid of the British. Magalia returned from the kitchen and overheard Osvaldo's comments.

"But India's a lot bigger than Puerto Rico."

"Size means nothing. Lots of countries are smaller than us."

Magalia maintained the British built roads and factories, curing diseases and civilizing them, as the Americans Puerto Rico. Cotto insisted the English took out more than they put in, just like the Americans. Magalia said at least they were citizens and came to America at will.

Osvaldo said that in the end, Puerto Ricans lost their dignity. "While other Latin America countries hold their heads high because of national sovereignty, Puerto Rico remains a colony."

"Then why do they sneak across?" Magalia protested. "If we don't guard the borders, those countries would empty out. They'd squeeze in through the back door, sovereignty and all. We come in through the front."

"You have a colonial mentality," her stepfather declared.

Goyo said nothing, although he agreed with Cotto Americanization was corrupting the youth.

Ana ended the polemics by announcing dinner. Goyo found the beef stew with white rice and beans delicious, as he did the plantains with garlic sauce. He thought Ana remarkable with a charm that made up for looks. It struck him odd how Osvaldo helped with the cooking and dishes. He surmised that Ana wore the pants in the relationship.

After dinner, the women excused themselves to watch television at the neighbors. When they left, Cotto gave him a paper with Consuelo's address. "It's in East Harlem?"

"Yes. *El Barrio*. I heard she's on welfare and works at the same time."

"She can get in trouble with the government."

"What happened between you?"

Goyo thought for a few seconds. "She disrespected me. Got up and left." He didn't look Osvaldo in the eye. "I made sacrifices for the party. She wouldn't do the same." Osvaldo studied him skeptically. "I wasn't the best husband." He paused. "There were other women."

But Goyo knew it had been murder, not his infidelities, that drove her away. She heard about the *Yaqui* engineer killed on an irrigation project and found Goyo's mysterious departure at the time no coincidence. He left that part out.

Osvaldo listened politely, and then chose his words carefully. "We Latinos think woman must serve us. But it's not the time of our grandfathers, Gregorio. Women are different now, especially here. They want a say in things. Here they can work and not depend on a man. Gregorio, think of this only as a *concejo*. But a woman needs to be confided in, and most importantly, respected."

"A woman must stick by her man," Goyo said, peeved. "That's what's wrong with Puerto Ricans today. We're too Americanized and forget our ways."

"Don't be offended, Gregorio," Osvaldo said. "But I've heard about your other women. I'm from Jayuya—I knew your wife's father. Went back a couple of years ago. A woman won't take cheating forever." Goyo said nothing. Osvaldo continued. "Respect doesn't guarantee respect in return. She left you. Worse happened to me. My wife played me for a fool. I heard rumors, but I didn't believe them. I followed her one day and discovered the truth. I'll spare you the details. She humiliated me. Some men hack the offending parties. Not me. I'd still be in jail. No woman's worth it."

"Is my wife seeing someone?"

"I don't know. And look, I tell you this only to show you I went on. So must you."

"I have to talk to her."

"Talk to her calmly. See your daughter. Give her money and a blessing. Then leave. Don't create a scene. She lives across from a police precinct. Remember you're a wanted man.

"But most important, Gregorio, there's a reason for life. Why are we put here? We're born, we eat, we procreate, satisfy our physical needs, and die. Is that it? No, Gregorio, we have a higher purpose. We were put here to free our country."

Goyo's head buzzed. Perhaps he could return home with his wife and daughter. He had the guns. He'd show Osvaldo how to use them, then disappear. "You speak nicely Cotto," he finally said, "but how are you going to pull this off? First, two of these patriots quit. The third sounds pretty shaky. They have another purpose. And you? How well can you use a gun?"

Cotto said he'd gone hunting upstate and had shot a .38, but never an automatic. The other fellow had served with the *Yanqui* army in Panama and knew weapons. They needed to practice and Goyo suggested they could at the end of the Hunt's Point Peninsula, where no one would hear gunshots. Osvaldo needed two days. He'd not told Ana and the girls but would say he was off to Puerto Rico to join the struggle. He'd need two days to take care of his affairs. If both Goyo and the third man dropped out, he'd go alone.

"How, Cotto?"

"I'll take a train and kill a president, no a man," Osvaldo corrected himself. "He's flesh and bones, shits and pisses. And he bleeds. He's no ordinary man, but a man. He killed 150,000 people at Hiroshima and Nagasaki and didn't flinch. Neither will I."

"We must think this out more carefully," Goyo said. "I'm going to see my wife now."

They agreed to meet on the peninsula in two days.

CHAPTER 29

For two days, Papo shadowed Consuelo Tejada. Friday, she left for work and returned after picking up her daughter. He ate at a greasy spoon *cuchifrito* joint that went by the exalted name Sea Winds Restaurant. He found the food tolerable and the buxom counter girl, Dora, cheerful and polite. The seat by the register offered a view of Consuelo's tenement. He watched her movements from there while eating his meals leisurely and chatting with Dora. The rest of the day, he loitered in the neighborhood and at night observed the tenement from his furnished room.

Consuelo shopped Saturday morning in *La Marqueta*, as Puerto Ricans called the stretch of shops from East 116th down Park Avenue under the elevated tracks of the New York Central Railroad. He kept his distance and his eyes in check, but he observed her carefully. Her beauty stunned him, and he found her green eyes captivating.

And reining in incipient passions, he understood why Gregorio had fallen in love. But why had she? Talking to Consuelo's parents and her employer confirmed she came from class and a Catholic home. This background should have precluded involvement with the criminal misfit, the murderer of his *compadre*, Martin Lanza. But Julito's description and the handsome photo he'd studied in the political files answered his curiosity. His looks removed the social barriers. A tinge of jealousy crossed his conscience.

He studied the unripe plantains, the rich mangoes, and coconuts in *La Marqueta*. A fat, unshaven, bald merchant measuring about five-foot-five in a dirty apron who looked like something that fell off a meat rack, came over.

"Cut me a stalk of sugar cane."

"About this much?" the merchant asked.

"Yes."

"A nickel, please."

Papo counted five pennies on the counter and sucked the cane's sweet juice with gusto. It all smelled of home and the tropics, and he longed for Marisol and the girls. He'd followed Consuelo back to her tenement and felt lonely when she went in.

A man appeared Saturday afternoon.

It was not Gregorio Tejada.

They emerged again Sunday morning. Consuelo and the girl dressed in Sunday best. Papo only imagined the fireworks should Gregorio also appear and almost hoped he wouldn't. How would Gregorio react? How would he himself react? Consuelo and the man returned later, holding hands, and went upstairs. After two hours, the man appeared alone and left.

Papo loitered in the neighborhood all day Sunday, venturing down a block where only Italians lived. He mistook one, a swarthy fellow for a Puerto Rican, who said something like *"queste"* and wrapped his vulgar gestures with dirty looks. Turning the corner, Papo removed his middle finger, as a gun from a holster. *"Este!"* he yelled and aimed it at him.

It was his second experience with ethnic conflict in the city. When he ordered beer in an Irish pub, the bald bartender walked away without a word. "Where'd he go?" Papo looked around at the other patrons, who looked away. It hit him in a flash epiphany: he'd not be served. And so he left. He stuck to his own kind after that.

He studied his rooming house neighbors. In the lobby by the mailboxes, he observed a *mulata* who always wore a kerchief wrapped around her head with four fatherless children open a letter from the home relief office. *Married to the government*, he concluded, which, like a husband, supported her. He'd observed a few unmarried women, not unheard of in Puerto Rico but more common here. The mulata's eldest son, a surly young boy no more than fifteen or so, dressed in dungarees and a black leather jacket. He was rude and disrespectful when his mother scolded him. It shocked Papo's senses when he overheard them arguing. "Shut up," he told her in front of others another time. Papo wanted to slap this young *sinverguenza* without shame and teach him proper respect for one's mother. He would've back home, but here, he thought it prudent to mind his own business.

The migration to New York did something to Puerto Ricans.

Another young man carelessly dressed in baggy pants and a loud Hawaiian shirt appeared dazed in the hallway one night, as if sleepwalking. He'd seen him another time under the train tracks on Park Avenue near *La Marqueta*, congregating with low lives with no apparent purpose in life. *Heroin addicts*, he concluded, unheard of back home, but here not uncommon.

Papo grew weary of his watch. His rat-infested rooming house reeked of urine and alcohol after the long weekend. And he endured the incessant rumbling of the El. Was it all in vain? Gregorio Tejada might not show. Maybe it was time to go home.

He now doubted the Puerto Rican police would call. Contacting them again seemed futile, as their hands were full with the troubles there. The papers said the nationalists had destroyed San Juan's telephone center. Was that why they'd not call? Should he go to the police and FBI? He had information, but he had nothing on Gregorio Tejada without incriminating his own brother. He called Chucho Cabranes, who was still away.

After a couple of days, he'd call again. If Gregorio didn't show, he'd confront Consuelo about his whereabouts. If nothing came of his efforts, he'd go home.

CHAPTER 30

Goyo took the Third Avenue El to 103rd Street in East Harlem and found the address, an old tenement that rattled when the train passed. The first time he came to New York and stayed in Brooklyn, he hated the fast pace of the city and the rude gringos bumping into him on the subway. A country boy, he thought it unnatural to pack so many together in one place. The dirt and constant noise of the el couldn't be good for one's sanity, he thought.

Goyo walked up two flights and knocked on her door. No answer. Second and third knocks failed also and he lost the count—and his patience—before hearing movement inside.

"Who's there," came a tired female voice.

"Me . . . Goyo." Waiting almost a minute, he knocked again. "Open the door, Consuelo. Don't leave me out here."

"What do you want?" The tired female voice opened up its fears, audible behind the closed door.

"You."

"Leave."

"Open."

"Go away."

He shouted and pounded on the door with his fist. Doors opened, and protected by door chains and peepholes, neighbors tuned in on the unfolding drama. A dog barked. Goyo felt anonymous stares and knocked more gently. "Open up, Consuelo," he whispered.

"Mami, Mami! Who's there?" A child's voice revealed its fears. Ivelisse's voice.

"No one, *Negrita*," he overheard Consuelo. "Go back to bed."

"Consuelo, open up. Let's talk."

"I'm through talking." He heard the child's sobs.

"*Carajo!*" he yelled, his fist again pounding the door, and in reflex, the foot. "Open the door!" The dog's whine grew into a growl, then loud barking.

"You son of a whore!" a tired, raspy voice shouted in Spanish behind the safety of his door. "You work tomorrow? I do. Beat her in the morning."

"Mind your business, *cabron*. I'll find you and shut you up for good." This quieted the neighbor, but not the dog, which barked and growled more furiously. "Open up, Consuelo."

"Let me get dressed." He waited a few minutes.

The door opened. Consuelo appeared. The girl clutched her, crying. Her dark eyes stared. His eyes, as was the light complexion and fine straight nose. Ivelisse trembled. Her mother kept her calm. A nervous silence followed. Goyo gazed on his wife. Fresh out of the shower, her hair dripped drops of water on to wet pajamas hastily slipped into. She tried in vain to button an open robe. But it was the eyes he tried to penetrate—the green eyes, averting his.

"You coming in?" she asked, still not returning his look. Ivelisse clutched tighter. They went in.

"Come here, *Negrita*," Goyo called his daughter, "don't you know me? I'm your *papi*." He pulled her to him, but she clung to her mother.

"Don't be afraid," Goyo said. "Call me Papi. I won't hurt you. I love you."

"Look, that's Papi. Say something," Consuelo coaxed. Ivelisse turned and stared.

"You're pretty," Goyo said, wrenching her free. "I missed you, *Negrita.*" He lifted her, stiff and apprehensive, and kissed her. Goyo sensed her relief when he let go.

"Go back to bed, Ivelisse. Give your father a kiss and ask his blessing."

"*Bendicion,*" she dutifully obeyed, kissing him stiffly on the forehead.

"God bless you," he mouthed a mechanical benediction.

Consuelo carried her inside the bedroom.

"Ask the Virgin for protection, *Negrita,*" he heard Consuelo say.

He peeked into the bedroom and saw Consuelo tuck Ivelisse in a small cot adjoining her own. He made out a picture of the Virgin on a wall with green peeling paint. From outside on the street, a faint noise came, growing louder. The building shook. He opened a grimy window and saw a procession of El cars rumble by and stop on the platform just a few feet away. Passengers got on and off and the cars pulled out of the station.

Goyo examined the apartment's second room, kitchen, dining, and living room combined. It boasted a small stove, a sink, and a small freezer crawling with cockroaches. An old sofa that had seen better days rounded out her possessions. A faded rug provided the only luxury. He urinated in the small, shabby bathroom, inspecting a still wet shower stall. An old creaky faucet and ancient pipes produced a loud cranking noise before reluctantly surrendering its miserly flow of water.

She returned. "You look good, Consuelo." He examined her wet hair and bathrobe draped sensually around a figure, grown fuller, the breasts swollen with maturity. "I've searched months for you . . ." The rumble of tracks outside drowned out his words. "How can you take that?"

"Don't hear it anymore. You get used to it." She enumerated the noise, dirt, large crowds of rude people. But she'd learned to bundle herself and her daughter against the cold, to stuff wet cloths into cracks in the windowsills to keep out the wind, and to ignore others like a native. The solitude and anonymity of the big city appealed to her, she said. "Unlike in Jayuya, no one knows my business here."

"Please, Consuelo. It pains me to see you like this."

"Don't live in luxury," Consuelo declined his pity. "But we don't starve."

"How do you manage?"

167

"I work." Surprised when asked if she received public assistance, her loud silence answered for her.

"I won't have it. Come back with me. I'm your husband. You're my responsibility."

"One you didn't take seriously." Although she confessed to taking public assistance, she worked off the books and vowed not to take it for long, growing fat like other women who stayed home. Soon she'd save and find a place in the Bronx.

"Is there another man, Consuelo?"

"No. Get that out of your mind." He gazed into familiar green eyes. They stared back at his, maintaining their serenity. "Don't need a man to bother me." Her look, and her eyes, grew firm. "Here in New York, a woman doesn't need a man. She can stand up on her own."

He offered money.

She refused. "I want a divorce."

"Don't talk shit." He grabbed her left hand and shoved the money in it.

"Don't push me, Gregorio!" She flung the money in his face. Two twenty-dollar bills floated down. "This is my house. Don't push me here!"

"I'll push—and more," he growled. "I'm the *macho*. I wear the balls—as it's ordained. Only in my grave will I stop."

"You're evil. I hated the life you gave me."

He picked up the money from the floor. "Take it."

"No."

Not his command, but his murderous look convinced her to take it. "Forty dollars solves many problems," she said. "It's only right you help feed your daughter. I'll take nothing. I'm no longer bound to you. Now leave."

"When I want. I'll leave when I choose." He stared long at her.

"Leave," she said, clearly growing uncomfortable with his eyes' desire.

He admired her shapely contours, marked clearly against the wet, clinging bathrobe. A scent of woman permeated her clean, moist body, and it triggered in him a primordial urge. "I want you." His manners softened as his penis hardened. He tugged at the bathrobe.

"No. No. No. Don't touch me. I'm not yours."

"You're my woman. I want you."

"You disgust me. Don't touch me."

He tried untying the robe, now buttoned firmly, and pulled her in to embrace her. Grabbing his throat with one hand, she pushed him back with the other. When he persisted, nails painted blood red raked across his right cheek, missing the eye.

"*Cabrona*," he screamed, feeling the cuts stinging his face. Rubbing it, he saw the warm blood on his finger. "What's wrong with you?"

"Hell do you think you are? Your toy? That stupid girl who fell for lies? Think you can come in after walking out, snap your fingers, and get me back?"

"I'm your husband."

"You cheated. I'm supposed to forget? Forget you weren't at my side when I gave birth to your daughter?"

"I'm your husband!"

"You're a petty bootlegger and a coward who shoots people in the back. You're nothing."

He grabbed her. "I'm somebody."

Consuelo sobbed. "You're nothing!"

"Shut up, Consuelo, shut up right now."

"You're nothing! A common criminal and a murderer."

A knock at the door loosened his grip. "Are you all right?" asked a female voice in English accented with Italian.

"Yes," Consuelo managed. "I'm all right."

"Leave. I'll scream. The neighbors will call the police. The precinct's across the street. They'll come fast."

The word police gave him pause. "What can they do? I'm your husband."

"Arrest you for the murder of that engineer."

"What?"

"Yes, Gregorio. You killed him. I know. I'm not stupid. You shot him in the back. I read it in the papers. That engineer in that irrigation project. I know."

"Don't talk shit, Consuelo."

"Leave, Gregorio, or I scream."

Furious, he smashed his fist against a wall. Then he thought. A fugitive, he mustn't get caught here. "Yes, I'll leave, Consuelo. It just occurred to me we really can't make it. But I want you to know I'm going to Washington."

"For what?"

"To do great things. You'll hear of me, Consuelo. The whole world will hear of me. You'll see I'm somebody."

CHAPTER 31

Hungry for company and food, Papo visited the Sea Winds Restaurant, empty now on a Sunday night. He slipped into his usual seat on the counter, studied the menu, and ordered the day's special of stewed pig's feet. It came with white rice and pinto beans. He mashed a ripe avocado with the rice and beans, took a bite, and washed it down with a Rheingold beer.

He'd picked up morsels of information in small talk with the waitress, named Dora, divorced, with two small sons, who told him she lived in a rooming house. Papo mentioned his wife and daughters but claimed to be separated. At first, Dora struck him fat and ordinary, with too much of a country *jíbara* about her. The stained waitress outfit she usually wore made her less appetizing still. But tonight she'd dunned a blouse and long jump skirt in fashion. A girdle reigned in her ample parts. His loneliness increased her appeal.

"When's your night off?" he asked.

"Monday."

"Maybe we can catch a movie?"

"Maybe."

Halfway through the meal, Dora revealed her fears for her sons in this country. The eldest often cut school and wandered through Manhattan aimlessly. And the younger became friendly with mischievous Negro boys. "I have nothing against Negroes, you know. Some of them are good people. But these little *Negritos* often run around wild and crazy without supervision. I'm afraid my boys will take after them."

Her long shifts precluded proper supervision and she considered sending them back to Puerto Rico to her mother.

Papo had neglected his watch, but a timely glance across the street revealed a man exiting Consuelo's tenement and walking briskly toward Lexington Avenue. Consuelo's boyfriend? He studied him closely. No. Gregorio Tejada. He remembered his mug shot.

"Got to go," he cut her off.

And your food?"

"How much?"

"I'll add it up," she grew indignant.

"Here." He threw five dollars on the counter. "Keep the change."

Outside he ran toward Lexington Avenue. Gregorio Tejada turned down Lexington and disappeared. Papo rounded the corner. Gregorio was gone. Either he'd turned right on East 103rd Street toward Park Avenue, or gone into the subway station. Papo looked down East 103rd on his right, then left. *The subway.* Descending quickly down the stairs, he looked around the platform and saw him across the tracks on the uptown platform, pacing up and down.

He rushed upstairs, braved the Lexington Avenue traffic, went quickly down the uptown stairs, and jumped the turnstile.

"Stop!" the token booth attendant shouted. "Stop! Police!"

Papo ignored his command and slipped into the uptown Pelham Bay Local seconds before its doors closed.

He rested on a yellow rattan seat and caught his breath. Three other passengers glanced at him, then turned away. He walked to the sliding back door of the car, opened it, and rode between cars. Peeking carefully into the next car, he opened the door, then entered. He inspected each car before reaching the last. Tejada sat somewhere up front. He worked his way back there.

In the second car from the front, Goyo sat, lost in thought. He loved Consuelo, the mother of his daughter, more than any woman, but now realized the impossibility of a life with her.

Even though he took responsibility for his infidelities, they no longer haunted him. He was a man and wouldn't apologize for the biological imperatives to love women, having no control over these impulses. And it'd become clear that after life in New York, Consuelo would never know her place again. These were the Nordic ways the party maintained corrupted Puerto Rican values.

Consuelo's words echoed in his psyche. "You're a nobody." He'd heard these words from his Uncle Justo, from the school missies, and from the priests. He'd prove them wrong. The world would remember him. As Osvaldo Cotto said, life held a purpose higher than satisfying animal needs. He had a cause— Don Pedro's orders. And as a boy, he took an oath to avenge a brother, a destiny fate, not him, chose. No woman would sidetrack him from this purpose.

He'd kill the President of the United States.

Papo made his way to the second car from the front. He peered in from his bumpy ride between cars, examining the passengers. Gregorio Tejada sat in the front seat, deep in thought.

When the train pulled into the next station, he could rush in, pull his gun, and order Tejada to put up his hands. The conductor would stop the train and call the police. If Tejada resisted, he'd shoot him. But he decided it'd be too dangerous and jeopardize other passengers. He'd exit, then pretend he'd just gotten on.

On East 125th Street, he entered with the new passengers. Tejada sat in the back, quite the fop in a brown pinstripe, still pensive. Papo studied furtively the high cheekbones and fine, straight nose Papo remembered from mug shots.

He'd get off with Tejada, following him out onto the platform, where he'd make his move. His eyes studied him as discreetly as New York's anonymity permitted.

After a stop, Goyo became aware of the man two seats down in a trench coat and a white hat and sensed the man, with a large build, large eyes, and moustache, was studying him. Less *Puertorriquenos* and Negroes now rode the subway after East 125ᵗʰ Street. After East 138ᵗʰ, only gringos did. This plantain stained face, obviously *Boricua*, felt out of place. Then it clicked.

It was the policeman man tailing him. He'd get off before Hunts Point, where he might be followed.

Three stops later, the train pulled into the East 143ʳᵈ station. The doors opened and two passengers got off. Goyo waited a few seconds. The doors began closing. He jumped up and bolted out in the split second before they shut. Peeking inside, he noticed the man get up and pull the door's rubber padding. The train began to move. Goyo walked calmly to the platform's middle exit.

Inside, Papo pulled the emergency chord, bringing the train to a screeching halt. He opened the rear door and between cars pulled the folding divider between cars and jumped onto the platform. He looked to the back, then ran to the exit, gun drawn.

Goyo reached the stairs, turned, saw the policeman, stopped, pulled his own gun, and got two shots. Hid behind a beam, Papo returned fire. Three commuters scattered.

They exchanged more shots until Tejada disappeared above the stairs. Papo walked cautiously toward the end of the platform, then, gun drawn, began to climb the stairs. The shaken, bespeckled female token booth attendant saw him and hid. He walked up one step at a time, eventually reaching street level.

He took a long hard look in all directions. There was no sign of Gregorio Tejada. He walked north on Southern Boulevard a few feet, then looked again. Nothing. Returning past the subway station entrance to East 143ʳᵈ Street, he looked again.

Tejada was gone.

Faint sirens grew louder. Police. Continuing to 138ᵗʰ Street, he climbed into a cab and ordered the driver to cross the Third Avenue Bridge to Lexington and 128ᵗʰ Street. From there he walked to the rooming house, angry and sore from his wounds.

He had Tejada and lost him. Furious, he smashed the headboard with a kick.

CHAPTER 32

Goyo ran to East 142nd Street, turning and zigzagging north through South Bronx streets to elude his pursuer. On East 149th Street, he took a cab to Hunt's Point. From there, he walked to the river and the cabin, thinking he'd let his guard down. It nearly cost him. There could be no more mistakes. Where had this policeman come from? Not chance but a stakeout of Consuelo led him onto the same train.

Now a higher mission called.

His dream found him back on the El. Consuelo and Ivelisse appeared in a tenement window. The train slithered into a tunnel and the vast, dark underground. His brother Arturo, on a yellow rattan seat opposite him, writhed in their mother's arms, her white dress soaked in blood. The American engineer and Howard Saunders sat next to them.

The motorman's cabin swung open and Harry S. Truman appeared at the controls. Goyo emptied his gun into the President. The rear door opened and the policeman appeared. The dream ended.

The next day the radio announced Governor Munoz Marin's declaration of a state of emergency, mobilizing elements of the National Guard, bound for Korea, against the rebels in Jayuya, where fighting raged. The Spanish language dailies *El Diario* and *La Prensa*, and especially the pro Nationalist *El Imparcial*, featured it on page one. The American media buried it in later pages.

He phoned Osvaldo from the Hunts Point plaza and told him of his brush with the policeman. Cotto agreed the policeman too had found Consuelo.

"Stay away from her," he urged. "We need to drop in on El Indio to coordinate the bombings and hit on president.

"And the others?"

"Bowed out. I won't think less of you if you do, too. I'll go alone."

"I'm going with you, "Goyo said.

Silence followed. "I'm glad, Gregorio," he finally said. "With you, we have a chance. Let's move fast."

Goyo related his meeting with Consuelo. "I know now my search has been in vain. It will never work. How will I get her to go back and be a good wife after New York has so corrupted her? No use. But you're right, Cotto. We have a higher purpose in life. I'll again answer the party's call. We will liberate our country from the *Yanqui* oppression."

"I'm happy, Goyo. Yes, we have a higher destiny in life."

Osvaldo broke the news of his leaving to Ana. Of all he'd do in the coming days, nothing haunted him more. "The day is here," he told her. "The people are ready and I must be there." He hid his real purpose, telling her he quit his job and headed to Puerto Rico.

"Go. You're not my husband," Cotto related. "I have no claim on you."

Cotto answered she did but implored she understand something bigger called, the cause—the only condition he'd placed on the relationship.

"The cause! Everything's the cause!" Ana had protested.

"I love her, Gregorio," he grew emotional, remembering casual girlfriends that never loved him, and a cheating wife. Only Ana truly loved him and a stability unknown before her was ending. He wept on the phone. He told Goyo after regaining his composure they'd drop in on El Indio later. Osvaldo needed to tie up his affairs.

Goyo suggested they shoot some rounds the following night, unsure of Cotto's abilities with a gun. Big Ears claimed he knew weapons.

Osvaldo picked him up later that afternoon, careful no one followed. Cotto explained El Indio worked as a superintendent in a Bronx apartment building. Goyo told him he found Indio's habits repulsive and Cotto confided tidbits he'd gleaned from others and Indio himself about Indio's past. He was born out of wedlock to a wanton mother who abused him, especially when the wayward child surprised her in bed with lovers.

She'd kept company in East Harlem with an old Sephardic Jew, a pharmacist who loved her and put Indio to work, teaching him chemistry's basics. Indio proved a good student and, dreamt of studying science, but the stepfather lost the pharmacy during the Depression. He quit school after his mother's illness and the old man's death, and worked odd jobs. He'd trained for demolition during the war, but drinking and brawling landed him not overseas but in the stockade. He hated the army, blaming *Yanqui* officers for his troubles and bouncing from job to job after the war. He considered the janitor job, though steady and secure, beneath him. A marriage failed, Osvaldo theorized, due to some sexual dysfunction.

"How do you know that?"

"Just a hunch."

Indio impressed Manuel Landia and Osvaldo with his knowledge after joining the party. They planned Operation *Huracan* with Don Pedro who stayed with Osvaldo when released from jail in Atlanta.

They staked Indio's building and, satisfied no else did, they went in, carefully examining the lobby. After descending the stairs to a lower level they rang the bell of a basement apartment and Indio let them into a cold, dark basement apartment with gray cement walls. Goyo examined an unmade cot with a coarse blanket, an icebox, a curtainless shower stall, and a toilet not properly flushed. The cot smelled of urine.

Bed wetter, Goyo suspected.

A sink in the filthy kitchen held piles of dirty dishes. Two stained workbenches nearby held unemptied ashtrays and bottles of chemicals. Boxes of nails, empty pipes, drills, caps, and watches lay strewn about. Goyo grew nauseous.

On a third workbench, like a sacred object on its altar, laid the pipe bomb.

"This it?" Osvaldo marveled.

Goyo gazed on it.

"Yes." El Indio, too, admired his creation, like a self-indulgent artist. He lovingly examined the finished masterpiece: a gray pipe mounted on a wooden board, filled with black powder, its ends sealed with matching gray caps. From a hole bored expertly into its center, two insulated wires ran to a red battery mounted on the board, and to a black timepiece connected to the battery. The total effect of the thing impressed Goyo.

"Sodium nitrate, sulfur, and charcoal," El Indio explained. Sharpened nails and shards of glass lay embedded in this black powder. Goyo imagined life's suffering and abuses also there embedded. Indio was crazy.

Perhaps they all were.

Osvaldo inspected the pipe bomb. Running his fingers through the wires and pieces, he admired the workmanship, enthralled by its power. "How does it work?"

"Simple." Indio lit a cigarette.

"Don't smoke," Goyo said.

"Afraid?" El Indio said with a smirk.

"Cautious." Goyo's eye filled with scorn. "I take chances, but I'm not stupid."

"I know what I'm doing." He crushed the cigarette against an ashtray.

"Show us," Osvaldo asked.

Indio pointed out a wire running to a battery from the center. Another extended from the battery to a clock, its little hand set to twelve and the big one to the desired time interval. When the two hands met, the bomb would detonate.

"That's all? Osvaldo further marveled. "Where will you set them?"

"The stock market, the post office downtown. And the El. Right on a train car."

"That's dangerous," Osvaldo said. Your best bet's an El station. Go in the rest room, set it for twenty minutes. Then put it in a trashcan. You can run."

"No! My carrier will set it off on the train itself for the best effect."

"How?" Osvaldo demanded. "Lots of people ride trains at rush hour. Somebody will see you."

"We'll do it. When the El pulls into Chatham Square and everybody gets off. It's the last stop. The conductor inspects the train, but he begins on the first car. When he reaches the last car, the bomb's set. The carrier has time to put it back in the briefcase under a seat and get off before the conductor comes."

"Suppose the conductor or the motorman sees the briefcase?" Goyo asked.

"Not where we'll put it—under the last seat by the dividing door. When the door slides, he won't spot it. Neither will the motorman."

"Risky," Osvaldo said. "But take the risk."

"Practice," El Indio told him.

Osvaldo caressed the pipe and fondled the wires running his fingers through the different components that bring a bomb to climax. Setting the timepiece for five minutes, Indio interrupted him.

"Forgetting something?"

Osvaldo thought.

"Wires all connected, right? " El Indio asked. "You have to first disconnect the detonator from the battery. More hazardous than smoking." He looked at Goyo, who said nothing.

"How stupid!" Osvaldo said.

"Takes practice."

They waited five minutes while the big hand moved. "It's quiet," Goyo said, expecting the loud ticking of anarchist bomb lore. "You can't hear it."

"I use only expensive timepieces," Indio beamed. "No one will hear it ticking. The briefcase muffles it more."

The loud click sounded in five minutes. It occurred to Goyo it almost aroused El Indio sexually. Its creator continued feeling and fingering, tightening and loosening the wires. Two of his carriers had picked up. This was his third. When they'd confirm the explosions, they'd call the press and say the colonized Puerto Rican people had set them off.

"Many innocent people will die," Osvaldo said.

"Many Puerto Ricans have died, too," Indio offered. "That's how war goes. We're at war."

They were silent for a few minutes.

Osvaldo broke the silence and filled in El Indio on the assassination.

They wished each other luck and Goyo and Osvaldo left, agreeing to meet midnight in Hunts Point.

CHAPTER 33

Papo slept late, dejected after his brush with Gregorio Tejada, reliving the moments on the Uptown Pelham Bay Local. Tejada had outwitted him. Luck had played a role, but so had the fact he'd let his guard down. He'd again flirted with unfaithfulness and he'd stumbled. From now on he'd be faithful to Marisol and to his purpose in life.

Dora again wore her waitress garb, though unstained, when he stopped for a late lunch the following Monday. She flung a menu, slapped down a napkin, and banged a glass against the counter, spilling water that soaked the napkin. She took his order last and served him last, without smile or ritual and radiated to other customers, although he felt her glances as she studied him furtively. Had he ignored her mischievous eyes, he'd have his man.

Lady Luck in turn abandoned him for Tejada, for he'd been unfaithful to vigilance. "Quite the lady's man," he thought, almost jealous of his finely chiseled features, so distinct from his own rough hewn mien.

How would he play his next hand? By waking Consuelo Tejada, late at night, when fatigue makes people most cooperative—and talkative. It was clear Tejada didn't visit often, perhaps only to see the daughter. This tie might reveal Tejadas' whereabouts. A secret boyfriend unknown to him might be the winning card.

At 11 PM, careful not to wake neighbors, he knocked on the door.

"*Policia*," he answered when a groggy voice asked.

"What do you want?"

"Consuelo Tejada?"

"*Si?*"

"*Policia de Puerto Rico.*" When she opened, he flashed his badge behind the chained door. "Where's your husband?"

"He's not here. Leave me alone." She tried closing the door, but his foot kept it open.

"Open, please," he said louder. "I must talk to you."

Reluctantly, she let him in.

Inside, Papo inspected the apartment. He saw mail on the table and recognized the letterhead of the Department of Social Services. She got welfare payments and worked off the books.

"I'm from the Puerto Rican police. We're looking for your husband. Where is he?"

"I don't know. He doesn't live here ..."

Despite her alleged ignorance, she admitted he'd shown up the night before after being separated for a year and had had no contact until he showed up unexpectedly. She planned to divorce him at the first opportunity. She knew only he wanted the United States out of Puerto Rico. She'd come to New York with her daughter and lived with an uncle and his arthritic wife. The uncle's wife had cared for Ivelisse, enabling Consuelo to work. But when the couple returned to Puerto Rico, she'd lost not only home but babysitter and job.

She managed to get the apartment, but even though her father sent money, she had experienced hard times. She'd met an old friend from Jayuya through her uncle, a nationalist, who made clothes in the South Bronx and offered her work off the books. She learned needlepoint from her mother and sewed a good hand at fifty cents an hour for forty hours.

"What did you talk about?"

"None of your business," she said, growing angry. "I don't know where he is. Now leave."

"I'm not finished."

"You have a warrant?"

He went over to the table and picked up the letter. "Here's my warrant. You're on welfare?"

"None of your business."

"It's the government's business. You'll be in trouble working and colleting a welfare check. You go to jail and who'll take care for your child?"

She cried, explaining her landlord, an Italian gentleman, motivated by pity and desire for steady rent, told her about Home Relief. She saw Congressman Vito Marco Antonio, at his behest, and the Congressman's staff got her on welfare. The money she received gave her breathing room.

"You'll tell the welfare people?"

"Not if you help me. Where is he?"

"*Ay bendito,* I don't know," she pleaded, in tears now, again explaining she'd not seen him in some time until he burst in just yesterday. A naive schoolgirl when he seduced her, she discovered only later about his bootlegging. But it was the infidelities that drove her to New York. She confessed to a boyfriend and feared Tejada would know. She pleaded for an end to questions and an understanding of her situation. She feared the neighbors would complain again to the landlord, who already warned her about the scene Gregorio had created.

Papo felt pity for this woman and promised not to tell welfare authorities. He asked about Ivelisse, who slept, mentioning his own daughters. Consuelo explained she'd lost two babysitters, although a friend now took care of Ivelisse. A sister was coming from Puerto Rico to live with them.

Close up, he found her more beautiful still. Her tan skin and green eyes captivated him and he tried not to stare. He thought of her marital troubles—and his own—and concluded the sexual drive to be humanity's bane. *We're prisoners of our dicks,* he thought to himself. Were he God, he'd find another way for people to make babies.

He urged her to remember anything else.

"Nothing. He got angry and left when I told him we were through. Mentioned something about Washington."

"Washington?"

"Yes. He mumbled he'd do something important."

"What?"

"I can't remember."

"Try!"

"I'm afraid of him."

"We'll protect you," he lied, having no such powers.

"He said he had a date with someone."

"Who?"

"Don't know. Said I'd hear about him. The whole world would."

"Why?"

"He didn't say."

"Mentioned names?"

"No."

He wished her a good night and left.

Outside, he walked around the block before slipping into his own building, lest he too came under surveillance. She'd said Washington, but not when and who. Where the nationalists planning something there? Or did Consuelo relate the mere boasting by a spurned husband?

He lay in bed, alone, and thought of Dora. And of Consuelo. But he slept with a failure that said *go home*. He'd leave flowers At Martin's grave and apologize to his spirit for that failure. One more lead remained: the homosexual Chucho Cabranes. Perhaps the party secretary/ treasurer had answers.

CHAPTER 34

Osvaldo showed up before midnight the following day. They examined the guns and cartridge clips. Osvaldo picked up the large Walther automatic, bluish black with a brown handle and weighed it in his hand.

"Makes my heart pound," he said. "Heavy."

"It packs power." Goyo took it from him. He pulled the base of the handle and the top carriage folded. He slipped in a clip and locked the handle. "Easy. Safety lock's on. Press this down, it's ready to fire. Careful with this safety catch. Try it." He locked it again and removed the clip. "It's like a woman: handle her right and she comes."

Osvaldo followed instructions, pulling the handle, inserting the clip, and locking it. Goyo pointed out the safety button and showed him how to push it in. He cautioned never to point it unless he was ready to use it and emphasized the importance of the safety catch, which Osvaldo pushed in. A gun needed oiling and cleaning, especially automatics, which jammed at the wrong times if dirty.

Osvaldo grew deft after a few tries. Goyo explained a cartridge held eight rounds and told him to remove the clips and fire it without ammunition. Osvaldo pulled the trigger.

Nothing happened. "It's jammed," he said.

"Forgot already? Safety catch is on, right?" Osvaldo put it on off and pulled the trigger, which then responded. Goyo pulled out his own gun and explained that pistols kicked, telling him to hold it with both hands, crouching and simulating a firing posture.

"Forget the bullshit in westerns. They use toy pistols—those cowboys that fire two at a time. Hold it so." He demonstrated with one hand. "You can't take good aim." Osvaldo took a firing position and tried it a few times.

"We need to fire from close. We got to be fast." Osvaldo repeated the motions, trying it several times against the mirror. "I wonder if we'll see Truman eye to eye?"

"Shoot him in the back if necessary."

"Not in the back," Osvaldo protested.

"You won't get another chance."

Outside, Goyo set up bottles on a railing along the river. Osvaldo fired off a few rounds at close range and missed. He slipped another clip, tried again and this time hit the targets. They fired more rounds and Osvaldo felt ready.

They walked and talked. Osvaldo again had visions of the land and his father and explained how *Yanqui* politicians in the pocket of the sugar interests passed laws wiping out the market for Puerto Rican sugar. His debt-ridden father, like other small farmers, lost the land to the Eastern Sugar Company and the *Yanqui* banks, which consolidated the small plots into huge, mechanized enterprises.

Osvaldo described the below subsistence wages paid by the new masters of the land.

Hard work awaited in the city—and a woman's infidelity. He vividly narrated his exodus on a ship of the Marine Tiger line to New York in the thirties. He mopped floors, washed dishes, and worked in factories under cold, impersonal bosses. He fell into deep thought.

"I'm cold," Osvaldo said. "For thirteen years I've dreaded this cool weather. Winter's coming. In Jayuya it's always warm. Delivery is near, although we won't see the Promised Land. I see my dead father, Gregorio, murdered by the banks." He wept.

Goyo mulled over these words. "I cry sometimes too, for my dead brother. I see him in dreams."

"We'll avenge them. Harry Truman will die. He's a decent man, Gregorio—a son of the land like us—but he leads this great empire that controls us. Like he says, the buck stops with him. We leave tomorrow. Jose Cabranes made reservations for us at the Harris there."

"How do we get there?"

"On the noon train from Penn Station. Let's meet there, but we should not ride together in case we're being watched by then."

"Where? It's a big place."

"Go in, buy a one-way ticket. We'll meet inside, in front of whatever gate the noon train to Washington leaves. Whoever's there first waits for the other. We'll board the same car, but we will not talk or sit together until the train leaves—if no one's following."

"I'll be there. It's not every day I set out to kill a president."

"A man, Gregorio, like you and me. A man who sweats, urinates, and bleeds. A man who killed thousands with a bomb and didn't flinch. A man who sends troops to far off Korea, denying its people the right to re-unify their land. He kills more and more Koreans each day and still doesn't flinch. Neither must we. Let's seize our country's destiny in our act, a triumph of the will."

They shook hands in a firm resolve. "I'm proud to die next to you, Osvaldo—for our country's honor."

CHAPTER 35

Papo pondered Consuelo Tejada's tip that her husband was headed to Washington. But where? Checking regularly with cousin Guillermo for messages, he got none, disappointed the Puerto Rican police never called and never would. Again considering going to the police and the FBI with his information, he finally decided he couldn't turn in his brother.

Papo got through to Chucho Cabranes after many tries.

"Obregon, how very nice to hear from you. What have you been up to?"

"Still working in the bodega," he lied. "Still looking to do better for myself."

"I've asked around, but I've been away. I'll try my contacts again. Why don't you come over tomorrow? We can have some drinks and maybe I'll have something for you."

"That sounds really nice, Chucho," Papo said, feminizing his voice.

The Party secretary sounded excited and invited him to his apartment on Manhattan's West Side the following night. Cabranes' tone betrayed no suspicions on the phone. Away on business, he perhaps knew nothing of a Puerto Rican cop tailing Gregorio Tejada.

Or maybe he was preparing a trap.

"I'm going home," he decided and began to pack his bags. Tired, he considered his self-appointed mission to avenge Martin Lanza's murder a failure. Back home, he'd visit Martin's grave and apologize to the spirit for his failure.

New York's daily grind exhausted him and every day Papo saw his people struggling. While some in the South Bronx lived well, most languished in the squalor of East Harlem's rat-infested firetraps, reeking of garbage and urine. Ethnic conflict troubled him, as did a welfare system he found degrading.

The migration, though an economic necessity, ate at the heart of *verguenza*, the self-respect and morality that glues people together. Besides Consuelo, the many unmarried women with children troubled him. Cousin Guillermo mentioned a woman with three children by three different men. Offspring disrespected parents, and husbands abused wives. Even more terrible was the sight of young Puerto Rican men addicted to heroin. He knew drugs in Puerto Rico constituted a tiny problem—a rich man's problem—hidden in privacy. Here, this poor man's problem lay open and visible.

Puerto Rico must care for of its people.

Dependency on America came at a price.

Papo finally accepted Guillermo's invitation for a meal. He took the el to East 138th Street and walked the two blocks to his cousin's tenement. Guillermo lived in a large, well-scrubbed, though worn apartment with his fat wife, Bienvenida, and two young ones, Ricardo and Allen. Guillermo had grown fat and bald like his father, Ciro, and now wore glasses. Bienvenida prepared a meal while the men downed some Rheingold beers. Papo brought Guillermo up to date on family and friends. The politics and violence on the island came up.

"Albizu Campos has a lot of fucking nerves and so do his crazy fucking fanatics. The people don't want independence. They want to be part of the USA. Nationalists talk about being in the same boat as Dominicans and Cubans. Sure—rowing hard to sneak in to this country. The first thing that'll happen if we become independent is that somebody will shoot Albizu Campos.

Then the new army will take over and set up a military dictatorship. It's what's always happens in Latin America. It's what's going to happen in a free Puerto Rico. Don Luis Munoz Marin sent out the National Guard. They're going to squash those motherfuckers—just you watch—and that fucking prick, Albizu Campos.

Bienvenida came in. "Guillermo, watch your language," she chided her husband. "Then you complain when the boys curse. And don't drink so much. Dinner's ready."

They sat down to a meal of greasy steaks and rice and beans.

"How's Marisol and the girls?" Bienvenida asked, eyes wide, chowing down a plateful of food. She wore her hair in a bun and looked ten years older than her actual thirty-five.

"Fine," Papo said. "Girls are big."

"You give them my best when you get back there." She got up to do the dishes.

I can't believe how the South Bronx has changed," he said, changing the subject.

"Latinos are spreading like plantains in a *platanal*," his cousin said. "Negroes, too. No white people left in Morrisania. Those *cocolos* keep coming from down South and spawn faster than mosquitoes. The Jews and Irish are moving out. It's like a second fucking Diaspora."

"Where do you go to school, Ricardo?" He turned to the eldest boy, missing his two front teeth and in a red plaid shirt."

"Call me Ricky. P.S.35." Papo saw in the brown eyes and straight nose his grandfather Don Bony.

"I went there," Papo said. "What's your favorite subject?" he asked his brother Allen, in a brown cowboy shirt."

"Lunch," the little one answered, flashing a mischievous smile. With light brown hair, he was the spitting image of his grandmother Mary.

Papo looked at Guillermo and they both laughed.

"We going to watch TV at Don Regino?" the older boy Ricardo asked."

"Yes. Eat up. Finish your plate."

Guillermo invited Papo to a neighbor's apartment to watch Milton Berle on television and Papo thought it a good escape. He'd seen television sets in store windows but never a whole show. Guillermo said the neighbor, Don Regino, owned the first set in the building, and Papo understood the high social status it conferred. Not everybody had the seventy-five dollars one cost.

Regino, a tall skinny man with a faraway look who resembled Don Quixote opened his door Saturday nights to the neighbors, who laughed at Sid Caesar and Imogene Coca's antics on *Your Show of Shows*. Weekdays, he and his tiny, plump wife, Modesta, invited only the family to watch the Milton Berle Show. Sundays featured Ed Sullivan's *Toast of the Town*. Guillermo and Bienvenida considered themselves family and so invited themselves and the kids for Milton Berle and brought Papo along.

Twelve people crowded into the tiny living room. No one spoke. All sat in silence, awed by the green metal box venerated on its stand. On its glowing screen, they followed religiously the black and white moving images. Only during commercial breaks did they grow sociable and exchanged pleasantries.

During such a commercial, Guillermo formally introduce him to his host and other guests, respecting the unspoken rule that one be quiet during the show. Ricky and Allen crawled in front of the television like two sleeping puppies and Papo marveled at their stillness.

They all laughed wildly at Milton Berle's jokes, antics, and large toothy laugh. Papo thought it all silly, even stupid, but he laughed out of courtesy.

A newsflash preempted the show. A pipe bomb, planted in a car, had exploded in the Wall Street area, shattering windows in the offices of the Marine Midland and Chase Manhattan banks and hurling garbage cans through the air. Nothing remained of the vehicle. The blast damaged several cars but injured no one. Regino's guests grew impatient with the interruption. Some talked, while others used the bathroom. Dona Modesta offered Coca-Cola and flan for dessert.

"Wonder who did this?" one neighbor asked.

"Another *loco* with a grudge," someone volunteered.

"I want my money back," another cracked, drawing a laugh.

When Milton Berle returned, they grew silent again.

After it was all over, Papo thanked his hosts and left, promising Guillermo and Bienvenida another visit before he returned home.

CHAPTER 36

Papo read in the *Daily News* the following day a *New York Times* communiqué received half an hour after the blast. A voice in heavily accented English directed reporters to a phone booth on Broadway and 181st Street, printed in the News Roundup.

"People of the United States, the Puerto Rican people implore you to withdraw immediately and completely from the internal affairs of our island. We have suffered under the domination of America and wish to become independent of your rule. We wish to achieve this end by peaceful means but will turn to violence and take the fight to your land. *Yanqui* go home."

He heard on the radio later that another bomb exploded at the Thirty-Fourth Street post office, killing no one but injuring several, some seriously. Another accented voice directed the United Press International office to another phone booth with another message demanding America withdraw from Puerto Rico.

That evening he heard of a third bomb exploding on the Third Avenue El. Glass and nails embedded in the bomb scarred and blinded a policeman and injured several, causing commuter nightmares and halting rush hour traffic. Yet another caller instructed the Associated Press to a phone booth in the South Bronx, where another waiting message read,

"A bomb has been detonated in the name of the liberation struggle of the Puerto Rican people. Get out of our island now or we'll rain terror on your land! Long live a free Puerto Rico."

Police and bomb squads descended on nationalists' offices in the Greater New York area, arresting dozens and looking for other suspects. Fear gripped New Yorkers, who now took note of Puerto Rico, although many still confused it with Costa Rica.

The bombings rekindled his resolve. It was now about more than just Gregorio Tejada and revenge for a death.

That nationalist fanatics would risk innocent lives shocked his senses. Although he understood better now the points they made, he thought these methods barbaric in the modern age, suitable only in India, Ireland, and Israel, with conflicts that were centuries older and much more difficult to solve. These methods did not become Puerto Ricans.

Papo called on Chucho Cabranes, his last card, hoping Chucho remained ignorant of Papo's true identity and would provide leads. He traveled across town to the party secretary's apartment building on Riverside Drive. A uniformed doorman pressed a buzzer and announced him. Seconds later, he heard Cabranes' voice giving the okay to let him in. Papo entered the plush marble lobby with its mirrors and fancy décor and looked around. Then he took the elevator up to the fifth floor and again he looked around.

Chucho let him. Quickly scanning the apartment, Papo decided they were alone. The place was scantily furnished, surprising Papo, who expected fancier décor.

"Come in, Obregon," said Chucho, wearing woman's makeup and dressed in a woman's nightgown." I just moved in. Haven't had time to furnish the place."

Cabranes embraced him warmly with more than a brotherly hug. He removed Papo's coat, rubbing his shoulders playfully. Papo masked his revulsion, hugging just enough to hold Cabranes' interest, and asked about the police raid on Party headquarters. Cabranes took his hand and said they'd arrested many and were looking for Landia and Cotto. They came after Chucho, who eluded them. Although he'd told people he was on vacation, he was really hiding the party files, keeping them up to date. He'd brought them into the apartment and they were all stacked in his bedroom; he suggested Papo help move them to storage in Brooklyn.

Papo smiled and preened.

Chucho put his arm around him and led him into the bedroom.

There, Cabranes crawled into bed. Brown cardboard boxes lay sprawled about. "That's what the cops want. We'll move them later."

"What's in there?" Papo stalled.

Membership files. Financial records."

"Can I look?""

"What for? This is what I want. Can *I* have a look?" He reached for Papo's private parts and pulled him toward him. Papo slipped into bed next to him, rubbing his hair and setting Chucho's goose bumps dancing. Cabranes rubbed Papo's leg, feeling a long, hard object. "What's this?"

Papo pulled hard on Cabranes' hair and banged his head hard against the headboard.

"Ay, *que pasa*, my love?" the stunned Cabranes said. "You *that* type?"

"It's over." Papo stood.

"Why do you do this?" Cabranes asked, hurt in his voice and tears in his eyes.

"Shut up. I want to see those files."

"What for? Who are you?"

"I'm this." He brandished his badge. "You felt this." He pulled his gun from his ankle holster. "I need something. I get it, nothing happens. Get in my way, you get hurt."

"*Maricon!*" the indignant Cabranes screamed and went for the gun.

"*Maricon, maricon?*" The angry Papo kneed him in the groin, pulling him to the floor.

"Stop, you're hurting me," Cabranes cried like a woman, the pleasure he had anticipated having turned to sudden pain. Papo flipped him on the side and cuffed him. "Oh this is terrible," Cabranes sobbed.

"Shut up, *cabron*. Act like a man."

"Terrible, this is terrible."

"Shut up, *maricon!*" Pressing his gun against Cabranes' behind, he threatened, "Like it up here? I'll go in—and come—if you don't shut up!" Cabranes' eyes shot up wildly. Dragging him to the bathroom, Papo tied his legs with a belt, taped his mouth with wrappings in his medicine chest, and locked the door. Then, he removed folders and papers from the boxes.

He examined the records, poring first over the membership files but finding no Tejadas. Next he checked accounting ledgers for the last three months, checking the money going toward rent, supplies, and sundry expenses—pens, paper clips, paper, and ink for pamphleteering. Most interestingly, he found recent entries for October 1950. Osvaldo Cotto got $250. A certain Jose Robles, $1000. A Rafael Lullanda received $500. This was Gregorio Tejada.

Most interesting was a receipt for a reservation at the Harris Hotel in Washington, D.C.

He found no address for Rafael Lullanda on the membership list, but he did for Jose Robles—a super's apartment in the Bronx.

CHAPTER 37

Osvaldo and Goyo checked into the Hotel Harris near Union Station. As they unpacked they listened to CBS Radio reports of the explosion on Wall Street the night before. In the morning and afternoon papers they eagerly followed the accounts and communiqués issued by the Party. Osvaldo practiced with the gun, slipping in the clips, locking the handle, unlocking it, removing and slipping in the clips again, and firing a few times on empty.

Pleased with the results, they were now ready.

They strolled through the capitol, on the second night from the Mall to 1600 Pennsylvania Avenue. They examined the scaffolding around the executive mansion and the construction equipment. "Think the President's there?" Goyo asked.

"Yes, he works there. Saw it in the newsreels. But he lives these days in Blair House."

They got their bearings from a bench in Lafayette Park. The iron streetlights provided good light, but a sparkling silver moon floating in the night sky outshone all else. Osvaldo studied a city map.

Goyo removed his new shoes and rested his feet.

He studied the Halloween throng in costumes celebrating October's final evening. The revelers milled about the park, laughing and playing pranks. There was a devil, a cowboy, a Frankenstein, and a ballerina. A Count Dracula wore a rich cape, and a Japanese aviator sported a leather jacket with rising sun on the back. A hobo spoke to a Sioux Indian. An Arab in a white robe passed alongside a buccaneer with an eye patch, hat, and wooden peg.

It occurred to him they all passed by two assassins masquerading as tourists.

Goyo next studied a statue of Andrew Jackson. "Notice all the military statues? Everywhere you turn, there's a gringo general on horseback."

"Yes, the *Yanquis* love their generals."

"And where does a President walk?"

"On the other side of the White House." He showed him the map. "Remember that big park? 'The Ellipse' it's called."

"That's where I'd walk, too." Goyo noted the circle of green on the map.

They too would take an early morning walk through there. Osvaldo mentioned he had once counted ten guards around the President in a newsreel. They'd charge from different sides, one creating diversion while the other went for the kill. They'd get close enough for a few shots. Osvaldo said most Americans came to the office by 8:00. A half-hour walk would put him up and out by 7:30. They figured by 7:00 AM they'd be in the Ellipse. They'd try it a few days and hope to chance on the President.

"We'll read the newspapers," Osvaldo added. "Presidents make news. We'll follow his whereabouts. We'll also stake out Blair House. Perhaps we can get him there."

They returned to the hotel, studying more statues of American generals on the way. Osvaldo explained that Andrew Jackson had killed many Indians before becoming President. Zachary Taylor too had killed his share—as well as Mexicans—to steal the South West from Hispanic people. "They stained the road to the White House with the blood of Manifest Destiny."

His knowledge amazed Goyo.

They ate a late dinner in the hotel and saw *High Noon*.

CHAPTER 38

Papo slept late, waiting for night before heading on the Pelham Bay Local to the Bronx.

He studied the large turn of the century apartment building, home to a Jose Robles, across the street on Intervale Avenue. He'd ask about vacancies if the super appeared, mentioning Cabranes and the Party. His gun would serve as reference if he aroused suspicion.

He checked the mailboxes in the empty lobby, finding Robles' name and a sign pointing in the direction of the super's basement apartment. He walked down a dark flight of stairs, where at the bottom a wooden door barred his way. He forced the lock and pistol in hand found himself in a dark corridor. He found a small sledgehammer among the implements in a tool shed in a storage area and picking it up, he continued down the corridor. From a heavy metal door with a lock, a thin, pale light escaped through a crack.

Slipping the gun in the holster, he lifted the sledgehammer and with all the force he could muster, pounded the door, breaking the lock. Seconds later, an explosion shook the basement and knocked him to the ground. He got up.

The metal door had saved him from the impact. He peeked inside, gun drawn, and entered slowly, coughing from the smoke and debris. Loud moans directed him to a mangled body on the floor, still conscious and speaking incoherently. Papo coughed again. A cigarette still smoldered on the floor.

He had found a bomb maker. Robles smoked. The sledgehammer had broken his concentration. Then the cigarette had fallen from his lips and its sparks ignited the gunpowder. The explosion blew off his hands, propelling nails and glass into his face. Papo coughed, then vomited. He wiped himself with the handkerchief. "Robles, can you hear me?"

Papo shook him.

"I'll be careful, don't worry. I'll be careful with the cigarette," he continued, dazed. "Who's at the door? They're coming. Be careful."

"Robles, listen to me."

Robles moaned hallucinations.

"Who are your carriers?"

He said nothing.

"Where is Gregorio Tejada?"

Robles moaned.

Papo pressed him. "Where is Gregorio Tejada? Is he in Washington?"

"*El Hombre* ..." he babbled a response. "He's meeting with *El Hombre.*"

"Which *hombre?*"

"*El Hombre Verdadero.*" His hoarse voice faded. "He's meeting with El Hombre Verdadero."

"Who is El Hombre Verdadero?"

"*El Hombre Verdadero* ... Tru ..." Robles uttered and died. Papo stared at the body.

He had to leave. The blast shook the building. Stunned neighbors milled about the lobby upstairs. More residents streamed out of apartments in panic and cast suspicious glances his way, motioning with accusatory lips.

He slipped out the front door. A large crowd grew bigger outside. He heard sirens and walked briskly down Intervale Avenue toward Southern Boulevard, then ran.

His overloaded brain mulled over the incoherent last words of the dead terrorist. "*El Hombre Verdadero,*" Papo repeated. "*Hombre Verdadero.* Washington,

D.C. *El Hombre verdadero.* Tru, tru, true," he echoed. "True … true and man—Truman. Harry S. Truman? The President?" Yes, the President. They were going to kill the President.

The police. Go to go to the police? No. No one would believe him and they would assume he was a bomber. Go to Washington? Call the White House? Take a cab to Guillermo's? No. The driver would report him. He continued walking, looking over his shoulder.

A police car approached and he hid in an apartment building. Inside he saw its reflection through the glass door and waited a few seconds as it passed. He peered out cautiously. It was gone. He left and continued walking.

At three in the morning, he no longer heard sirens on the empty streets. At the next intersection, before a bar still open at the hour, he stopped. A blue Ford pulled up to the corner and a woman in her fifties got out. She went inside the bar and, through the large glass window, Papo saw her enter a phone booth. Papo looked inside the car and saw the keys in the ignition.

He got in and drove south on Southern Boulevard until East 138th Street, then across the Third Avenue Bridge to East Harlem and the rooming house, parking on the side street. He packed his bags and wiped the room clean of fingerprints.

Then he drove southwest and headed for the tunnel. Crossing it took him into New Jersey and south for a few miles. Stopping for gas, he bought a road map and after filling the tank, studied the map.

He headed for Washington, D.C.

CHAPTER 39

The retinue of reporters and anxious secret service men strained to keep up with the President as he walked through the Mall, across from the National Gallery. The G-Men's eyes searched every face and scoured every blade of grass and tree leave in the park.

A. B. Howland too searched for an imagined assassin behind each bush, scrutinizing anyone coming near the President. The Chief joined these walks but he was all business, taking none of the pleasure his charge did. He wiped his brow with a handkerchief already damp with perspiration.

Mr. Truman let the way, walking briskly, with his usual gusto, clasping the cane firmly in one hand. The Chief remembered Inauguration Day 1949, when the Missouri doughboys of Battery D, 129th Field Artillery of the 35th Division, presented the black and gold tipped cane to their Captain Harry. The President turned left on Fourth Street and headed for Pennsylvania Avenue.

People turned and looked at the smartly dressed, elderly gentleman in an elegant light blue suit and wondered a few seconds before his identity registered. "It's the President." Mr. Truman tipped his big Stetson hat and smiled, continuing his energetic walk. The reporters struggled to keep pace.

"Mr. President," an eager journalist with a sign reading press on his hat asked, "your comments on the violence in New York and Puerto Rico?"

"We'll catch the cowards who did this. These fanatics will not stop the march of the Puerto Rican people toward self-determination."

"Mr. President, have the Chinese mounted an offensive into North Korea?" one asked, pencil and notebook at the ready.

"No comment at this time. I'll have more for you at tomorrow's press conference."

"Mr. President," another pushed forward, brushed back by a G-man. "You have reason to doubt General MacArthur's assessment at Wake Island that there's no Chinese threat?"

"The Joint Chiefs are assessing the situation. I expect a briefing from General Bradley this morning."

"Is bombing the bridges on the Yalu River an option?" ventured another.

"No comment."

"Mr. Truman, you're a betting man," another said, changing the line of questioning. "Your odds on next week's elections? The polls predict the Democrats will go down to defeat."

"They're wrong. They were wrong in '48 when they proclaimed Governor Dewey the new president and pronounced my political death. Yes, we're going to win. Now I'm calling it quits for today, boys. Tomorrow's press conference day. I'll have more then."

Chief Howland gave the signal and the secret service formed a ring around the President and Chief, shooing away reporters. The Truman party reached the southeastern tip of the Iron Triangle, where Constitution and Pennsylvania Avenues bisect, and there crossed Pennsylvania. On their right, the white dome of the Capitol Building came into view.

"You know, A. B.," the President said, turning to him, "I often wish I was back there." He pointed with his cane. "Nobody bothered me there when I was the unknown Senator from Missouri."

The Chief said he understood and added he sometimes wished he was back driving a cruiser for the Michigan State Police on a highway far from here.

"I'm constantly on a stage, an engineer on a train that can't leave the wheel for fear it'll crash."

"You can't go back to the Senate, I can't go back to a beat. It's the circumstances of our lives."

"Yes, circumstances—and luck. That's how I recall '44, when I learned I was Roosevelt's running mate. They sentenced me to this prison."

They took Constitution Avenue, past the round colonnaded facade of the Federal Trade Commission Building. Mr. Truman acknowledged the *ooh* and *ahs* from the people with a tip of the hat.

The Chief pressed closer. "Interesting metaphor." He wiped his brow and scanned the crowd. "The presidency as prison."

"Sweating already, A. B.? Healthiest set of sweat glands I've ever seen."

"Always something to sweat about." The Chief took this cue to explain his latest worry after a union official at the CIO building on Fifteenth Street called the secret service. One could see inside Margaret Truman's window in Blair House from a room there.

"What?" The President stopped.

The Chief said workmen would install a bulletproof screen immediately. He knew Margaret Truman, at home for a change, would hate it, but it'd be a temporary measure. They'd seal the room in the union building and cement the windows. Nobody used it except two colored janitors on the late shift.

"I'll leave it in your hands. Take care of my little girl."

The retinue continued up Constitution, past the Internal Revenue Building, reaching Twelfth Street and the Interstate Commerce Commission. There it turned right, reaching Pennsylvania Avenue, still free of pedestrians. The light traffic slowed down and the secret service drew tighter around Mr. Truman.

"Good luck, Mr. President," a woman pushing a baby carriage shouted.

"Thanks, I'll need it," the President smiled.

"Give 'em hell," a Negro construction worker in a hard hat shouted.

The President acknowledged him with his raised cane and continued to the White House.

CHAPTER 40

The sights of Washington, D.C., appeared like a moving diorama from the window of the cab cruising down F Street. While it waited for the red light at an intersection, Goyo sensed the tall, gaunt driver with a yellow cap studying them through the mirror, staring at their clothing. Osvaldo wore a brown chalk-striped suit with a maroon tie and a large, brown fedora. Goyo sported gray pin stripes with blue shirt, white tie, and matching white hat. They'd make a good impression on the President, he thought.

"Where you from?" the driver asked after pointing out landmarks. Osvaldo said Cuba, their fake Cuban identity being part of the masquerade. The driver said they picked a good time to come during this unusually warm November day. Goyo joked it felt like home.

The name on the taxi license read Spiro Agadamaris and Osvaldo asked where he was from.

"From here." Agadamaris explained his grandparents came from Greece, although he didn't speak Greek. Osvaldo lamented the lost language and identity.

Agadamaris argued living in America entailed speaking English.

On the next street Agadamaris pointed out the theater where an actor had shot Abraham Lincoln. "Want to see it?"

"No. We have our own drama to perform."

The driver laughed and drove to the White House. "Gonna meet the President?" he joked.

"*Si*," Osvaldo went with it. "Don't have an invitation, but we'd like to see him on his morning walks. I hear he walks around Washington in the morning."

"You're too late. Gets up early. Saw him once—around six. By now he's in White House. Or Blair House."

"Blair House. That's where he lives," Osvaldo said.

"Yes. He works in the Oval Office. But while they fix the rest of the White House, he lives in Blair House.

"Yes, we saw the scaffolding around the White House yesterday," Osvaldo said in Spanish. "No chance of seeing him?" He turned to the driver, casually.

Agadamaris suggested they wait until noon, when the President returned to Blair House.

"He walks?" Osvaldo asked.

"No, they drive him in a big limousine. Took a fare near there once and stood five cars behind him. Some people go in style, eh? You should've gotten here early. You probably would've seen him."

"Missed him," Osvaldo said in Spanish. "Show us Blair House," he added in English to the driver.

Agadamaris cruised and pointed out more sights. On Pennsylvania Avenue, he turned left and pointed out Lafayette Park and the North Portico of the White House. Blair House appeared on the right. He slowed down and the two passengers stared at the small mansion, taking in its details. Goyo counted four entrances and four guards, three posted in the guardhouses and one on top of the steps beneath a long, green canopy.

"Where do I leave you, *senores*?"

"The White House. We wanted to see the President, but probably won't. We'll see the White House."

"Okay," Agadamaris said. "You tell the folks back in Havana you saw it." He made a sharp left on Seventeenth Street, pointing out the ornate building on the left he called the Executive Office Building. Driving around the block, the White House came into view again, and they turned up Fifteenth Street.

"So you say Truman's in the White House now?" Osvaldo asked nonchalantly.

"I assume so. He doesn't give me his schedule of course, but I think he works there 'til twelve, then goes to lunch. What do I do?"

Leave us in front of the park." Osvaldo said, "On the other side of Blair House."

The meter read 95 cents when the car stopped on the corner of Jackson Place. Goyo handed the driver two fresh, unwrinkled dollar bills, which put a sheen on Agadamaris' eyes. "*Gracias, senores*," he beamed and dropped them off.

They crossed Pennsylvania Avenue, walked to the Executive Office Building, and on a bench, studied Blair House across the street. In the guardhouse on the left, two policemen in blue uniforms talked on top of the main entrance steps. In the other guardhouse on the right, a fourth cop studied carefully all passersby.

"What do you think?" Osvaldo asked.

"Hard."

"I count four entrances. Four guards. See the people? They just walk by. We could too, undetected, and slip in through one of those doors. See the one on the left?"

"No guard. It must be locked. We could blow it open."

"Truman wouldn't be down there," Goyo said. "He probably has lunch upstairs. Our best bet's up the stairs. But the other guards," he sighed. "One of us has to take care of them."

"We could attack the limousine," Osvaldo suggested. "We'd position ourselves around the garage and hit it when it came in."

"We won't get the chance. We'd be lucky to be in position when it pulls in. We can't loiter here four or five hours. We got to charge the house."

"Or wait 'til tomorrow morning," Goyo urged. "We'll be up early and wait in the park."

"It's big. We'd be lucky to bump into him."

"Let's do it today. We'll come back at twelve."

"Yes. Let's take a walk," Osvaldo suggested. "We can't linger."

They headed east on Pennsylvania Avenue and crossed to Lafayette Square, reading the inscriptions on the statues of Kossuth and Pulaski. Goyo protested they couldn't look at statues for five hours. Osvaldo suggested they go to church.

"Why?"

"To pray—and light candles for the saints. It's November 1st—All Saints Day. Tomorrow's All Soul's Day."

Goyo knew the next day one remembered the dead. Its implication dawned on him. "Who'll light a candle for us?"

"Or my parents," Osvaldo said ruefully. "I'll light one for them—and us."

They walked up Pennsylvania Avenue toward a church they'd passed in the cab.

CHAPTER 41

From the front pew of St. Francis of Assisi Church, Goyo gazed at the tortured body of Jesus Christ on a sculptured wooden cross, his serene eyes transfixed on the heavens above. Below the crown of thorns, the face exuded a tranquility divorced from the agony of the flesh. He studied the twelve Stations of the Cross lining the sides. The stained glass windows, decorated with saints and scenes from the New Testament, filtered the sunlight. He watched the candles in the chancel, their flames dancing. The church smelled of incense.

Only a handful of worshipers dotted the other pews. A priest prayed in the chancel. Osvaldo knelt next to Goyo, his hands clasped in meditation. Osvaldo looked up at the figure of Christ. "I am the light and the resurrection; he who believes in me shall not die," he said aloud. Goyo admired his faith in the spirit. He buried his face in his hands and prayed.

Goyo himself felt a stranger to God and stopped attending church long ago. Once a nun pulled him by the ear in a church for talking to a girl. Another time, he asked a Spanish priest, "If Jesus's so tough, why'd He let them nail him to a cross?" The priest beat him and complained to his mother, horrified at the son's blasphemy. His knees refused to kneel.

Osvaldo finished his prayers and rose, genuflecting and making the sign of the cross, rose, and went to the chancel.

The priest finished his prayers. "Good morning, Father."

"Good morning, my son. Did you wish to talk?" he asked in a colorful Irish brogue.

"Yes. Want to light a candle for my parents and the saints."

"Very well, my son. We ask a ten-cent donation for the small ones, twenty-five cents for the large ones. Just a suggestion. Give what you can."

"Thank you, Father." Osvaldo watched the bright flames consume the colorful wax.

"We have a mass later to celebrate All Saints' Day, if you wish to stay." The priest's ruddy face, Celtic and benign, radiated warmth.

"Afraid not, father. We have an engagement."

"Some other time, then. And your friend?" he motioned to Goyo.

"He's not religious."

"Too bad. Let's both pray for him. God bless, you."

"Thank you, Father. Good-bye."

When the priest left, Goyo rose and joined his partner.

"Irish priests are our friends," Osvaldo said. "They befriended Don Pedro at Harvard when others shunned him." He explained that Don Pedro's religion, opposed to the Protestant religion of his host country, became a political statement. The priests bolstered Don Pedro's faith and filled him with tales of the Irish struggles against the Protestant English monster. Don Pedro drew parallels between the Irish struggle and their own people's war against America and even traveled to Dublin in the 1920s to help draft the Irish constitution upon Ireland's independence.

Osvaldo slipped five dollars into a money slot, picked up the wick, and lit it. "For my mother," he said, lighting a candle. "She died when I was young." He lit another for his father. He lit two more. "These are for us. We'll need light through Purgatory's darkness. Tomorrow's, All Soul's Day, when one remembers the dead." He lit one more. "For Harry S. Truman." He knelt and prayed. He rose and at the font, Osvaldo anointed himself with holy water and crossed himself. "Take some."

Goyo hesitated.

"It won't hurt."

"Goyo dipped into the cistern. "I've forgotten how to do this." His hands reflexively made the sign of the cross.

"You don't forget."

CHAPTER 42

Papo arrived in Washington at 11 AM, numb after ten hours behind the wheel. He'd covered a distance three times the size of Puerto Rico and realized the smallness of his homeland. He wiped the blue Chevy of his fingerprints and left it in the Union Station parking lot, feeling relief from the steering wheel's bondage, like an unfettered galley slave in days of old. He removing his luggage and left it in a locker inside the station. A cab took him to the Harris Hotel.

By now police would be looking for Fulgencio Obregon, and he registered under Martin Lanza, paying for one night's stay in Room 14G. "The maid's getting it ready," the swarthy desk clerk said. "If she's done, you can go up." *Not all blond and blue eyed, these gringos,* he thought. This one had jet-black hair.

"I'm looking for a friend," he told the clerk. Rafael Lullanda. Is he here?"

The desk clerk checked. "Yes, sir. Room 14B, three rooms down from yours, on the second floor. He left early with another gentleman. Any messages?" The clerk's alert black eyes waited for the answer.

"No, thank you. Want to surprise him. I'd like to see the sights."

The clerk pointed out the landmarks on a map.

"I've always wanted to see the President of the United States."

"Go to Blair House.

"Blair House?"

"That's where Mr. Truman lives. They're fixing the White House. It's right here, across Pennsylvania Avenue from the White House."

Papo studied the map.

"Go around lunch time."

"Thanks."

Papo got his key and went to the room, stopping first at 14B. Pressing his ear to the door, he heard nothing. He saw the cleaning car outside his own room.

"It's almost ready, sir," the matron, an elderly woman in glasses and a maid's cap said. "Give me a few minutes."

"Take your time." Papo noticed several keys on the cart.

"Have you cleaned 14B yet? I'm looking for friends staying there."

"Yes sir. They left early," She went back inside his room.

The key marked 14B on the cart's rack felt right for the taking. But he decided he couldn't return it unobserved. Finished, the matron wished him a good afternoon and left. He showered and took a cab to Lafayette Park. He called the Office of the Resident Commissioner for Puerto Rican Affairs form a pay phone and was connected to Nelson Jurado, the Police Attaché.

Papo remembered Nelson Jurado from long ago, a career bureaucrat without any credited arrests in years. Jurado supported the Governor early, when Munoz, still a long shot, rewarded him with nice political plums, the latest, the attaché job in Washington. Although nominal Head of Security, an attaché did little, like most bureaucrats. He performed largely ceremonial functions, though occasionally he did help FBI and other police organizations with Puerto Rican criminals on the mainland, and gringo fugitives on the island.

Papo knew Jurado's real job was advancing his career back home. Jurado sought high office in the autonomous government, and becoming the future Police Commissioner offered only one step for the vain Jurado.

Papo told him about Martin's death and the search for Gregorio Tejada, then explained the pipe bomb explosions and the plot to kill the President.

Silenced born of apparent disbelief followed. "Get over here right away," Jurado ordered. "Don't speak to anybody," he warned sternly.

Papo hung up. He called the secret service and told a female receptionist two assassins in the capitol would shoot the President. He declined to leave his name and headed for Blair House.

CHAPTER 43

The north gate of the White House opened and the presidential limousine pulled out past the crowd, held back by guards and secret service men. A cheer rose when the bubble top rolled onto Pennsylvania Avenue for the short trip across to Blair House. The President waved to the crowd from inside and joked with his secret service escort. The car sped off.

The Chief declined the President's invitation for lunch, explaining he'd inspect his daughter's window, then get a haircut. He assured the President there'd be no noise during his nap.

The usual crowd gathered on the sidewalk, but it now watch the presidential limousine enter the driveway to the Blair House garage. The Chief got out first, followed by two other agents, then the President, who led them through the garden and up the stairs.

Bess Truman greeted them. Hayes wheeled in Mrs. Truman's mother, Mrs. Wallace, to the dining room. The President placed a kiss on the First Lady's cheek.

"Hello, Mother Wallace." Mr. Truman turned to his mother-in-law and repeated the ritual kiss. "How's the hip?"

"Terrible. It hurts like hell!" Madge Wallace then lashed a long tirade against Yankee doctors. The accumulated wrinkles of ninety years each bent in a scowl, sharpened by the dislike for life in Washington.

"And Margaret?" Mr. Truman asked for his daughter. "Upstairs rehearsing," Mrs. Truman answered. Said she'd skip lunch."

"Not right a proper young lady should tripsy about cross country singing like that," Mrs. Wallace complained.

"Or skip lunch. But what's a fellow to do?" the President protested. "Next time I see Joe Stalin, I'll ask his advice."

The Chief still marveled at the sturdy, Midwestern constitutions of the Wallace women and admired their simplicity and lack of pretension. He took his leave and began his inspection. He greeted Agents Lolley and Stacks and took the elevator to the second floor.

Margaret Truman, passing through for two days, occupied the end room, with her accompanist, rehearsing for upcoming recitals across New England. He then inspected every detail in Margaret's own room. The bulletproof window satisfied him. From this leisure room came strands of the Mexican song "Cielito Lindo" in broken Spanish.

De la Sierra Morena, Cielito Lindo yo vi bajando
Un par de ojitos negros, Cielito Lindo de contrabando ...

Only the music critics could take pot shots at the first daughter now.

The smile less Stanley Stacks greeted him. Stacks' lifeless eyes met his, and he bowed his head indifferently. The Chief nodded and went across the hall and up the stairs. The six-foot-five Stacks made him uncomfortable. But he liked his closely cropped hair, dull eyes, and cold, steely presence. It was Stacks he wanted closest to the President's room.

Marc Lolley waited in the conference room, his long brown hair, parted at the side, longer than the Chief liked. Lolley reported all well and the Chief lauded his effort. Lolley struck him as a high priced lawyer in expensive gray pinstripe suits to match his manners. He believed agents should be inconspicuous in crowds. But inside Blair House, Lolley's efficiency earned him his flashiness.

Outside, Officer Eagleton on the front steps turned alertly and saluted smartly.

"At ease, Jim. Everything all right?"

"Yes, sir. Normal."

"Take care."

The Chief walked down the front stairs slowly, protected from the sun by the canopy. He walked toward Guard House West, blending into the flow of pedestrians, to where the handsome, blond hair, blue eye Lindley Cottel did duty. Cottel's alert posture satisfied him, aware of Cottel's livelier side.

"Afternoon, Chief."

"Afternoon, Lindley. Everything all right?"

"Yes, sir. Busy," he said, keeping his eyes on the pedestrians.

"Fine. Keep up the good work."

Eagleton scanned the crowd at the main entrance, from the front steps. At Guard House East, the cherubic Bill Loring talked to his superior, a sour face Joe Droz, and both saluted. Howland acknowledged him with a raised hand. Then he checked the garage.

He walked toward Lafayette Square, rounding Fifteenth Street, then relaxed. The men's alertness calmed him.

Although the violence in Puerto Rico concerned him, the police in New York seemed to have things under wrap. The National Guard seemed to be gaining ground on the rebels in Puerto Rico itself.

His men in the Midwest had in custody the author of the unsigned letter from Iowa scolding the President for recognizing a Jewish state and threatening to finish off "Harry Jewman." They were closing in on one letter sender threatening the President for Hiroshima and another who'd addressed correspondence to Harry "Stupid" Truman and also hinted at retribution.

And for the first time in a long time his mind was at peace, satisfied he could not have stopped President Harding's assassination. Mr. Harding had arrived at the Palace Hotel after a long train ride from Seattle, where he delivered a final speech, then developed what attending physicians called pneumonia. He died suddenly after a conversation with his assassin. One doctor called the death a stroke. Some pointed to a sudden loss of pulse due to something called arrhythmia. Still others held he'd shown no signs of cardiac insufficiency. A plain heart attack?

No. The Chief knew his wife, Florence, killed him. She'd been in the room with him. As she left, the Chief noticed a bottle quickly slipped into her purse. Poison. Mrs. Florence Harding, sick of his philandering, murdered him. She later refused an autopsy. Many so maintain, and one historian even said so in a book, later repudiated by the cover-up.

The Chief himself kept quiet. It wasn't his job to opine on the matter, only to protect. And though he failed, he realized he could not have prevented it. No one ever knew when an assassin would strike. One could only do one's best. He'd done his best to protect his presidents and would continue to do his best.

His biggest fear now was his short gray hair approaching the length of Agent Lolley's locks. He headed for his barber.

CHAPTER 44

A taxi pulled into the corner of H Street and Jackson in front of Lafayette Square and Osvaldo stepped out first, followed by Goyo who paid the fare. The two walked briskly through the park, passing statues of Steuben and Rochambeau. On Pennsylvania Avenue, they crossed Jackson Place and passed the driveway to the garage. There, Goyo's alert eyes saw the limousine and two men protecting the garage entrance.

"The limousine's there. See it?"

"No."

"It's there, I saw it. He's in."

They melted into the crowd strolling past Blair House and approached Guard House West where two officers talked. They passed under the canopy and met the glances of a policeman on top of the steps. They walked by the officer in Guard House West on Seventeenth Street, then crossed back to Pennsylvania Avenue. They sat on a bench with the noon-hour crowd eating lunches out of paper bags in front of the Executive Office Building.

"What do you think?" Goyo asked.

"He's up there somewhere."

"But where? In the dining room?"

"It's not a big house," Osvaldo said. "The dining room must be on the second floor, not the first or the basement."

They decided Goyo would enter through the bottom entrance on the left, past the guardhouse. If the door were opened, he'd get in while Osvaldo stormed the main entrance, shooting the guards in front. Once inside, it'd be easy surprising and picking off the guards.

Osvaldo would blow his way through the front. If he didn't find Truman, he'd create a diversion while Goyo got inside through the side and found a staircase up.

"All set with the pistol?" Goyo asked.

"It's a machine. I know machines. I'll draw their fire. You slip in by the side." Osvaldo would start first and once across Fifteenth Street, wait for Goyo, to cross Sixteenth Street.

When he saw Goyo in position, he'd begin shooting.

"Let's start," Osvaldo breathed harder. "And shake hands. We won't again in this world."

"*Adios*, Osvaldo." Goyo took his hand. "Long live a free Puerto Rico."

"*Adios*, Gregorio." Osvaldo gripped his. "Long live a free Puerto Rico!"

They embraced.

Three blocks away, at George's Capitol Barbershop, George had cut half the Chief's hair and lathered his sideburns when the phone rang.

"It's for you, Chief," the barber said.

The Protective Research Bureau had received an anonymous tip from a caller that two assassins lurked in the capitol gunning for the President. The bureau had notified the White House police and the White House Detail. The Chief bolted from the chair, ripped off the barber's sheet, then dashed out, lather still wet on his sideburns. He ran the three blocks to Lafayette Park.

Goyo watched Osvaldo cross Pennsylvania Avenue and approach Blair House. When Osvaldo got to the other side, he began to cross. Osvaldo took out his gun and pointed it at the policeman on the steps, who jumped to the ground and rolled down the stairs. He bounced up after hitting the pavement and removed his revolver from the holster in one agile motion, holding his fire to avoid the pedestrians, who scattered. Osvaldo banged his fist against the Luger.

Jammed, Goyo thought. Osvaldo's unsteady hand shook with fear. The gun discharged and a bullet flashed out.

Osvaldo's hand steadied, took aim, and then fired. A bullet ripped into the policeman's leg. He fell on one knee and returned fire on Osvaldo, now in control of the front stairs.

Goyo crossed the street and approached the alley on the left. The policeman in the guard house saw him and went for his pistol, but Goyo fired first and struck the policeman, who fell back dead in the guard house.

Chief Howland arrived at Lafayette Park and sized up the situation from behind a tree's cover. A gunman had shot Eagleton and controlled the front steps. The Chief's eyes searched the windows upstairs. The President was taking his nap, he knew, and with luck, wouldn't wake up. He imagined the Truman women panicking by now and hoped they'd act sensibly.

Bess Truman's head appeared at a window. "Harry! Someone's shooting our policemen! "Harry! Wake up!" Marc Lolley appeared from behind her and pulled her in.

The Chief knew the noise and shouting would awaken the President. He imagined Mr. Truman's instinct and military training pushing him out of bed after recognizing the sounds outside, the same sounds he'd heard in France on the Western Front. And the Chief prayed he'd not rush to the window. He crossed the street toward Blair House.

The gunman leaped up the steps. Bullets stopped him. One blew off the brown fedora from his head. Eagleton, wounded on the ground, continued firing, and from the guard house on the right, other officers trained their guns. The gunman turned to fire, but the gun clicked. He reloaded. The tall iron picket fence, its black paint chipped by bullets, protected him from the fire. He reloaded calmly, indifferent to the bullets coming closer. The Chief could

TO KILL A PRESIDENT

tell he was hit. Blood oozed from his ear. The Chief aimed his revolver and fired a shot that missed.

The gunman rose and lunged for the front door. The Chief aimed and fired. The shot found the assassin's chest. He fell and rolled down the stairs, landing on the pavement in front. His face pressed against the sidewalk, turning red from the blood flowing from his chest and ear. The Chief inched forward.

Goyo reached the side. The bolted door on the side didn't give way to his kicks. Reaching a dead end down the alley, he hit the ground and crawled back unseen to the front, passing the dead guard he'd killed. Goyo paused some seconds to watch the blood ooze from his lifeless body. The firing stopped.

He peeked around the picket fence. Two officers inched their way on the blood stained sidewalk toward the motionless Osvaldo.

"Look out, there's a second one by Guard House West!" Frank Eagleton shouted. "He shot Lindley!" He turned, hobbling on one leg, but Goyo shot the other leg, felling Eagleton once more, both legs now bleeding.

Goyo discharged once more, taking down Droz, who clutched his arm in pain. Goyo rose and fired again, and Loring fell, a large red stain fanning out from the point of impact on his large stomach. He writhed in agony on the ground. Goyo grew bold, made drunk, it seemed, by blood's scent. He jumped the picket fence and moved recklessly on the soft grass, gun ready in his unerring hand.

The bedroom window on the second floor opened and the President appeared.

"Mr. President! Get away from the window!" Chief Howland shouted, his six bullets spent. Goyo saw the President. Their eyes met. And for a few seconds that seemed to Goyo an eternity, they were locked together in a mutual stare.

Papo saw them from across the street in Lafayette Park. He'd witnessed the shootout in the minutes after his arrival, pulled out his gun, and braved the traffic halfway across. And when Gregorio Tejada aimed at the window,

Papo too took aim. His gun rang out first. Its bullet found its mark: Gregorio Tejada's head.

The Chief saw the second gunman's face register a stupid, quizzical expression. The gun fell from his hand and he dropped to his knees, rolling lifeless to the ground. Papo backtracked across the street to the park.

"There's another one! In the park!" someone shouted. Papo felt all guns trained on him and he dropped to the ground. The passing traffic blocked their view, as did the park's lunch crowd taking cover. No one saw Papo, who slipped his gun into his holster and ran across Lafayette Park, then slowed down to avoid attention.

He came to G Street.

CHAPTER 45

It was all like a dream, running from Blair House and eluding capture in the confusion of Lafayette Park. Everyone scattered. No one stopped him—no one even looked at him. He'd had no sleep in the last twenty-four hours, and his mind grew indifferent to all around it.

Except for a pay phone on G Street he used to call Nelson Jurado at the Office of the Resident Commissioner. He told him everything.

The police attaché railed and shouted and demanded he not show up at the office. Jurado stressed the Resident Commissioner must not know. He gave Papo an address and cautioned he not write it down. Jurado ordered him there, stressing he not be followed. He'd help but would deny knowing him if he were caught.

He found the address four blocks away and the anxious Jurado. Papo repeated his story. Jurado shouted that he'd been stupid. "Every cop in America is looking for you." The bombing charge alone might fry him, Jurado warned. A White House policeman was dead and three were wounded, the radio was reporting. The least charge for sure was car theft. "Get out of Washington—out of this country."

Papo waited his turn. "You listen to me, bureaucrat. I save the President's life; you scold me like some goddamned kid. I got ten years with the force."

"No, you listen to me, Officer Oregon. We follow orders. The Puerto Rican police looks bad because of what you did. That's your biggest crime."

"I killed the *cabron* who killed my best friend, your fellow officer, Martin Lanza. Suppose I give myself up to these gringos?"

"Nobody would believe you. Go out there and I'll deny you. Obey or go to jail. We'll help you—get out of the States."

Papo grew delirious. "Home, take me home."

Jurado softened his tone. "You got *cojones*, Obregon. You have honored your island and your department. But you're in deep shit." The attaché explained that if he was caught, Papo would do time. The government of Puerto Rico would clear him, but it would take time. Jurado gave his word the Governor himself would take care of it, and the Resident Commissioner and the Commonwealth office in New York would help clear him.

"Take me home."

"You're better off in bed with your wife than sleeping in an American jail with angry convicts that think you tried to kill their President and bomb their country."

Papo missed Marisol and the girls and wanted to go home. He shaved his mustache, donned glasses, and put on a new suit of clothes. Jurado gave him papers and he assumed the identity of a clerk in the Office of the Resident Commissioner. After retrieving his possessions from the locker in Union Station, Jurado drove him to Norfolk, Virginia, where another car waited to take him to Florida. Outside Miami he was put on a plane to Puerto Rico.

Four stone faced types whisked him away unceremoniously into a car. They drove him not home, but to a hacienda in Caguas. Only when they took his gun and badge did it dawn on him that he was a prisoner.

They told him he was forbidden to call his wife and that the brass would soon speak to him. They did bring him a good breakfast and a newspaper.

A Sherman tank flanked by National Guard troops entering Jayuya appeared on page one, below headlines of planes bombing nationalist strongholds in

Jayuya. The press praised the "plantain stained *jibaro* army clad in American khaki" that suppressed the "anti-democratic forces." Police and the National Guard held hundreds of prisoners after the battle for the post office, the attack on the Governor at La Fortaleza, assaults on police precincts, and other scattered acts of rebellion. Police rounded up leftists, writers, and artists.

On the radio he followed accounts of a siege at the Plaza San Jose in San Juan and another outside nationalist headquarters. The police and National Guard fought a ferocious battle with nationalists barricaded inside a barbershop in the plaza. The attackers lobbed tear gas inside and ended the siege.

Embarrassed police and national guardsmen found not an army, but a lone gunman inside in a blood-soaked barber's tunic. Shattered glass and broken bottles of hair tonic lay strewn about. One source said a National Guard sergeant fired at the crazy barber's head, identified as Arcadio Diaz. The bullet reportedly glided off the temple of the un-killable barber, who was then hauled off to jail.

Papo also followed the radio accounts in front of Pedro Albizu Campos' headquarters on the corner of Tetuan and Cruz where another gun battle raged. The guardsmen pumped automatic fire into the house and the police lobbed tear gas through the shattered windows. They ordered through a bullhorn that the defenders give up.

The radio reported that one hobbled out carrying a white towel on a broomstick. The police held their fire. Three more came out, throwing their guns in front of the street and raising their hands. The police stormed the house and hauled out more prisoners, including a coughing woman. They finally removed the nationalist leader himself, slumped and unconscious, on the arms of two soldiers, his eyes closed and his arms listless. Jeeps whisked him away.

Papo learned elections took place and that the people voted for Commonwealth and continued ties with the United States. The Popular Democratic Party of Governor Luis Munoz Marin won by a landslide.

The investigation into the New York bombings and the Blair House attack also made constant news.

They brought in his grandfather Bonifacio, who told Papo they'd tracked his brother to Cousin Nicolas' house in the mountains. After a severe beating,

Julito told them everything. The police still held Nicolas and Uncle Ciro as accomplices.

The Governor sent two men to Don Bony and one explained Julito's role in the death of the two policemen and the wounding of a third outside Santa Isabel. They'd be prosecuted for murder. The second hinted all government contracts would stop—unless the Obregon family cooperated.

"And what do they want from me?" said an outraged Papo.

"To keep quiet. You'll embarrass them if it comes out you warned them about Gregorio Tejada and they didn't act. Tejada nearly killed the President." Don Bony added the Governor needed to control the damage by silencing Papo. Police were labeling Howard Saunders' death a simple robbery, and they couldn't have it otherwise. Americans would stop coming after the disturbances and the attempt on the American President. News about assassinated American businessmen could cripple the economy.

Papo felt dazed. "Bullshit. All bullshit. I did something there. Killed the *cabron* who murdered my best friend and saved the President of the United States. I won't be quiet."

"Yes, you will. You talk, your brother's dead. We're all ruined."

"I hate them. Hate them all. Look what they do to truth. Manipulate it—for themselves, not for the people."

"Necessary evil in an imperfect world. They think of themselves—you think of *us*. Your brother was stupid. He'll suffer. But does he die over your bruised ego? Your uncle, my son, your father's brother? And your cousin, my nephew? They'll go to prison. It's not about you, but us."

"The world must know this story."

"And give you a medal to wear with your ego?"

Two men came and took the old man away.

Papo, alone, felt scared.

In New York and Washington, the papers reported, authorities searched for an escaped bomber and a third assassin. They were looking for the same man: Papo. If the Puerto Rican police abandoned him, he'd be arrested, placed at the scene of the bombing and in Lafayette Park.

And Marisol and the girls? Who'd support them until the evidence cleared him? Not his brothers—dead or in jail. Not a grandfather too old to support great grandchildren after raising sons and grandsons—without money once government contracts ended.

Circumstances required neither truth nor pride. Too many had died for Pedro Albizu Campos' bruised ego. Papo decided he could afford the price of silence, satisfied he'd avenged Martin Lanza.

They released Cousin Nicolas and Uncle Ciro. Later, they freed Julito, too. Policemen's blackjacks had cracked against his face and pliers had ripped out his budding mustache, his upper lip now like raw pork. Although he told all—and more—unsatisfied, they'd kicked him savagely about the groin for the dead comrades.

Papo finally was reunited with Marisol and the girls. He embraced her and told her he loved her. "Me too," she said, tears in her eyes and more in her voice. Absence multiplied his appreciation for this woman who'd stood by him.

He fancied Natalia and Carla had grown in his absence.

"*Bendicion*," they said, asking for their blessing.

He kissed and hugged them. "May God bless you and the Virgin guide you."

The world could fuck itself, he decided. He'd not leave them again.

CHAPTER 46

Chief Howland watched the clouds hover above from the front steps of Blair House. The long Indian summer lifted, and a belated cold autumn breeze blew through the capital. The curious crowds, swollen after the assassination attempt, ebbed with the cooler weather, and he sweated less. He inspected the security cordon guarding the residence, triple its original size since the House of Representatives, in a special appropriation, approved the increase.

They voted the same day they blew taps for Lindley Cottel in Arlington National Cemetery in a wet but moving ceremony. The Chief and most of the men attended, except for Loring and Eagleton, who were still recuperating from their wounds. The sobbing widow and three children stood solemnly throughout the ceremony, their groans etched permanently in his memory. He played those sobs often in his thoughts, like a phonograph record.

President and Mrs. Truman also attended. Great sadness filled the President, whom the Chief knew held a new appreciation for the dangers facing him and a greater gratitude for the risks taken. He promised to make their job easier at Blair House.

Mr. Truman took lunch inside, but not the nap.

He got less sleep these days, the Chief knew. His string of luck, once taut, had snapped. Fifteen thousand miles away, the Chinese Army had crossed the frozen Yale River into North Korea. The congressional elections cast another disaster, and everywhere it counted, Republicans won.

Mr. Truman couldn't stop to dwell on his near assassination, and he had no time to consider a rebellion in Puerto Rico, which by most accounts was over. Nor was there time for the petitions pouring into the White House, seeking clemency for the surviving assassin, Osvaldo Cotton, whose trial began soon. A conviction and death sentence seemed sure. Congress called for a special investigation, and everything would come out at the hearings.

The nasty war escalating near the Chinese border would occupy the President's time. The bridges over the Yalu, the Chief knew, began to cast long shadows over Mr. Truman.

But the assassination rested very much on Chief Howland's shoulders. A vanished third assassin still lurked. A second was dead.

He was summoned when the first assassin, Osvaldo Cotto, finally opened his eyes and regained consciousness the day after the assassination.

"Oswald, who sent you?" the Chief pressed.

"Nobody," he moaned.

"Did Pedro Albizu Campos send you?"

"No."

"Who's the third gunman?"

"There were just two of us."

Cotto held to his story under sharp interrogation.

The New York police, the bomb squad, and the FBI questioned a long list of suspects and arrested every active and inactive member of the Nationalist Party in the Greater New York Metropolitan Area. They questioned Osvaldo Cotto's common law wife and the estranged wife of the dead Gregorio Tejada. A sister claimed his body at the morgue.

His special investigators in Puerto Rico found the Puerto Rican police cordial, but the Chief remained dissatisfied with their cooperation. The investigation in Washington shed no light on the third assassin, like Cotto and the dead Tejada, checking into the Harris Hotel under the name Martin Lanza. This same Martin Lanza identified himself as a policeman to the dead assassin's widow. Yet the only policeman by that name died earlier in a battle with nationalists. Investigators uncovered no fingerprints.

The ballistic tests raised more questions than answers. The bullet removed from Gregorio Tejada's skull at the autopsy came from the same .38 service revolver his men carried. Yet none of their guns fired it.

The loose ends gnawed at him.

CHAPTER 47

Weeks later, the Chief attended opening arguments at Osvaldo Cotto's trial.

"Your Honor, and ladies and gentlemen of the jury," the US prosecutor said, pointing accusingly at Osvaldo. "We have irrefutable evidence that nationalist fanatic Pedro Albizu Campos sent this man and his dead confederate to execute this fiendish plot to murder the President of the United States."

"I acted alone!" Osvaldo shouted. The judge ordered him to keep quiet, and guards restrained him.

The courtroom buzzed with excitement. The prosecutor mentioned the violence in Puerto Rico, which he claimed the extremist Albizu Campos instigated, citing letters found on the dead Gregorio Tejada with the nationalist leader's signature to be introduced as evidence. "This is conspiracy," the prosecutor finished his presentation. Cotto's court appointed defense attorney entered a plea of innocence.

Chief Howland followed the trial in the coming week, though not attending every day. The prosecution presented many witnesses. A co-worker of the defendant at the Achilles Metal Company told the court of Cotto's anti-

American outbursts in the shop before supposedly heading for Puerto Rico, mentioning anti Anglo Saxon comments.

Solomon Rifkin, his boss, took the stand and spoke well of him, citing an excellent work record but also Cotto's patriotic outbursts. The taxi driver testified that the defendant and the other passenger showed great interest in the President's whereabouts the morning of November 1.

Officer Jim Eagleton, still recuperating from leg wounds, hobbled to the stand on crutches and identified Osvaldo Cotto as the man who'd shot him and other White House policemen who were on duty that day. Eagleton also fingered the defendant as the man trying to force his way into Blair House. Forensic experts produced the gun, smeared with Cotto's fingerprints. The Chief himself took the stand and identified Cotto as the man he'd shot with his .38 service revolver.

The Chief also attended when Osvaldo Cotto took the stand over his attorney's objections. The assassin took the prosecutor's drilling, secure in his beliefs and convictions. Knowing the world watched, he grabbed this forum to put before it his country's plight, expounding his political philosophy and dropping names like Jose Marti, Simon Bolivar, and Miguel de San Martin.

"I bear the American people no ill will. I admire you. But you, too, had a liberator." He unfolded a crisp dollar bill and displayed George Washington. "Would you put *him* on trial as you do me?"

The prosecutor ignored his comments and grilled him during the cross examination about his past associations with the American Communist Party and its leader, Earl Browder, who spoke at a Nationalist meeting Osvaldo chaired in 1947.

Cotto denied being a communist, proclaiming himself a Puerto Rican patriot seeking help for his subjugated country. When asked if he'd received money and support from Russia, Cotto denied it. "But if you know of Russians with money, send them to me. You had your Lafayette."

Cotto called Puerto Rico an occupied country and insisted America had no legal control over it. Under an act of the Spanish legislature in 1896, Puerto Rico became an autonomous country with the right to conduct its own foreign policy. "We are at war with the United States. I am a prisoner of war. You have no jurisdiction over me."

The judge repeatedly warned him during the trial to answer only questions put to him, calling his political rhetoric irrelevant.

Cotto insisted it related to the trial and several times shouted and fought with the prosecutor and the judge, who at one point told the bailiff to restrain him. At trial's end, the judge asked if he felt sorry for what he'd done.

"No. I'd do it again tomorrow if I could. You have no jurisdiction over me."

Unconvinced, the jury found him guilty. The prosecutor asked for the death penalty, citing the clear and unequivocal evidence of his participation in the attempt on the President's life and the murder of White House policeman Lindley Cottel. The defense pleaded for mercy, stressing the ballistic evidence showing it was the late Gregorio Tejada's bullet that killed the dead officer.

On sentencing day, the judge cast stern gray eyes on him and spoke about the democratic process, triumphant in Puerto Rico. "The people of Puerto Rico have proclaimed their will. They've repudiated your program of violence, hatred, and murder and have voted overwhelmingly for ties with America. I feel sorry for you and your kind. For the heinous crime you have been convicted of, I sentence you to die in the electric chair."

"Long live a free Puerto Rico!" Cotto shouted. His common law wife and stepdaughters wept when they took him away.

Harry S. Truman, by executive order, commuted his death sentence to life in prison.

"This will show Joseph Stalin, Russia, and the world the capacity for clemency in the American system," the President proclaimed.

The Chief knew of Stalin's severity with plotters and presumed plotters. Many commentators opined that the commutation proved a propaganda coup and sensible politics. But the Chief knew compassion also moved the President, a good Christian, shown not in outward ritual, but in his sincerest practice of forgiveness.

His love and respect for Harry Truman grew.

CHAPTER 48

Papo took Marisol and the girls to the thermal springs of Coamo for a long vacation. The warm mineral waters worked their curative effects on mind and body as he reflected on his experiences. Although cheated out of fame, he found satisfaction in avenging Martin Lanza and the respect it bought him from the few who knew.

After his stay in America, he understood more clearly that Puerto Rico couldn't cut itself off from America. His visit only magnified his countrymen's poverty, more stark after seeing how others lived. Puerto Rico needed technology and knowhow, and America offered a ticket into modernity from which geological forces cut it off eons ago.

He still condemned his brother Julito's foolishness and the nationalists' abstractions of liberty and nationhood. His people needed a better diet and toilets to replace latrines, not vague abstractions imposed through a gun's barrel on an unwilling people. And he considered killing a President to win independence mere hubris.

He now knew freewill as an illusion—for nations as well as people. Forces beyond its control, not people, moved humanity.

Yet curiously, after his stay in the States, he appreciated the more nationalist belief that Americanization would erode traditional Puerto Rican values. He knew the vice and crime growing here on the island and among the expatriates in New York, as well as the breakdown of families, to be by-products of Americanization and modernization.

No, Puerto Rico couldn't shrink inward into itself; it needed to reach out to the world. America was a bridge. But neither could it rush blindly into a permanent union. It needed to progress materially *and* keep its soul.

He rethought his shaken certitudes.

When he returned home from the mountains, he learned he'd been assigned traffic duties in San Juan. Needing to earn a living, he had to live with the indignity. But closer to home, his hours became regular, leaving more time for Marisol and the girls.

He knew his days with the police department were numbered after its lies and cover-ups. He felt empty without Martin Lanza. He had few friends in the department, and Martin wouldn't be there to smooth the way.

Julito paid a great price for his ideals. But Papo wouldn't forget how the police took his manhood. No more Obregones would flow from that source, forever dried by the kicks to the groin his colleagues had meted out. His grandfather grew ill and frail from the experience.

And he came to hate the police, the brass, the bureaucrats, and the government. This hatred became the first thing he felt in the morning and the last thing he felt at bedtime.

He reported for duty outside the Plaza Colon. Putting on a uniform again constituted a step down after working undercover for so long. He found traffic duty an insult this late in his career. But he wore his service gray with dignity, and with great pomp he directed the flow in and out of San Juan. With a wave of his hand, all movement ceased in the capitol, and with another, it moved again.

He accepted his lot for now, knowing himself to be capable of great things.